FOURTH
DIMENSION

ERIC WALTERS

PENGUIN RANDOM HOUSE CANADA
BOOKS BY ERIC WALTERS

FOURTH DIMENSION

ERIC WALTERS

PENGUIN TEEN

an imprint of Penguin Random House Canada Young Readers,
a Penguin Random House Company

Published in hardcover by Penguin Teen, 2018

1 2 3 4 5 6 7 8 9 10 (RRD)

Manufactured in the U.S.A.

Library and Archives Canada Cataloguing in Publication

Walters, Eric, 1957-, author
Fourth dimension / Eric Walters.

(The rule of 3)
Issued in print and electronic formats.
ISBN 978-0-14-319844-4 (hardcover). —ISBN 978-0-14-319846-8
(EPUB)
I. Title. II. Series: Walters, Eric, 1957- Rule of 3 series.

PS8595.A598F69 2017   jC813'.54   C2017-901305-X
                                               C2017-901306-8

Library of Congress Control Number: 2017933732

www.penguinrandomhouse.ca

Penguin
Random House
PENGUIN TEEN CANADA

*For Christena Gay—my grade 5
teacher who told me I could be a writer
when I grew up—and for all the
teachers who make a difference every
day. Their words change lives.*

1

"Emma, it's almost 1:30. If we want to get out of the city before the traffic gets bad I'll need you to put down your phone and help get us packed," my mother said.

Reluctantly I lowered my phone and sighed. I wasn't really looking forward to this weekend camping trip with my mother and brother—especially now that it was May and the mosquitoes would likely be out in full force—but at least we'd been allowed to take the day off school. Not that anybody would even notice I wasn't there. Being the new kid in a new school starting most of the way into the year had meant that it was too late to make any real friends. Not that I wanted new friends. I just wanted my old friends back.

"If you didn't want bad traffic we shouldn't have moved here," I answered.

She chuckled. "The traffic is definitely a lot worse here."

"Everything is worse here. *Everything*." I repeated it for emphasis, and my mother stopped chuckling and gave me a scowl that almost matched mine.

"You know, wherever you go, there you are," she said.

"And that's supposed to mean . . . ?"

"You make your own happiness. A negative attitude can only create a negative atmosphere."

"Have you thought of giving up being a nurse and writing bumper stickers instead?" I asked sarcastically.

"Maybe I'll do both—and be happy doing both."

"I was happy before we moved."

"Were you?"

That caught me by surprise. The last couple of years had not been easy, with my parents going through all the fighting and drama and then finally separating. But at least I'd had my home and my friends. I'd thought that their separating might make everything better, or at least quieter. Little did I know then that their separation was going to mean a new start in a new city for me.

"I was *happier*. Happier than I am here."

"Give it a chance," my mother said.

The way you gave my father another chance? I almost blurted out, but didn't. She didn't need that. She wasn't the one who had found somebody else.

"This is an amazing city. It will grow on you."

"Cancer grows. Mold grows. I don't want anything to grow on me."

"Attitude . . . it's all attitude."

I heard the door of our condo open and my younger brother, Ethan, appeared. He'd already brought a load down to our car. At eleven he was still young enough to be excited about a camping trip.

"Help your brother with the rest of the bags that are ready to go," she said, and disappeared into the bedroom before I had a chance to argue.

I turned to Ethan. "I know how to speed this up. How about you go down below. I'll drop our gear off the balcony and you can catch it."

"Would that work?"

"Why not? It's only seventeen stories down. I'm sure you can break the fall."

"Do you think I'm an idiot?"

"I know you're an idiot. What I can't believe is that we're actually related."

"I keep hoping one of us is adopted," he said.

He picked up one of the big packs. I didn't have much choice. I slipped the phone into my pocket and picked up the other. It was heavy. We were only going camping for four days but the way my mother had packed you'd have thought it was four weeks.

"What's in these packs?" I asked.

"You know Mom, probably everything."

Our mom was an ER nurse, and a former Marine nurse, and probably a Girl Scout when she was young, so she was always really, really prepared. It was one of her most irritating qualities. That and the fact that she thought she was never wrong. Okay, what was most irritating of all was that she hardly ever was wrong.

My father had said—more than once—that my mother and I fought so much because we were two of a kind. Did any fifteen-year-old girl ever want to be compared to her mother? I would have rather spent the weekend with him, but that wasn't possible. It wasn't simply that he lived where we used to live before they separated—halfway across the country—but right now he was stationed on the other side of the world on a six-month tour with his company. My mother had been a Marine—that's where they met—but he was still a Marine. Then again, I'd heard them both say more times than I could count: "Once a Marine, always a Marine."

I lugged the bag to the door. My brother dragged his out the door and down the hall to the elevator, which opened as soon as he pushed the down button.

"You coming or what?" he demanded.

"Just hold the door. It's not going to bite you . . . or is it?"

He gave me a dirty look. He didn't like elevators, and I knew living on the seventeenth floor was hard for him. In our new city we'd moved into a brand-new condo. It had been two months but I still couldn't get over the teeny tiny space we were crammed into. The whole place wasn't much bigger than the main floor of our old house on the base. It was so small that my old bedroom furniture was too big for my new room.

Sure, it was nice to live in a new building, but new also had its downsides. There was still some construction going on to finish up the last units and to fix the things that were still going wrong. We'd had power and water problems—my mother called them "hiccups"—and today the lights had gone out twice, and the water once. It was getting better, but it still felt like living in a construction site.

My brother kept trying to be cheerful, which was irritating, so I needed to irritate him in response. Bothering my brother was one of the things that made me feel like we were back home.

I stopped at the door, holding it open with one hand.

"You sure you want to do this . . . take the elevator . . . didn't you notice that it was, I don't know, a little iffy today?"

There had been some ongoing problems with the elevators. They were slow and sometimes bumpy, and a few people had actually got stuck. It was only for a few minutes but, still . . .

"We won't get stuck."

"It *has* happened."

"Emma, do you remember when you used to be nice to me?" he asked.

I shook my head.

"Neither do I. Would it hurt you to try not to be so mean all the time?"

"It's not all the time. I do sleep."

I stepped into the elevator, dragged the bag after me, and pushed the button for P3, the third below-ground parking level. The doors closed. As we started down I jumped into the air, and as I landed the whole elevator shook, and my brother gave a little gasp.

He quickly realized what I'd done. "You really are mean."

"Suck."

"Loser."

"Bigger loser," I said.

The doors opened and we dragged the bags out.

My brother didn't like elevators. For me, it was parking garages. I'd seen too many murders and assaults and abductions take place in underground parking areas. Well, at least I'd seen them on TV and in movies. Lately I'd been watching a lot of horror movies. What else did I have to do? It's not like I had any friends here.

At least our parking spot wasn't too far from the elevator. That meant that there were fewer places for the murderers to hide.

Right beside our car on the concrete floor was our long red canoe. We'd moved it out of our storage unit, and it would have to be carried up to the street and then strapped on the roof. It was wide and stable and big enough to hold all three of us plus all this junk my mother had packed. It was part of our history of camping together. Trips my parents took before I was born and then with me, and then all of us together. There were good memories in that canoe.

We stuffed the two packs into the trunk of the car. Now, with the exception of a few last-minute additions, we were basically packed. That was good since there wasn't going to be much space left once the three of us piled in.

I took out my phone to text Liv—my best friend from back home—and there was no service. I don't know what I was expecting down here, buried under the ground. That was yet another reason to hate the parking garage. Maybe that's why murderers liked them so much. They were not only dark and deserted but you couldn't call for help.

I was suddenly happy to have my brother with me. Strange to think he might defend me from anything or anybody, though. He was small for his age and, well, a little goofy. I knew if push came to shove I'd be the one to have to protect him. I had before. New kids in new schools often get bullied, and we'd been in a lot of new schools. Military life was like that. Nobody ever tried to bully me, though. Maybe I was my mother's daughter.

My father was so different from Ethan. He was big and

strong and acted and looked and talked and thought like a Marine. From the brush cut down, he was a take-charge, take-no-prisoners sort of guy. My friends—especially my friends who were boys—all seemed a little afraid of him. Little did they know that the one they should have been afraid of was my mother. She wasn't nearly as big, or physically strong, but she was a Marine too. Because she was much friendlier on the surface, they usually didn't realize how tough she really was underneath.

"You sure you don't want to walk back up instead of chancing the elevator again?" I asked Ethan.

"Getting stuck in the elevator isn't what makes me afraid."

"It isn't?"

"No, I'm afraid of getting stuck in it with *you*."

"How do you feel about getting stuck with me in a canoe and a tent for the next four days?" I asked.

"Not good either, but at least there's a chance one of us will be eaten by a bear. I'm hoping it's you."

We got back into the elevator. I'd lay off him for this ride.

"If it had to be one of us, I think Mom would rather it was you," he said.

"It was me what?"

"Eaten by the bear. You know I'm her favorite child."

Although I knew he was joking, there was a kernel of truth in what he said. I had been giving my mom a hard time about the move—okay, even *before* the move—and Ethan had been taking it pretty well. She probably *did* like him better. But I had more to complain about. I had been halfway through sophomore year at high school with my friends when we moved here, whereas Ethan had only been in sixth grade. Starting a new high school halfway through the year was much harder than starting at a new elementary school. Something my mother obviously didn't even consider when she accepted the job at one of the new hospitals here.

When we got back to the apartment, I could see my mother checking the last few items off her list. She was, as always, organized. It drove her crazy when I forgot things. What she didn't know was that sometimes I did that deliberately just to make her nuts. After all, if she could force me to move across the country, I could at least cause her a little bit of grief.

"Is the car all packed?"

"We were supposed to put that stuff in the car?" I asked. "We put it down the garbage chute."

"Funny. Nice to know you haven't lost your sense of humor completely," she said without looking up from her list.

"You know, if there isn't enough room in the car I'm willing to volunteer to stay at home."

"Responsible parents don't leave their fifteen-year-old children alone for four days."

"I'm almost sixteen and I'm not a child. I'm basically an adult."

"Not according to the law."

"If we hadn't moved I would have had lots of friends and their parents to stay with and you could have gone without me."

"I don't want to go without you. Besides, you love camping."

"I used to love camping . . . when I was little."

"As opposed to how old you are now?"

"I'm not a baby."

"I love camping," my brother said.

"I guess that just reinforces my point about it being for babies. Look, if you did leave me I'd be okay. It's not like I'm going to invite *all* of my friends over for a party. I don't know if this apartment is even big enough to hold all of them."

"I know it's not easy," my mother said. "But it's not like it's the first time you've changed schools."

We'd lived on or near nine different army bases. They were in different corners of the country, and one was in a different country altogether.

"Moving is just part of the military life," she added.

"That was military. We were ordered to move. This move was all about you."

"Yes, this was for my career, but also for our future together and—"

I pulled out my phone and started texting Liv again to tell her how much my life sucked, and to show my mother how little I cared about what she had to say. My mother very gently put her hand on my arm, and I looked up.

"I've said it before, but I'll say it again. I'm sorry. It wasn't fair to you, and if this doesn't work then we can look at going back."

"But I like it here," my brother said.

I felt like screaming at him.

"How about we just put everything aside for the next few days?" my mother suggested. "It'll be us and nature. We'll be doing something as a family."

I was just going to ask, "Oh, is Dad going to be joining us?" when the lights went off. Another power failure.

"Again?" Ethan said.

The floor-to-ceiling windows let in more than enough light for us to see.

"I'm sure they'll be back on soon," my mother said. "They always are."

"It feels like we're already camping," I said.

"We're going away anyway, so what does it matter if there are no lights?" my brother asked.

"Always seeing the bright side, aren't you?" I asked.

"Well . . . the semi-bright side, really."

I laughed in spite of myself. "Not bad." He always did seem to be able to look on the positive side of things.

I pulled up my phone. The screen was dark. I fiddled with it . . .

"My phone is dead!"

"No surprise there," my mother said.

"She means because you use it so much," my brother added helpfully.

I shot him a look. "Yeah, I get it. I can't even charge it because there's no power."

"It sort of sucks being you, doesn't it?"

"You can use the charger in the car," my mother suggested.

"Then what are we waiting for?" I asked. "Let's go camping."

2

We went slowly down the stairwell. Dusty cement stairs meeting dusty landings dimly lit by the yellowy glow of the emergency lights. This was almost as unnerving as the parking garage—wait, would the emergency lights be working down there?

"Are all the flashlights in the car already?" I asked my mother.

"All of them except this one," she said. A beam appeared, leading from my mother's hand and down the next flight of stairs. Sometimes having an annoying organized mother had its benefits.

"I'm just glad we weren't in the elevator when the power went off," my brother said.

"I think we're all glad about that," I said.

"Mom, what would have happened if we'd been in there?" he asked.

"There'd be nothing to worry about. There'd be emergency lights in the elevator and—"

"If they were working," I said, cutting her off.

"They would have been working," she said. "As would the emergency call box. It would have been a short time until either the power came back on or they got us out."

"The lights have been out almost fifteen minutes," I said.

"And will probably be back soon," she said.

We heard voices coming up the stairwell and then caught glimpses of light coming ahead of the voices. It was two or maybe three male voices, and I was happy that our mother was with us.

"Hello," she called out cheerfully, and they answered back.

There were two of them wearing hard hats and vests. I recognized them as construction workers who were putting the finishing touches on the building.

"Do you know how long the outage is going to be?" my mother asked.

"No idea," one of them answered.

"This one isn't our doing," the second added. "It's more than just this building."

"Do you know how far it's spread?"

"The surrounding buildings for sure, and the traffic lights are out at the top of the street."

"That must have snarled traffic," she said.

"It's basically gridlock out there."

"Maybe we shouldn't go," I suggested hopefully.

"It probably won't be long," one of them offered.

Great, now strangers were conspiring against me.

"It can't be soon enough for the people stuck in that elevator," the first guy said.

My brother gasped. "People are stuck in the elevator?"

"Two of them are in Elevator 3," he answered.

Even in the dim light I could see my brother go pale, and I suddenly felt sorry for him.

"Look, that hardly ever happens," I said, trying to make him less worried for his future elevator trips.

"Oh, you'd be surprised," the first worker said. "Between the power outages and getting the elevators running right, we've had a lot of people stuck."

I pictured Ethan taking the stairs forever. That was funny and pathetic and sad.

"We're just walking down. No elevators needed right now," my mother said.

They started up, and we'd continued down a few steps when my mother stopped and called out, "Is the garage door to the underground parking open?"

"We manually opened it," one of them said. "You're good to go."

"Thank you. I appreciate that."

Probably just as much as I didn't appreciate it. I hadn't even thought that no electricity might stop us from using the automatic doors and leaving. If we could have delayed a day we probably wouldn't have had to go at all.

"Mom, do you think this is a good idea?" I asked as I trailed her and Ethan.

"I think it's a great idea."

"But with the power out and everything, and the traffic thing, wouldn't it be better to just stay here until the problem is fixed?"

"I'm sure when we drive four blocks away it will all be fine."

We reached P3, and I was relieved there were emergency lights working down there.

"That's strange," my mother said as we approached the car. "My clicker isn't working." She held up the remote. "The batteries shouldn't be dead this soon."

"All part of the power failure," my brother said.

"Batteries," I said, shaking my head.

"Joking," he answered.

My mother used the key to manually open the driver's door and then hit the door release button to open all the rest. My brother climbed into the passenger seat—as always. He got a bit motion sick so he needed to be up front. I really didn't mind. In the back I didn't have to talk. It would just be me and my phone and my distant friends. And that reminded me, I had to power it up. I reached over the seat and plugged my phone into the cord so it would start charging as soon as the car started. We were going to drive up, park, and then come back down for the canoe.

"Oh, that's just great," my mother said. She sounded angry.

"What's wrong?" Ethan asked.

"It won't start."

She tried again, and there wasn't even the sound of the car engine trying to turn over.

"The battery is completely drained. There's no power at all." She turned to my brother. "You didn't leave the lights on when you started to load things this morning, did you?"

"I didn't touch the lights."

"But if you left the door open then the interior light would have been left on and—"

"The door was locked when we got here—you opened it yourself! And it was locked when we brought down the last load," I said. "It's not his fault."

I think me defending him caused my brother to be more confused than pleased.

"I guess the only thing we can do is call the Auto Association and have it boosted."

She started to rifle around in her purse for her phone.

"There's no point. You can't get phone reception down here."

"Are you sure?"

"Look who you're arguing with," my brother said. "Emma is the queen of cellphones."

We all got out of the car and started to walk up the ramp leading to the next level. Up on P2 it was darker. Some of the emergency lights weren't working, or they were so dim already that they were giving out more of a glow than actual light. Were they already running out of battery power?

"Excuse me!" a man called out, and I practically jumped out of my shoes.

He was standing by a car, with the hood up, holding booster cables.

"Do you think you could jump my car?" he asked.

"Sorry, but we have the same problem," my mother answered.

"That's a real coincidence," he said. "You don't think kids are doing something with the cars, do you?"

"Like stealing batteries?" she asked.

"I still have a battery," he said, pointing under his hood. "I guess I'm just being a little paranoid."

"We're just going up to call for a tow truck. Maybe he can do two cars when he comes," my mother suggested.

On the next level there was light coming from the open garage door. There was a nice breeze blowing, and the fresh, normal, above-ground, free-of-car-fumes-and-construction-dust air flowed down the ramp and into my lungs. It didn't just smell wonderful, it almost tasted wonderful. I let out a big sigh of relief as we exited the garage and entered the world.

"Wow, look at the traffic jam!" Ethan exclaimed.

The cars on the street had come to a stop. Nothing was moving. It was bumper to bumper. I thought how there was no way a tow truck could get through this to help us. We circled around along the street toward the front door of our building.

"This must be bigger than I thought," our mother said. "The power must be out and the lights down for a long way out from here."

"Does this mean we're not going camping?" I asked.

"This might mean that we're not going camping."

I tried not to smile too much. Being here wasn't great but camping would be far worse.

"Why isn't there any sound?" my brother asked.

"What do you mean?" my mother questioned.

"The cars aren't running. I don't hear the engines going."

He was right.

"They might have turned their cars off to save gas," my mother suggested.

"All of them?" I asked.

Many of the drivers were out of their vehicles and standing beside them. Some of the cars had been abandoned completely. Looking up and along the street I saw that there were half a dozen vehicles with their hoods up. Traffic lights being out wouldn't cause people to look at their engines, and neither would a traffic jam. Something else was going on.

"My phone still isn't working," my mother said.

"No phones are working," chipped in a man who was standing at the side of the road.

"None, or just cellphones?" my mother asked.

"I don't know. I haven't tried a landline. They might work."
He rushed off.

"What's happening, Mom?" Ethan asked.

"I don't know. I really don't. Let's just get back up to our place."

I wanted to get up there and off the streets. Whatever was happening here was getting stranger and stranger. And bigger and bigger.

3

We all stood at the window staring down at the cars below. My mother had got her binoculars out and we'd been able to see pretty far in three directions: east and west along Lakeshore Boulevard, and south toward the lake and the island airport. And as far as we could see it was the same everywhere—nothing was moving except for the people who had abandoned their vehicles. Actually, that wasn't quite right. There were a couple of cars and trucks that were slowly weaving between the immobile vehicles that filled the streets. The ones that were moving seemed to be older— much older. Did that mean something? I'd have thought the newer cars would be the ones still running. And there were more and more people out there as well. The office towers and condos were emptying out in response to what was happening. Or I guess, actually, what wasn't happening.

Out on the lake, white and red sails were still being pushed around by the strong winds, and there were also a few little motorboats making their way across the waters of the harbor. The big boat—the passenger ferry—that brought people back and forth from the city to the island was docked at the mainland terminal. Was it able to move?

I didn't like much about this city but I did like the view

from our condo. We were on the north side of Lakeshore Boulevard, looking practically right down onto the lake. We could see the whole inner harbor, out over the island, and across the lake until it disappeared at the horizon.

The island itself wasn't that big—really it was three larger islands joined by little bridges, and then a bunch of little ones scattered in the lagoons. I could see the bigger ones quite clearly—green patches surrounded by blue. The view was beautiful, even today.

On Main Island—the biggest island, in the middle—was an amusement park. I'd heard there were rides for little kids, a petting zoo, places to picnic, flower gardens, a marina for pleasure boats, and open spaces to play. On the weekends we could see the lineups at the ferry docks of people waiting to be taken over. There were always lots of people, pushing strollers and pulling wagons full of the stuff they'd need, holding onto their bikes as they boarded. From what I'd been told, over on the island bikes were the only way to get around.

The island on the left was mainly woods, but on its far east side was a group of little houses or cottages, maybe a hundred or so. That's where I found myself looking. I tried to imagine what it would be like to live out there, so close to the city but so far away. They'd clearly be able to see the city, and I guess even hear it, but they were living in their own little world, separated by a strip of blue.

The final island held a little airport. The planes were small—mostly private, I guessed—except for some bigger four-engine planes with some airline called Frontier. I could see the logo on their tails as they landed. Some of them came in so close and so low that I had to look down to see them as they passed our building. When my mother was on the night shift and trying to sleep during the day, the sound of the planes buzzing by woke her up. Wait . . . what about the planes?

"Have either of you noticed any airplanes?" I asked.

My mother gave a quizzical look. "I hadn't thought to look . . . but I don't think so. If there's no electricity the control tower might be out of operation."

"Don't places like airports and hospitals have emergency generators in case of emergencies like this?" I asked.

"They do. At least, every hospital I've ever worked at did. I wonder how they're doing with all of this."

I had a terrible thought. "You're not thinking of going there to check, are you?"

"They have lots of capable people. I think my place is here with you two."

I almost let out an involuntary sigh of relief.

"Do you have *any* idea what's happening?" I asked.

She shook her head. "I've heard about the possibility of a . . . no . . . that's just science fiction."

"What's science fiction?"

"Well, not science fiction, but not really science, either. It's just that some people think that a massive solar flare could fry electronics."

"So, no phones or electricity, but how would that affect cars?" I asked.

"A car is nothing but a rolling pile of electronics," she said. "The military went to great expense to make sure their electronics are hard-shielded to avoid that."

"But why would the military do that if they didn't think it was a possibility?" I asked.

"I think they're more worried about a concentrated electro-magnetic pulse being used as a weapon against us."

"Has that happened?" my brother asked. He sounded scared.

"Of course not. That really is science fiction. The government and the military spend money on all sorts of crazy possibilities. But I don't believe that could really happen."

"Then what did?"

"I don't know, but whatever it is, it will be taken care of. What we have to worry about is the fact that we have just a few hours until dark and we'd better get going," she said.

"Going where?" I asked.

"Camping."

"We can't even get out of the parking garage."

"We're not going by car. We're going by canoe. We're going there," she said, pointing across the lake to the island.

"We're going to camp out there?" I asked.

"Yes."

"Is that even allowed?" Ethan asked.

"I don't think anybody's going to object."

"That's crazy. We can't go camping while all this is happening!"

"It might be the only thing we can do. Here in the condo we have no light except flashlights. We can't cook, and we can't get any water because the pumps aren't working. Over there we can break out the propane stove and cook. We can use our lanterns to see, and we can take all the water we need from the lake and use our water-purification system to make sure it's safe. Doesn't it make more sense to be there instead of here?"

It made too much sense for me to argue with her, no matter how much I wanted to.

"Look," she said, "it's only going to be for a day or two—"

"Do you really think it could take two days?" I questioned.

"Oh, less than that, I'm sure. It might be fixed before we even get the canoe to the lake. If that happens, we just strap it onto the car and go back to Plan A. Okay?"

I looked at my brother, and he looked at me.

"Okay, I guess it makes sense."

My mother balanced the canoe on her shoulders. My brother had a pack and the paddles and two fishing rods. I was carrying a pack, and a bag holding the propane stove and the two lanterns. All three of us were wearing life jackets. I could feel sweat running down my back already.

We struggled across the road through the stalled cars. This was just eerie. People were standing by their vehicles, not able to drive them but still not wanting to leave them, and they all seemed to be staring at us. We did look pretty strange. A couple of people made comments about the canoe.

We passed over the paving-stone walking path and my mother put the canoe down on the pavement with a clunk. "Either it's getting heavier or I'm getting older."

"Nice canoe," a man said. He looked normal enough, middle-aged, and he was wearing a suit and tie. I imagined that a few minutes before he'd been either up in one of those offices working or driving in his car.

"We like it," I said.

"I imagine there isn't room for a fourth person?" he asked.

"Sorry," my mother said coldly.

"Thought I'd ask. I've got a long way to walk tonight so I'd better keep moving."

He started walking away, and my mother gave us both a look. "Let's get the canoe into the water quickly," she said.

There was something about her voice, about this situation going on around us, that made me think getting on the lake would be a good idea. I helped her get the canoe into the water, then held it in place as my brother climbed in the middle and my mother put the packs on either side of him. I climbed into the bow next, and finally my mother got into the stern and pushed us away from the shore.

"It feels good to be on the water," she said.

It did. I was glad to have an ever-widening swath of water between us and everybody else.

"How far is it across the harbor?" I asked.

"At the far end by the airport the gap is only a few hundred yards, but we're closer to the middle so it's probably about two miles," she said.

We were paddling at an angle toward the island, which made it an even longer trip. It did, however, give me a view to my left, back toward the city. With each stroke of the paddle the panorama became larger and clearer. There were dozens and dozens of office towers and condominiums stretching up to the sky. Each held thousands of people who either worked or lived there, and it seemed like nearly all of those people were out on the streets.

The wind was getting stronger and it was whipping up the waves. We were catching a lot of spray. I was grateful for my life jacket. I started digging in deeper, trying to move us closer to the island. I knew my mother was working hard as well.

"It's really pretty," Ethan said.

"We should have come out in the canoe before this," my mother said.

The island's shore was a combination of rocks and sand and places where the trees and the brush came right down to the edge of the water. I looked back over my shoulder at the city towers. They were so close but so far away. How could two places that looked so different be so close together?

"I don't see anybody," I said.

"That's good for camping," my mother said. "Let's head in there and look for a spot to put ashore."

We paddled into a lagoon. It was sheltered water with no waves. There were some Canada geese, a few ducks, and a pair of swans, but there was no sign of people.

"Do you think there are fish in here?" my brother asked.

"It's a lake, so there are fish," my mother said.

"If I caught something, could we eat it?" he asked.

"If you catch it, I'll clean it and cook it," my mother said.

"I'm just going to have some noodles."

"More for us!" my mother said.

"Assuming he can catch anything."

As we continued to paddle we passed through smaller channels that separated even smaller islands. From high up in our condo, I hadn't realized how many of them there were. It was calm and quiet, and the city was now out of sight completely, which made it feel even calmer.

"Let's put in right there," my mother said, pointing with her paddle. "Then we'll have our own little island. We can be away from everything and everybody."

Somehow, that didn't seem like such a bad idea.

4

My brother had fished all day and caught nothing, so we ended up having a chicken stir-fry cooked over an open campfire for dinner. I liked the food. What I didn't like was sitting around all day doing nothing but watch my brother not catch any fish.

After dinner I sat on a log looking back across the harbor at the city. It was the one spot on our little island from which part of the city could be seen. Not that there was much to look at. The towers were just darker silhouettes against the dark horizon. There were so many stars, though. It felt like being somewhere up north away from the city, instead of just across the open harbor from it.

There were still a few lights visible. Were they from emergency generators? Some of them were moving—those must have been the old cars and trucks that were still working.

For the hundredth time, I turned my phone on, hoping to see it light up, to see that everything was normal again. So far it was as dark as the city. More than anything else I wished that I could just call Dad and let him know that we were all right. Even if he was halfway around the world I was sure he'd have heard about this. I just wanted him to know.

Actually, what I really wanted was for him to be sitting here on the log beside me.

I heard a twig snap and spun around. A flashlight was bobbing toward me. It had to be my mother. There were only three of us on this little patch of land. I knew that because we'd checked out the whole thing before we'd set up camp. It wasn't that big, but big enough that where we set up our camp—in a clearing in the very middle, surrounded by trees and bushes—we were hidden from all sides.

My mother sat down on the log beside me.

"Is Ethan asleep?"

"He was practically asleep before his head hit the pillow. Do you see anything over there?"

"Nothing. I can't see anything except some flashes of light," I replied.

"That's certainly something. Could you see our condo before it got dark?"

"There are so many buildings and they all blur together." I held up the binoculars that were still hanging around my neck. "These were good until it got dark."

"Night-vision goggles would have been useful, but even they need some light to work."

"There is some light," I said, gesturing skyward. "Have you thought about why this is all happening?"

"I've thought a lot but I don't have any answers. The power I understand, but the cars and the phones . . . that just doesn't make sense," she said.

"If the electricity is gone then the cellphone towers might not have power to relay messages."

"But that still doesn't come close to explaining why the

apps, and even the flashlight on the phone, don't work. And what about the cars and trucks and planes not working?" she asked.

"So you don't know."

"All I know is that we're here, together, and safe," my mother said. "We have warm sleeping bags in a waterproof tent. We had a good meal and, with our water-purifiers, we have a lake full of water that we can drink."

"But for how long?" I asked.

"I packed for four days of camping. We're good for that long."

I nodded. Whatever it was, it wouldn't last four days. We had nothing to worry about . . . but still I worried.

"I was wondering, why did you make us bring the canoe right up to our campsite?"

"I didn't want it to potentially drift away."

"Normally we just tie it to a tree. That would be enough. You know that."

She nodded. "I wanted it really safe."

"Were you afraid somebody would steal it?"

"There are lots of people looking for a way to get around. I don't want our canoe to be that way."

"We could have set up camp by the canoe instead of in the middle of the island if you wanted to watch it. You didn't want anybody to see us either, did you?"

"I'd prefer that nobody knows we're here."

"But why?"

"If I told you, you'd think I was a little crazy."

"Look out there," I said, gesturing to the darkened city. "Is any of this *not* crazy? Just tell me."

She hesitated, as though she was gathering her words. "I've been in some pretty desperate parts of the world."

"The Marines don't usually send people to resorts."

"Yeah, Club Iraq and the Syrian Sandals are not among their most typical locations." She laughed. "You do a tour of duty in a place where bad things are happening and you see things that you can't believe are possible. War can bring out the very best and the very worst in people . . . usually the worst."

"But this isn't a war."

"Of course not. Look, I shouldn't even be talking about any of this. It isn't like I have any information to go on."

"But you have been thinking," I said.

"Maybe too much."

I waited for her to go on. Was she thinking about what to say, or if she should say it to me?

"I want to know what you're thinking," I said. "Please tell me."

She let out a big sigh before continuing. "The world is a three-dimensional place—things that you see all around you."

So far that only sounded a bit silly.

"But I've seen another dimension, to the world and to people. There's a fourth dimension to people that you don't normally see. Normal, nice people in normal and nice circumstances become different when bad things happen. Desperate situations cause people to do desperate things."

"But this isn't desperate . . . is it?"

She shrugged. "We had a nice meal tonight. We have water to drink and a warm place to sleep. We're safe. How many people aren't going to have all of that tonight?"

"A lot."

"And what if it goes on for two or three days, or even more?" she asked.

"Do you think that's possible?" Now I was getting more worried again.

"Like I said, I have no information to base anything on. All we have to go on is what we see, and what I know about people," she said.

"Now you're sounding like you expect them to turn into zombies or something," I said, trying to joke around.

Her answer was simple and chilling. "They can turn into worse."

She put an arm around me and pulled me close.

"I shouldn't be burdening you with any of this," she said. "It's not zombies, not a war, probably nothing at all. We'll wake up tomorrow and all of this will be fixed."

"Do you really think so?"

"Of course."

She pulled me closer still, and I felt a lump against my side and instantly realized what it was.

"You're wearing your holster and gun!"

She moved slightly away. "I was going to take it camping to protect us from wild animals. There's always the potential for bears."

"There are no bears out here. The wildest animal is a swan or goose."

"I didn't want to leave it in the condo. I thought it was more responsible to bring it along. You know, just in case."

I wanted to ask her *Just in case of what?* but I didn't.

My attention was caught by something on the far shore,

in the city. It was a small spot of light in the darkness. Was it a generator, or had some lights come back on . . . ? No, it was a fire.

"Emma, let me have the binoculars," my mother said, looking across the water.

She brought them up to her eyes and stared at that spot. It seemed to be getting bigger by the second.

"It looks like it's a fire on the edge of the water," she said, answering my unasked question. "Probably just a big bonfire. That's all."

Even though I couldn't see that far, for a second I thought I could sense what she was talking about—out there was the fourth dimension.

5

_____

I smelled fire and sat bolt upright in my sleeping bag. The tent was empty. Light was flowing through the thin nylon material so I could see perfectly. For a second I didn't know where I was, but then the burning odor of the fire brought it all back.

Last night my mother and I had sat on the log and watched across the harbor as that little fire in the city became bigger and bigger and bigger. It wasn't a bonfire. It was a building that had caught fire and ultimately, we thought, burned to the ground. At its height it had thrown off enough light for us to see through the binoculars what it was—a warehouse right on the lake. Finally, as the flames died, around 3:00 in the morning, we went to bed.

It was hard to believe that the smell of the fire had drifted this far. No, wait, it wasn't just a fire. Something smelled good.

I climbed out of the sleeping bag, unzipped the tent, and crawled out. My mother and brother were sitting on stones around a little fire, and she was cooking fish!

"Good morning, sleepyhead," my mother said.

"Morning. Ethan, you caught a fish?"

"I caught three fish. And I'm prepared to share this one with you," Ethan said.

"That's very nice of you."

"I *am* the nice one, remember?" he said.

My mother forked it onto a plate and handed it to me along with utensils. She also added a piece of buttered toast and scrambled eggs that were in a little bowl staying warm by the fire.

"Thank you so much."

The fish tasted the way only a fresh fish grilled over an open fire could. Delicious.

"So what are we going to do today?" I asked my mother.

"I thought we might go for a paddle."

"Back to the city?"

"Over to Main Island to walk around. We can talk to some people and see what they know."

"Could I stay here and fish?" my brother asked.

"There'll be time for fishing later on, and probably a swim. But right now I just want us to have some quality time together."

Was this about spending "quality time" together or not leaving him alone? I knew that in every horror movie I'd ever seen the worst thing anyone ever did was go off alone. We'd be staying together. Even if my mother didn't insist on it, I would.

———————

We paddled to the big island and then hid the canoe. It took a long time but my mother cut branches and brush with her hunting knife, and we piled it on until the canoe was invisible even from a few feet away.

As we walked along the manicured paths, I noticed that there were little green shoots just breaking the soil in the recently planted flower beds. We stopped at an intersection, peering at the posted signs. In one direction were the ferry dock and the marina. A path led another way to the amusement park and a petting zoo. The third sign pointed toward the community, which was called Ward's Island.

"Which way do we go?" I asked.

"I vote for that direction," Ethan said, pointing toward the amusement park.

"It won't be working," I said.

"I don't think the petting zoo needs electricity."

"We'll go to the ferry dock," our mother said.

"Are we going . . . wait, the ferry isn't working, is it?" I asked.

"No, but there might be people there who can give us information. I don't think the animals at the zoo will know much."

We came up to the dock quickly where dozens—no, hundreds of people were standing and sitting on the benches and grass nearby. They had obviously spent the night out here and were probably tired, cold, and hungry.

Off to one side was the marina. There were thirty or forty boats, ranging from small motorboats to big yachts that looked like they were not only worth a fortune but could sleep a lot of people. I was wondering why those people hadn't just taken over the boats, and then I saw the answer. The docks holding the boats were blocked off by a high metal fence and a gate. Standing at the gate was a guard.

Just then a little boat came chugging up to the docks,

belching black smoke, the engine sounding loud and rough. There were two men on board, one of whom threw out a line, which was hauled in by a man on the dock. In unison the crowd got to their feet and surged toward the incoming boat. I had a vision of them all rushing the boat and sinking it.

Crack! A gun fired, and the crowd suddenly stopped moving.

My mother grabbed me and my brother by the arms and pulled both of us off to the side.

One of the men on the boat was standing at the bow, and in his raised hand was a pistol. He started to speak—loudly.

"I can take ten people over to the city every trip. I can make enough trips to take you all, but if you're pushing and shoving I'm just leaving."

The crowd settled to silence. Despite the gun, he was trying to do the right thing and be a good guy.

"The first group I take will be those who can offer me enough money to make it worth my trip . . . you know, my time and gas."

So much for him being nice. This was a business deal.

"How much?" a man asked.

"Yeah, how much for a ride?" another yelled.

"There's no set price. It's like an auction. I'll take the ten highest bidders," the man said.

"You can't do that!" another man yelled.

"It's my boat, my gas, and my *gun*. I can do what I want. I'm not forcing anybody to do anything. Feel free to take another boat."

"The other boats are locked up," a woman said, pointing to the marina.

"I noticed that too. Basic supply and demand. I have the supply and you all have the demand. If nobody wants to get back to the city then I'll just—"

"I'll pay!" a woman called out. "I have a hundred dollars!"

"I have two hundred and a watch! It's a really nice watch!" a man called out. He took the watch off his wrist and held it out.

More and more people started calling out offers. Voices got louder and then some people started arguing and shoving each other. Mom moved us farther back and to the side.

"I want to see but I don't want to be caught up in it," she said.

"What's going to happen?"

"This could get ugly fast. It's better for us if they all get back to the city."

"It is?"

"The fewer people here the better for us. I want to talk to that marina guard. Come on."

We bypassed the crowd—which was starting to feel more like a mob—and went to where the guard was posted on the other side of the high chain-link fence. He was wearing a uniform with a matching hat, and he had a gun holstered at his side.

"I can't let you in," he said as we approached. He was younger than I had expected—maybe in his early twenties— and the hat couldn't hide longish, curly brown hair.

"I wouldn't expect you to," my mother said. "I just wanted to know if you have any idea about anything that's going on. Oh, by the way, I'm Ellen and these are my two kids, Emma and Ethan."

"Um . . . I'm Sam, but I'm afraid I don't really know much . . . well, I know a bit. Some of the boats here have people living on them and two of them have old shortwave radios."

"And those are working?" my mother asked.

"That's about all that is working. Anything new is down, including all cellphones."

"So what are they getting from their shortwave radios?" my mother asked.

"This is happening as far as the radios can connect. Everything within four or five hundred miles has been shut down."

I knew that wasn't good.

"I hope that idiot doesn't fire his gun again," Sam said.

"Do you know him?" my mother asked.

"Unfortunately, I know them both. I went to school with both Johnny and Jimmie. At least until they were kicked out in eleventh grade."

"I think the bigger idiot would be the person who let him have a gun," I said.

"You have to understand that things are different out here on the island," he said.

"You mean there are lots of guns?" I asked.

"You can get a gun, but it's not like there are that many people with guns. It's just that the rules are different."

"I don't understand what you mean," I said.

"It's hard to explain. People are just more free to make their own decisions. There are city rules and island rules."

"You make it sound like it's another country," my mother joked.

"Yeah, that's it," Sam said. "It's like a different country. As long as you're not harming anybody you can pretty well do whatever you want."

My mother looked skeptical. Marines liked rules even more than mothers and nurses.

"I see you're carrying," my mother said.

"I'm trained and licensed."

I noticed that my mother didn't mention that she was carrying as well.

"There's no way those two idiots should be carrying that many people over open water in that little dinghy . . . Come to think of it, neither of them even owns that boat."

"I don't think I'd want to get into that boat with them," my mother said.

"Smart, but don't you have to get back to the city as well?"

"We have our own way back," my mother said. "We came over by boat."

"I understand people wanting to go home," Sam said. "It couldn't have been easy sleeping in the open. I wish I could have let them in to sleep on some of the vacant boats, but I have my orders."

"I understand following orders. So you're from here too, right?" my mother asked.

"I'm an island boy. My grandmother raised me. She has a place here on Ward's Island." He gestured off to the east. "I hope she's doing okay but I can't leave my post to find out."

"Do you want us to check in on her?" my mother asked.

He looked unsure.

"We'll see how she's doing and come back and tell you if there's a problem."

"That would be great. Thanks."

"Are there any police on the island?" my mother asked.

"There's a marine detachment that comes over from the city now and then, but they aren't here now."

I thought that explained why the rules were an option here.

"Right now it looks like I'm as close as you get to law enforcement around here," he said. "There is a volunteer fire department, though. You pass by the fire station on the way to my grandma's. Her house is a little gray cottage two doors down from it. Her name is Chris."

"Sure. And if there's any problem whatsoever we'll let you know right away."

"Thanks. She's almost eighty but she doesn't miss a trick. Just tell her that Sammy sent you."

"We will."

We angled our way around the crowd. It was still noisy, but the shoving and yelling had basically ended. Three people were already on the boat and, as we left, we could hear negotiations continuing to see who would fill the remaining spots.

6

The streets were more like paths. The houses were almost all small and wooden and cute, and I almost expected to turn a corner and run into Hansel and Gretel nibbling on a gingerbread cottage. These homes seemed to be from another time and place—fairy-tale land.

"There are a lot more of these houses than I thought there were," my mother said.

"There's the fire station. So that must be Sam's grand-mother's house . . . right there," Ethan said.

It was just as cute as the others.

"Remember, she's old, so you'd better knock really loud," I said.

My mother raised her hand to knock, but just then the door opened and an older woman appeared.

"Hello, are you Chris?"

"Yes, I am."

"I'm Ellen. Your grandson Sammy sent us to check on you."

"That's so sweet of him. I was going to send somebody to check on him. And he's doing well?"

"He's just fine."

"Would you like to come in for a glass of lemonade?" she asked.

"That's a lovely invitation but we really have to get going," my mother said.

"Going where? The world seems to have stopped. Please, join me for that lemonade, or even a cup of tea."

"Please, Mom?" Ethan asked.

"I guess we could stop for a while, and lemonade would be nice."

She ushered us inside, and as she did so she put down a baseball bat that she'd been hiding behind the partially closed door.

"Were you expecting a baseball game to break out?" my mother asked.

"One cannot be too careful right now."

"I understand," she said. "Better safe than sorry."

The little cottage was small and very tidy and crammed with framed photographs, on the end tables and walls. She had us sit at the table and she hurried off to the kitchen.

"So, how are you three holding up with all these problems?" she asked when she returned, carrying a tray with four glasses of lemonade.

"We're doing the best we can," my mother said.

"You must be anxious to get back to the city."

"We're staying over here," my brother said.

"Here, on Ward's Island?" Chris asked.

"No, elsewhere," my mother said.

"I didn't think it was here. I know everybody, and I would have heard if anybody had been taken in . . . not that people haven't been approached."

"So, is it just you and your grandson who live here?" my mother asked.

"Just us. It's been that way for a long time. His mother—my daughter—died when he was only five."

"I'm so sorry to hear that," my mother said. "It must have been very hard for—"

Suddenly there was a loud noise and the front door flew open. Two men came rushing in and—

"It's all right!" Chris exclaimed.

The two skidded to a stop. They were big and bearded and looked as much like a couple of grizzly bears as they did men.

"I invited them in," she explained.

"Okay, good. We were just checking."

Chris went over and gave each of them a hug. "I appreciate it. You are both wonderful friends and neighbors. Do you two want a glass of lemonade as well?"

"I think we're going to pass for now, but thanks. We're going to stay on watch."

They were gone as quickly as they'd appeared.

"It seems like a lot of people are checking on you," my mother said.

"We have a few people out walking, sort of a community watch. We're a very tight-knit community of about eight hundred people. Some of us have family connections out here going back almost a hundred years. I myself was a little girl when my family first set up a tent right on the spot where we now sit."

"This was a tent?" my brother asked.

"Oh no, but we lived on this lot in a tent at first. Soon my father built our first little cottage right here, and over the years things just kept getting added on. So, you said you were staying elsewhere. There really isn't much elsewhere on these islands," she said. "So where exactly are you staying?"

"We're in a tent too," my brother said.

I glanced at my mother. I knew she wouldn't want Chris to know that. There was a reason we were hiding out.

Before my mother could say anything, Chris reached over and hit a switch and a light came on over our head.

"It's over!" I exclaimed. "The power is back!"

My brother shrieked excitedly.

Chris put her hands up, as if to calm us. "Oh, my goodness, I'm so sorry. No. This is solar power. I have panels on my roof."

I felt deflated.

"There are often power failures here on the island, especially in the winter months, so many of us have solar panels and batteries. I'm afraid whatever is happening out there is still happening. Do you have any news?" she asked.

"We left the city when things started going wrong. We paddled out and stayed in a tent last night," my mother explained. "We thought it would be safer out here."

"It's strange how we can see the city but we're so separate from it."

"Your grandson said it's like a different country here," I told her.

"A better country. I guess because we know and depend on each other, we behave in a more civil manner."

That made sense. It was the way it was when we lived on military bases, too.

"I haven't been to the city for over a year," Chris said.

"Really?" I said. "How do you shop for food?"

"We have people who make grocery runs and we stock up. Everything else I need is right here. So, you have no more idea about any of this than we do?" Chris said.

"We don't know much. Your grandson told us he'd heard that it's an extensive and long-range problem. Sort of like a big power failure."

"A power failure wouldn't explain the failure of cellphones, Internet, airplanes, and all motor vehicles," she said.

She obviously knew as much as we did.

"It sounds like something that might take some time to fix," she added.

"It might. I hope you'll be all right," my mother said.

"Oh, dear, I'll be fine. We grow most of our own vegetables out here, and water is free for the taking. And as you've seen, we do look after each other. I'm more worried about you."

"We're all set," my mother said.

"I'm sure you are, but it's important that you take care of your children . . . which I imagine is why you're carrying that pistol." She pointed to the slight bump under my mother's sweater. It was hardly noticeable, even though I knew it was there.

"It's my service revolver. I'm a former Marine."

"I suspected you were former military. You just have that way about you."

"I'll take that as a compliment," my mother said. She tipped back the glass and finished her lemonade. I knew I should do the same because I was sure she wanted to leave.

"Thank you so much for your hospitality," my mother said as she got to her feet. We joined her.

"It was my pleasure. Please come again. If this doesn't pass in the next few days, I need you to come back so that I know that the three of you are all right. Can you promise you'll come back?"

"We'll come back. I promise," my mother said.

7

After letting Sam know that his grand-mother was all right, we went back to our little island and stayed put for the next day and a half. My brother caught our lunch and dinner, and it was still pretty cold but we even went swimming. We were working hard to pretend that nothing was wrong and that we were just at a strange campsite overlooking the city.

Of course, just looking over at the mainland we could tell that things weren't right. My mother spent a lot of time with the binoculars staring at the city—as did I. From what we could see the only changes were for the worse.

We didn't need binoculars to see the fires burning—especially at night. That first night there had been just one, but on the second night we'd seen three, and last night I'd counted at least half a dozen. Now, during the day, there was still a bit of smoke rising up into the air. Mostly the wind was blowing in off the lake, but when it shifted and came from the city we could smell the fires.

We'd originally brought food for four days, and my mother was working to make it last. My brother was also having luck catching fish, and Mom had been digging up some roots and dandelions and other greens and using them to create meals.

She explained that Marines were taught how to "live off the land" when they were in hostile territory. Was that where we were, in hostile territory?

My thoughts kept whirling about: no power, wanting to be home, not wanting to be home, and wondering if this was happening to my friends back in our old city, or even to my father overseas. If something like this happened where he was, well, there was no place better to be than stationed with hundreds of Marines.

My mother had remained calm, but that meant nothing. That combination of Emergency Room nurse and Marine meant that she was trained not to panic, and certainly not to show it, no matter how bad things were. She had been relentlessly cheerful, upbeat, and positive. Maybe that was what worried me the most.

Out here, things had become so calm it was boring. We sometimes heard voices from over on the bigger island but we hadn't actually seen another human being. Realistically, unless we were on the edge of our island we couldn't see anybody on the water or walking by on Main Island. We were isolated and pretty well hidden from view.

Today was going to be different, though. My mother had decided that we needed two things from the city—food and supplies from our apartment, and to talk to people and find out what was happening. It wasn't enough to stare at the city through binoculars from across the harbor.

I walked along the little path that we'd worn down from the edge of the beach to the edge of our campsite. I was surprised to see her breaking down the tent.

"Are we moving home?" I asked.

"Not moving, just making our site less conspicuous."

"What do you mean? Nobody can see us."

"Unless they come out here to our little island," she said.

"Why would they do that?" my brother asked.

"For the same reason we did. I want to make sure nobody stumbles across our cache of food or our camping gear."

"What are we going to do with everything?" I asked.

"Put it all back in the packs. And we're going to hide the packs in the thick brush down at the west end of the island."

Part of me thought she was being paranoid, but another part of me understood. We had tents and sleeping bags and camping gear—what would it be like for us without them? I didn't want to find out.

We weren't alone crossing the harbor. There were other canoes, a couple of old motorboats, some sailboats, and, strangest of all, a paddleboat that looked like a big swan. Had that come from the amusement park? Some of the people on the little vessels waved to us, and we waved back. It was like we were part of a special little club made up of only those who had a way to move over the water. I thought back to those two guys charging people to get across and figured they must be out of business. By now, everybody would have either paid to cross or found another way back to the city.

We paralleled the shore, wanting to come in as close to our building as we could. As we came near, I was reassured to see that our condo was just as it had been. In fact, all the towers looked just the same. The whole city looked the same. Except it was all frozen in place and—

"Look, there's a truck!" my brother yelled out.

An old panel truck moved along the road that paralleled the shore. It was slowly weaving around the abandoned vehicles that littered the street. It was the only thing moving.

As it drove along it was the focus of everybody's attention. People seemed to materialize out of the buildings and the side streets and they stared at it, or ran toward it, or tried to wave it down. It kept moving, sometimes swerving over to the wrong side of the road, and finally it raced away, leaving the gathering crowd behind.

"That was an old truck. That's the pattern," my mother said. "Old things, whether they're trucks or cars, seem to be working."

"I don't know what that means," I said.

"Everything new has computers, or at least digital chips," she said.

"So you think this is some sort of computer virus?"

"I hope so."

"Why would you hope that?"

"If it's a virus then they will find a cure that will potentially work just as quickly. Everything might just turn on in a second."

I could only hope that was true.

As we paddled even closer, I started to notice how many people there were. They were everywhere, sitting on benches, sleeping under makeshift tents made of tarps and pieced together chunks of wood and plastic. The park along the lake had become a shantytown. I suddenly appreciated the value of our tent and camping gear and the need to hide it all.

"Why are these people out here instead of in their homes?" Ethan asked.

"They may not have homes, or those homes could be far away," she said. "Think about all the people who drive a long way to work, and those who would have flown into the city on business. They could be from anywhere and have no way to get home."

"Or they could be from one of the buildings that was set on fire," I added. Instantly I wished I hadn't said that.

"But why are they all right here, all together?" Ethan asked.

"Partly because there's water, but partly because we're herd animals," my mother said. "They're together because they feel safer when they're together."

"Safe from what?"

"Other people," I said, answering for Mom. She nodded.

"Maybe we should just go back to our camp," Ethan said. He had that anxious going-into-an-elevator look about him.

I was thinking the same thing but didn't want to say it.

"We'll go back, but first we have to stop by our place and gather more things that we might need."

We continued paddling past the camp. A couple of people called out to us but we were far enough away from the shore that we could just ignore them and pretend we didn't hear. Past the shantytown, we came up to the shore right across from our building.

"I was thinking that we'd pull in to land just long enough for you to drop me off, and then the two of you would push off and go back out into the harbor and wait for me to come back," my mother said.

"I think we need to stick together," I said.

"I won't be long. I'll move fast and be back in less than an hour."

"I think Emma's right, we should stay together," Ethan said. He was sounding worried and a little scared. I didn't blame him at all.

"Why can't we take the canoe with us?" I said. "Ethan and I can carry it so that you're . . . you're free."

I didn't say free to do what, but it was just assumed. She did have her gun. That was reassuring. She was re-assuring.

Mom could take care of us, although I couldn't help thinking about how much better it would have been if our dad had been with us, too. He'd never let anything happen to us . . . but what was happening to him? How was he doing? I'd been so focused on us through all this that I hadn't given much thought to him since that first night.

Mom thought for a second. "Okay. Say nothing about where we've been and where we're staying," she said as we glided toward the shore, where people looked like they were waiting for us. They didn't look anything except friendly, but I was still worried.

We got into the shallow water and I jumped out to pull the canoe in.

"Let me help," a man offered as he waded in. Before I could say anything he grabbed the tip of the canoe and dragged it to the shore.

"Thanks for your help," my mother said. She offered a big smile as more people started to gather around. "Can you tell us what's been happening here?" she asked.

"Nothing good," another man said.

"No power, no phones, no transportation," a woman said. "Is it different where you came from?"

"The same. Although we came from just down the lake. We've been paddling for the last two hours." I stared down at the ground, trying to keep a neutral expression while listening to my mom make this story up.

"And it's the same there?" the first man asked.

"Exactly the same. We were visiting with my aunt when this happened. We had to leave our car there but we wanted to come back to our condo," my mother said. She pointed to our building.

"Has there been any violence where you were?" the woman asked.

"What sort of violence?"

"There's been a lot of looting, people smashing windows and breaking into stores," she answered.

"But that's just been to get food and water," the first man said. "People have to eat and drink. You can't blame them."

"There are lots of other things you can blame them for," the woman said. "People have been fighting, taking things off each other. Has that happened where you came from?"

"It's touch and go, but we haven't seen anything yet."

"Then it might have been better to just stay there. People are leaving the city in droves. I'm getting ready to leave," the woman said. "It's a long walk to my house but waiting here isn't good."

"We should probably get going too," my mother said. "We'll check our place and then we'll head back ourselves."

"Is there room for anybody else?" the woman asked.

"Sorry. This canoe is really too small for even the three of us. We have to go."

"You can leave the canoe here if you want," another man offered. His friend nodded. "We'll watch it."

There was something about them that I didn't like, and I think our mother saw it too.

"We're going to take it with us," she said.

"You can trust us," he said.

"Thanks for the offer but we're going to take it."

"No, you need to leave us the canoe," the second one said.

They came forward threateningly. One of them placed a hand on the canoe and tried to grab it. I wouldn't let go.

"Leave us alone!" my brother yelled.

"It's their canoe," another man called out, defending us.

"Yeah, leave them alone!" the woman shouted out.

"Look, we need it!" the man yelled, still trying to wrestle it away.

"And so do we," my mother said. She pulled the pistol and aimed at them. The two men looked shocked but backed away. Everybody backed off.

"You're pulling a gun on us?" the first man asked.

"You haven't given me any choice. Go," my mother said.

They hesitated.

"Go, now!" she ordered, and they stumbled away, looking over their shoulders as they moved.

I felt frozen to the spot. I had never seen my mother pull her gun on someone—or look so fierce. I glanced over at my brother, who looked just as shocked as I felt.

"Come on, Ethan," I said. "We got this." My brother and I flipped the canoe up onto our shoulders. Water splashed out and onto my head as the weight settled in.

Our mother picked up the two paddles and led the way, still holding the pistol. Still wearing our life jackets we crossed the road and went up onto the sidewalk. We circled around the building toward the underground parking area. The door was still wide open. We started down the incline and gravity was now working in our favor, although the light wasn't. It was getting darker with each step and—there was a beam of light. My mother was shining a flashlight to show us the way. What else would I expect?

"We're going to put the canoe back in our storage locker. It should be safe there, at least for a little while."

We circled down and past our car. "Can we take some of our stuff from the car?" Ethan asked.

"There's some canned food that we'll take for sure. We'll take things from the car and from the condo but we'll have to decide what's most needed out on the island. We can't carry everything so we'll take what's most important."

———————

With the canoe locked up we climbed up the stairwell. It was dark and empty and smelled of concrete dust, which didn't seem any different from the last time we'd walked down. We finally reached the seventeenth floor, where some light filtered into the hallway. Where was that coming from? That question was answered as we passed by the open door of one of the units. The front door handle was shattered and the door splintered.

"It looks like it's been kicked in," my mother said.

We passed by a second and third condo that were the same.

"Both of you behind me," my mother whispered.

She pulled her gun back out of its holster and led us down the corridor. We came up to our condo. I don't know why I'd expected anything different. The lock was smashed and the door hung limply on the hinges. My mother pushed it open and light flooded into the corridor from the big picture windows. Things were scattered all over, furniture pushed over—

"The TV is gone!" Ethan yelled. "And my Xbox!"

"Those aren't the things we care about," my mother said.

"*I* care about them!" Ethan exclaimed.

"Emma, go and get sheets from the beds."

"Why do we need sheets if we don't have beds?"

"Sheets make a big bag to carry things," she explained.

I pushed open the door to my room. It had been trashed. Every drawer had been opened and things strewn about and smashed. My computer was gone from the desk and my clothes were scattered everywhere. Somebody had gone through all of my things. The covers were sort of off the bed—not like it had been searched, but like it had been slept in. Somebody had slept in my bed. I felt disgusted and upset and afraid, but I didn't have time to think about anything. We had to just grab what we could and get back to the canoe and back to the island. I didn't want to be here if they came back.

I struggled under the weight of the bundle as I dragged it across the floor to the door of the condo. We'd cleared out all of the food from the kitchen cupboards. There were cans and bottles, boxes and containers. Then we'd added in matches, a lighter, kitchen knives, a big jug of bleach, three blankets, an extra pair of shoes each, a couple of pairs of socks, a change of clothes each, another fishing rod, and an old bow and a dozen arrows that had been stuffed into the back of my closet, unseen by the people who looted our place. The fishing rod made sense. The bow was more about feeling like it wasn't just my mother who had a weapon.

Just after I put the rod in, my mother told me to take the folding jackknife from the utility drawer and tuck it into my sock. It was weird, having your mom ask you to carry a weapon.

Each of these items on its own was light. Together they were a heavy burden to carry—physically and psychologically. We were taking away parts of our lives—the parts we needed to survive—and leaving behind everything that was personal. All my clothes, my shoes, the things I'd been given, presents, little treasures that had been so important to me. Was I supposed to take my dolls, my birthday figurines, the cards I'd saved? They had once meant everything, and now it was better to take a knife and a can of sardines.

What choice did we have? We could only carry so much. But I knew that whatever we didn't take this time might not be here for us when we returned. We couldn't very well lock the door or bar our apartment in any way—and anyway, the lock hadn't stopped them the first time.

"We'd better get going," our mother said.

"I'm ready," I said. "As ready as I can be. This is just, well . . . I don't know what to say . . . it's just that I can't . . ."

"Believe any of this," she said, and I nodded. "Stepping through the door into our condo was a step into the fourth dimension I told you about."

"It felt . . . it *feels* unreal."

"I feel the same way. I've been in war zones before. I just never thought my home, my city, and most importantly my children would ever be in one of them." She paused. "I just wish I hadn't brought you to this city."

"Isn't it happening back home as well?" Ethan asked.

"Probably. But there we had friends. Even with your father stationed overseas we had people who could help us. Here we have nobody."

"We have each other," I said. "We're here to take care of each other."

She wrapped an arm around both of us and we hugged her back. We did have each other. I just didn't know if I believed that would be nearly enough.

8

It was easy enough to pretend that we were simply on an extended camping trip, especially when we were paddling around, just the three of us in our canoe. For days now we'd been living out in the woods, sleeping in a tent, drinking filtered water from the lake and eating over a campfire, fishing, swimming—just the way we had planned to before everything happened.

These islands had never seemed very big when I'd stared out at them from our condo window. Now, paddling around them, they seemed like a lot of new territory to explore. As always, my mother was in the stern, my brother in the middle, and I was in the bow. Ethan had argued that he didn't want to come along on this expedition, that he should just be left on the island. Part of me would have been happy to leave him behind—nine days on a small island together had been more than enough punishment for me—but I knew it wasn't smart to leave him alone.

For days it had just been the three of us. Occasionally we'd hear a boat passing by, or see a sailboat out on the harbor, and a few times we'd heard or seen people pass by on Main Island, but we hadn't had any contact with any of them. We'd stayed hidden behind the bushes and trees in our own little hideout.

Ethan spent a lot of time at the edge of the lagoon fishing, and we were all grateful for his success. At least one meal a day was from his fishing rod. We'd had pan-fried fish for breakfast, lunch, and dinner on different days. I spent my time trying to be productive as well. I used the jackknife I now carried everywhere to clean the fish he caught. I brought water from the lake to our campsite and made sure that it went through the filter and was ready to drink. We were taking water from the lake side of the island, where it was open and more free-flowing, instead of the lagoon side. It was also the opposite side from where we'd built our latrine. My mother had used the camping shovel to dig a little hole in the ground that we used to go to the washroom. This was something we always did when we camped.

I also gathered wood from around the island for our campfires. I knew that sooner or later I'd have to start paddling over to the big island to get more wood. We still had a good supply of deadwood available, but how long would that last? Fifteen days, twenty days . . . how long would any of this last?

We still had our propane stove, but the fish did taste better over a real fire. Besides, we might need that propane later on. So far the weather had been good, but if it rained it would be hard to cook over an open fire.

I was also spending a lot of time with the bow. When I was younger I'd used it for target shooting in our backyard. Now I'd fashioned a target on a big tree away from our campsite and was re-learning to shoot. It gave me satisfaction and made me feel somehow just a little safer. But safe from what?

We'd developed a ritual. Each day as the sun started to go down we went and sat or stood by the log that overlooked the city. We waited, hoping beyond hope that tonight it wouldn't vanish, that instead the darkness would be pierced by the lights from thousands of office and condo windows. Each night it didn't happen. And as the sun set and darkness came we'd see the stars come out. Brilliant in the darkness. There had to be millions of them. It felt peaceful and calm, until I started thinking about what those stars being visible meant.

It was hard not to think about it. Of course, here there were no distractions—no computers, or TV, or social life, or social media, or phone. For the first few days I'd kept pulling my phone out—it felt strange not to have access to the outside world. What were my friends doing? But now all I did was go over the same things in my mind, trying to make sense of what had happened, how it was possible, what was going to happen next, and, most troubling, how long this could go on. It was spring. We could live out here for the next four months if we needed to, but what if it went even longer than that?

I'd finally put my phone away completely. I'd stuffed it into the toe of one of my extra shoes, out of sight, useless but somehow still precious.

"It's really beautiful out here," my mother said, snapping me out of my thoughts.

"What? . . . Oh yeah, it's beautiful."

We were paddling in and out of all the little inlets and lagoons, and we'd circled more than a dozen small islands, some of them much smaller than the one we called home.

As far as we could tell there was nobody living on any of them. Then again, anybody paddling by our island would have thought the same thing.

While my mother and I paddled, Ethan fished. I wasn't complaining. He'd already pulled in a couple of small perch.

I'd put my bow and a few arrows into the canoe with us, which didn't really make sense, but I liked having them close and didn't want to leave them at the camp. In some strange way they and the jackknife had replaced my phone. I guess I could have hidden them away. We had hidden a lot of things. My mother had made a series of what she called "hidey-holes." She had dug a dozen small depressions where we put things wrapped in canvas, and then she'd covered them back up so nobody would know they were there. She said it was a "Special Forces thing" to keep a campsite hidden. It was a lot of work to put everything away, but I understood. There was a fine line between being careful and being paranoid. I thought we were just being careful.

While the little islands still seemed deserted, we had seen people on the big island, some of them even riding strange-looking bicycles built for two people to sit side by side. Mom mentioned that they were probably from a bike rental business on the island. As we'd paddled we'd been waved at, yelled at, and two guys had tried to convince us to come in to "talk" to them. Instead we'd gone out even farther.

Now we were coming up to the part of the island where the airport was located. From our condo I used to watch as planes took off and landed, dreaming about flying home for a visit. The single runway had looked so narrow from that distance, flanked by small buildings and anchored by the terminal, with its control tower, I assumed, on top.

The shore near the airport area was lined by large boulders and a high concrete break wall. With the waves crashing up against it, it would have been almost impossible to land there. Making it even harder, even if you could put ashore, there was a chain-link fence topped with a few strands of barbed wire.

"It looks like a jail," Ethan said.

"Airports are always high-security," my mother explained, "especially since they've become potential targets over the last few years. It's probably completely encircled with a security fence."

"That would be even better than being on an island," Ethan said.

"Even better, it's fenced in *and* on an island," my mother pointed out. "If you had a few strategically placed guards then it would be completely secure."

Almost as if they'd heard her speak, two people appeared behind the fence, both carrying rifles. My mother changed our course slightly and we paddled farther out to try and get more distance from them. I looked over my shoulder as they watched us.

"What do you think's going on in there?" I asked.

"Probably just some people trying to make sure that they're safe from the outside world."

"Do airport guards usually have rifles?" I asked.

"At bigger airports they have their own little SWAT teams."

"SWAT?" Ethan asked.

"It stands for Special Weapons and Tactics. Is that who you think those guys with the rifles are?" I asked.

"They certainly look like they're guarding the perimeter."

"I wish we had perimeter guards," Ethan said.

He hadn't said much today. In fact, he had been pretty quiet for the past few days. Usually I wanted him to shut up, but now I was grateful when he did talk. I knew that just because he wasn't talking didn't mean he wasn't thinking or worrying.

"You've got me and your sister," Mom said.

"Yeah, her bow and arrows make me feel really safe," he said.

"Mom has a gun," I said.

"And Mom sleeps. Who's watching us then?" he asked.

"I don't sleep that much."

"You snore all night long," Ethan said.

"There aren't enough of us to take shifts," she said.

"That's the problem." I'd been thinking about this. "Three of us isn't enough."

"I have to agree," our mother said. "But I'm not sure what we can do about it."

Unfortunately, neither did I. If my father had been here we would have been four. Plus his girlfriend, that would have been five—until my mother shot her. I decided I shouldn't even joke about things like that—not now.

"I think we'd better turn around," Mom said. "The winds are picking up and it's a long way around a whole section of the open lake."

"I'm good with going back."

"We can explore the other direction tomorrow."

That was toward the marina, the ferry docks, and the settlement on Ward's Island. There would certainly be more to see in that direction.

We started back around, going much farther out from the shore to pass by the airport. We didn't want to worry those guys with the rifles.

"What's that?" Ethan asked. "There, sticking out of the water."

"Probably just some rocks," I said.

"It's not rock . . . it's shiny . . . like metal."

"It could just be garbage or—wait, I see it too," I said. "Mom, can you steer us to the right?"

As we got closer it was more obvious that it was metal and it wasn't floating. Maybe it was some sort of navigation buoy marking rocks below the surface.

Then, all at once I knew what I was looking at.

"It's an airplane," Ethan said. "The tail of an airplane."

We stopped paddling but continued to drift. There was no question. The logo of the airline—Frontier—was vividly displayed on the side of the tail. I followed its shape with my eyes, down through the wavy water, until I could make out the blurry, silvery outline of the rest of the plane. We were floating a few feet above a plane wreck.

9

The next morning we got up with the first rays of light, and after we ate, we broke down our site, hiding away our tents and sleeping gear, and got into the canoe. We decided to go to Ward's and try to find Sam, the guard, and Chris, his grandmother, to see if they had heard anything new. It had been more than a week since we'd met them, and since they had access to a shortwave radio they might know something more.

Ethan couldn't stop talking about the crashed plane, but I just didn't want to think about it. I had realized that there were no planes up in the sky anymore, but I hadn't really stopped to think about the planes that were already up in the air when the power went out. Why would they be any different from cars? Engines stalled and cars rolled to a stop. Plane engines stopped working and planes crashed to the ground . . . or into the lake.

The plane looked as though it had plunged into the water as it approached the runway. If it had been ten seconds earlier, would it have made it safely? All those people were gone because of a few seconds.

"I can see the marina," Ethan said.

At Mom's request, he was using the binoculars to see

ahead of us instead of fishing. It seemed like the smart thing to do. Besides, I was getting a little tired of fried fish.

"Do you see many people?" our mother asked.

"I don't see any people, but there are lots of places they could be hiding," he said.

That was a chilling thought. We were in a game of hide-and-seek. Most of the time we were the ones doing the hiding, out there on our island, hoping that nobody would find us. Now we were out here in the open doing the seeking.

Closing in, the marina seemed so tranquil, so normal. The boats were still sitting there, bobbing in the water. Farther out was a cement breakwater protecting the marina and the boats from the worst waves of the harbor. We angled to the inside of the wall and instantly the water was calmer.

I scanned the marina looking for somebody—Sam, I hoped—but there was no movement except for the gentle rocking of the boats. Either he had successfully kept people away from the boats or, because it was still early, they were there but still asleep. Sleeping in a boat would have been a luxury compared to sleeping on the grass, or even in a tent. I was tired of sleeping in the tent. I wanted my own bed back—I wanted my own life back!

"I see somebody!" Ethan exclaimed, just as I spotted a man on shore.

The man was quickly joined by three other people. Before we could react further, one of them called out.

"Ahoy, people in the canoe! Ahoy . . . come in for a docking!" he yelled out.

"What do we do?" I asked.

"Go in closer but we're not docking. They have the short-wave radio so they'll potentially have the most information."

As we paddled closer they were joined by other people. There were now seven or eight of them waiting. Two of them were women—that made me feel less anxious—but then I realized that two of them were carrying baseball bats and another had a knife strapped to his belt, and my anxiety level rose. We came toward the dock, but stopped with fifteen feet of water between us.

"Good morning," one of the men said.

"Good morning," my mother called out. "We were hoping to talk to Sam."

"I don't think there's anybody here with that name."

"He was the guard," I answered.

"There was no guard here when we arrived three days ago," the man said.

"I was wondering if you've heard anything more about the outside world from the shortwave radios on the ships," she said.

"There were no radios. A lot of things were stripped away before we took over the boats."

"Took over?" my mother asked.

"We needed a place to sleep. We've come together, about fifty of us—"

"Fifty-three," a woman said, correcting him.

He didn't look happy.

"Did you all know each other?" my mother asked.

"We came alone, or in pairs, or groups of a few," the woman answered. "It's better to be in a group . . . safer."

It would be safer. I wondered if they had room to make it fifty-six.

"And were you stranded out here on the island, or did you come from the city?" my mother asked.

"A couple of guys were from out here. Others came out after everything collapsed," one of the women said.

"Where are you coming from?" the man asked.

"We just paddled over from the city ourselves," my mother answered.

"What's it like over there?" one of the women asked.

"Not good. We've basically been sleeping under our canoe," my mother answered.

"Just so you know, there's no room here," a man snapped, and three others nodded.

So much for that fleeting fantasy.

"And even if there was room, it's not like we have any food."

"We just want information, and it sounds like you don't know anything more than we do. We'll get going."

"Wait!" one of the men called out.

We turned.

"Those binoculars you have are pretty nice," he said.

"They are," my mother said. "Military grade."

"I bet you can see the city well, even from here. And that's why you should leave them." He pulled back his jacket and revealed a pistol.

Before I could even think to react I realized that my mother had her pistol in her hand. I reached down and pulled out my bow, slipped an arrow onto the string, and brought it up to aim directly at the man's trunk. I'd hit smaller targets from farther away than this.

"You should stand completely still," my mother said. Her

voice was so calm, so quiet, like she was asking him the time rather than threatening him. I felt terrified.

The entire group froze. One, then another put his hands in the air until the whole group had their arms raised.

"I'm hoping I don't have to shoot you," she said. "But I will if I have to."

"My gun's not even loaded!" he exclaimed.

"I actually don't care if it is or isn't. I'm going to ask you to take two fingers of your left hand and remove that pistol from your belt," she said. "I want you to hold it by the barrel and you need to do it slowly. If I get concerned, I will shoot."

The man did what he was told.

"Now I want you to drop it into the lake," she said.

"You have to be kidding."

"Does this gun make me look like I'm joking around? Do it now. You can dive down and get it later."

"But it'll be ruined!" he protested.

"If it doesn't have bullets it won't make any difference. Do it now, or I start shooting."

"Just do it!" another man said. "I don't want any bullets flying around me!"

The first man cursed under his breath but released the gun, and it dropped into the water with a plunge and a splash.

"We're going to go now," my mother said.

I lowered my bow and arrow and placed them back in the bottom of the canoe, grabbing my paddle.

"You made yourself an enemy here," the man—now without a gun—said.

"I didn't make anything. My friends don't usually threaten me with a gun and try to rob me," she answered.

"That was his idea!" a woman protested.

"We didn't even know he was going to do that," another man added.

"If he's with you then what he does comes back on all of you. Keep in mind anybody stupid enough to pull an unloaded gun is going to get somebody killed before too long."

She lowered her pistol to her lap and picked up her paddle and we started away. I dug in my paddle and we pulled away quickly. I wanted to look over my shoulder but I knew that would only slow us down. I started counting the strokes in my head. Every stroke brought us farther away. They couldn't get us. And even if they came after us, we still had a gun and they didn't—or did they?

"Mom, what if they have rifles?"

"They don't have rifles."

"How do you know that?"

"They were standing guard with bats and knives. If they had rifles the guards would have had them out. Not just to use but to let people see so they'd be discouraged from launching an attack," she explained.

"That makes sense." I felt as if a weight had been lifted from my shoulders.

"Well, at least that's what I figure. We should still get as much distance from them as possible."

So much for lighter. I dug in deeper, while at the same time I slumped in my seat to hide behind the gun wall as much as possible.

"Get down," I hissed at my brother, and surprisingly he did.

10

———

Rounding the point, we lost sight of the marina, and more importantly they lost sight of us. Now we were safe. And then a man appeared on the shore—and he was holding a rifle!

"Mom," I gasped.

"I see him. We have to get closer to the shore."

"But, I don't understand."

"Up close we can talk to him. Up close I can use my gun. From this distance he has us at a disadvantage."

"So we're just going to paddle up to him?" Ethan asked.

"Paddle and wave and smile. I want you both to act really friendly."

She turned the canoe toward the shore and straight toward him. I was in the bow of the canoe so if he was going to shoot somebody it was going to be me.

As we closed in he was joined by a second man. He also had a rifle.

What we were doing was crazy. But what was the choice? I was certain they could have picked us off just as easily from out there if they'd wanted to. We closed in until I could see them clearly, the way they were dressed, even their expressions, which were partially hidden behind beards.

The shore was marked by stretches of boulders, some breaks, and a beach covered with stones. Behind that were the peaked roofs of houses. The men had now moved down to the beach and we moved toward them. Finally, we got close enough, and my mother spun the canoe so that we were parallel to the shore and she could see them.

"Hello," she called out. "We were wondering if—"

"I'm really sorry, but there's no room here!"

"Yes, could you please go back to where you came from!" the second man called out. "We'd appreciate it." They were no more welcoming than the marina people, but they certainly were more polite, and a little bit pleading, like they just wanted us to go away peacefully.

"We will go back," my mother said. "But we were asked to drop in to see somebody."

"Who?"

"Chris," she said.

"And her grandson, Sam," I added.

The two men turned toward each other and they were talking, but we couldn't hear what they were saying.

One ran off then, and the second man called out to us, "You can put in to shore right here, but I want you to basically stay right by your craft."

We paddled in until the canoe grated against the rocks on the bottom. I climbed over the side and sloshed into the cold water and a shock went up my legs. I should have taken off my shoes first but I didn't think about it. With me out, the canoe lightened and I pulled it forward until I skidded it up the beach. My brother jumped out without even getting his feet wet.

"You were at Chris's cottage a week or so ago, right?"

"And you were one of the men who came to check on her," I said.

"That was me. We take care of each other around here."

"Are the people at the marina part of that?" I asked.

He snorted. "Not likely. They just took over those boats. Us here, we belong here. This is our place, our home."

"They tried to rob us," my mother said.

"Figures. Some of those people can't be trusted."

"Does that include Johnny and Jimmie?" she asked.

Those were the two guys who had been selling boat rides back to the city. I'd forgotten about them until now. Were they the "couple of guys from out here" that the marina people mentioned?

"Yeah, I heard the two of them are living at the marina. You do know a lot of people."

The second guard returned, along with Chris, who rushed over to us. She moved incredibly quickly for somebody her age. She gave us all a big hug, like we were long-lost friends. I noticed my mother had tucked her gun away out of sight.

"Please come up to my house," Chris said. She turned to the guards. "Could you bring their canoe off the beach and secure it?"

My mother looked unsure.

"They'll make sure it's safe," Chris said, reading her expression. "It will be fine."

Ethan still had the binoculars around his neck. I considered reaching into the canoe to pick up my bow and arrow, but thought better of it.

"I was hoping that you've been doing well," Chris said, as we started walking.

"As well as can be expected under the circumstances," my mother answered. "Is there any news?"

"We have family members who have returned to the island with stories about what's been happening in the city, and farther away."

"We know about the fires," my mother jumped in, "and our condo was broken into and things stolen."

"I've heard stories about robbery, assaults, and even murder. There are things happening that I never thought people could be capable of doing to each other," Chris said.

That was the "fourth dimension" my mother had talked about. I was starting to understand the concept better with each passing day. Even scarier, I'd started to wonder what I was capable of doing.

Chris shook her head slowly. "There have been reports of people—mostly men—coming together in gangs and taking advantage of the situation, taking what they want and doing what they want."

"I was afraid that it was going to get much worse if things didn't get better quickly," my mother said.

"What about the police?" I asked.

"They seem to have disappeared, from what I've heard."

"They're probably busy taking care of their own families," my mother explained. "Besides, with no communication and no transportation there's not much they could do to control the situation. And how are things out here?"

"Things have always been different out here. You'll see."

We turned down one of the little paths that led between the cottages, some with laundry hanging out on clotheslines. Two kids—younger than Ethan—rolled by on their bikes.

They both said hello to Chris. There were other children out, and people sitting on front porches. An older couple was gardening, and another couple was drinking from mugs and having a discussion over the fence. Almost without exception they waved to Chris, and she waved back.

"It seems so normal here," my mother noted.

Chris laughed. "'Normal' is a word that has hardly ever been applied to this community. I think we pride ourselves on being different."

"Right now, isn't 'normal' actually pretty different?" I asked.

"Point taken. We really are a community here," she said.

"We've lived on military bases so we know what it's like to live in a community," my mother said.

"But in important ways, we're the farthest thing possible from a military base. Many of the people here are sculptors, painters, writers, actors, woodworkers, jewelry-makers, musicians, weavers, and potters. And we have a rather strong collection of yoga instructors, Buddhists, and pacifists of all sorts and kinds."

I could imagine my father's response to that. He didn't have much time or tolerance for people who weren't prepared to fight for what they believed in.

"There's a goat!" Ethan exclaimed.

I turned to where he was pointing. There was a goat, and there were a couple of sheep in the other corner of the yard.

"Yes, we have some guests—about a hundred of them," Chris said. "They were part of the petting zoo and we thought they'd be better off here."

"That's just smart," my mother said. "You can get milk from goats."

"A surprisingly large amount. Not to mention the three cows that came along. They were part of the little operation that was run to show city kids what a farm is like. There were also almost a dozen chickens and a rooster. We haven't needed an alarm clock with all his crowing in the morning."

"So you now have goats, sheep, cows, and chickens," my mother said.

"And a few other animals—I won't ruin the surprise. Keep your eyes open."

Both Ethan and I looked around. I didn't see anything, but I wasn't sure what I was expecting. Maybe there were a couple of horses, or a mule?

"Here we are," Chris said as she ushered us inside her cottage.

The table was set with dishes, and there was music! There was a record player in the corner and it was playing an old vinyl record. I didn't recognize the singer, but still, it was music to my ears!

"I see your solar panels are working well," my mother said.

"Quite well. Please sit, and I'll get you something to drink and a bite to eat."

"Do you have any more of that lemonade?" Ethan asked.

"Ethan," my mom started to chide him, but Chris just smiled and went into the kitchen. We could see her through a little opening in the wall between the living area and the kitchen.

"When the power goes out here, the city has never been in any hurry to fix it," she continued. "You probably don't know the history between the city government and our little community."

"We just moved to the city a few months ago, so really don't know much at all," my mother said.

"These islands are all technically park land," Chris explained. "And about twenty years ago the city decided that nobody should live in the park."

"I guess that makes sense," I said, and then caught myself. "But what do I know?"

"Your opinion was the same as that of most of the people in the city. So they decided to try to evict us."

"But you're still here," my mother said.

"Did I mention that we're stubborn?" She laughed as she poked her head through the opening. "We met every legal challenge with our own legal answer. It's not like we just stumbled here overnight. We were here long before this was ever a park."

She brought out a tray that had steaming drinks—it smelled like coffee—two glasses of lemonade, and a plate with crackers and cheese and slices of bread covered with jam. I couldn't believe it.

"The cheese is from our goats, the jam is from crab apples that were picked last year, the bread is baked here from ancient grains."

"I don't imagine the coffee is local," my mother said.

"Or the lemonade," my brother said as he took the glass and had a sip.

"Not quite, but we do have locally grown tea, if you'd rather," Chris offered.

"No, coffee is wonderful. We're almost out of coffee."

"I'm surprised you're not out of most everything."

"We brought out everything we had, and we're being careful and adding from local sources."

"I've caught a lot of fish," Ethan explained proudly.

"A good fisherman hardly ever goes hungry. Now dig in."

None of us needed a second invitation. I started with the crackers and cheese while Ethan went for the bread and jam.

"This is all so good," my mother said.

"We're a very self-sufficient little community. It's amazing what you can harvest if you know what's right under your feet. If you'd like, I can show you some of the root vegetables you can dig up, leaves you can eat or brew, nuts and herbs that are natural to the island and good for your health to boot."

"I think I'd really appreciate that."

I made note that my mother didn't mention that we were already doing some of that because of her Marine survival training.

"I was wondering, when the city tried to remove you from your houses, did they try to evict the boats from the marina as well?" my mother asked.

"Oh, goodness no. Those people with the boats have money. People with money can do practically what they want."

"I don't think that works right now," I said.

"Nothing works. It bothered my Sam when he had to abandon the marina."

"Where is Sam?" I asked.

"He's out on patrol. Although some of our residents are opposed to us even having a patrol. Our more vehement pacifists find it distasteful to need to be protected by men with weapons."

"Isn't that what a police department normally does?" I asked.

"That was our argument, and they finally seemed to agree. I just think it's a wise precaution."

"Better safe than sorry," my mother said. "Yesterday we paddled by the airport and they had armed guards."

"They've always had armed guards, and fences with barbed wire ringing the whole operation."

"We saw that. Did the city want them out, too?" I asked.

"Part of the reason the city wanted us out was so that the airport could be expanded."

"I thought it was because you were on park land," I said.

"That's the excuse. The airport is on park land just as much as we are, but if they could expand the runways they could land jets. There was even talk of building a tunnel from the city out to the island to get those plane passengers to and from the airport."

"But that didn't happen, right?"

She smiled. "I told you we were a pretty stubborn group out here. We managed to stop them, at least so far. We think the airport itself is a danger to the quality of our lives, to the ecology of the island, the animals and aquatic life."

"And what do they think of your community?" I asked.

"Oh, they probably think that we're a bunch of tree-hugging, organic, earthy hippies, and come to think of it that does sound like us." She paused. "But speaking of flight and natural life, it won't be long before the ducks and geese start laying eggs. You should mark nests now so those eggs can be gathered when it's time. Not much difference between a chicken and a duck egg."

"I thought about that," my mother said. "You really do like to prepare. You might have been a pretty good Marine."

"Oh, goodness knows I'd be a terrible soldier! I was an elementary school teacher."

"Isn't that sort of like being a drill sergeant?" Ethan asked, and she laughed.

"I think there might be a bit of similarity there."

"Our mother was a Marine," I said.

"But now I'm just a nurse. I work at the Emergency Department at Eastern General Hospital."

"A nurse," Chris said. "That's interesting."

"What are you doing for medical care out here?" my mother asked.

"We have a naturopath, a massage therapist, a veterinarian, two psychotherapists, two midwives, a practitioner of reiki, and a psychic."

"A psychic?" I questioned.

"I know, I know. If she was any good she probably would have seen all of this coming," Chris said with a little laugh. "Maybe it's better that we can't see the future right now, though."

I didn't agree. I always wanted to know what was going to happen, even if it was something bad.

"But there's no medical doctor," my mother said.

"No doctor and no nurse," Chris said.

"You know, if you need medical advice or assistance, if anybody does, I can help," my mother said.

"That's a wonderful offer, and perhaps we will have to take you up on that." Chris leaned in closer and lowered her voice. "And I have something I'd like to offer to you. I'm going to give you some seeds."

"What sort of seeds?" I asked.

"Carrot, some lettuce, radish, and tomato. You do have a secure, safe place to grow them, don't you?"

"We're out on a little island," my mother said.

I was surprised she'd give away even that much information, but really there were dozens and dozens of islands.

"Good. Being isolated might be better than being here."

I thought about what she'd just said. Was that her way of saying we weren't welcome to come here? Was she trying to make us feel better about it? Was that what my mother was angling for when she offered to help? And then I had one more thought. If we were going to plant seeds, was it because we were still going to be here in the middle of the summer when those seeds would become something we could eat?

"Neither of you think this is going to end soon, do you?" I asked.

They exchanged a look like neither one of them wanted to be the one to say that Santa Claus wasn't real.

Finally Chris spoke. "I know that it's better to plan for the worst and be pleasantly surprised if it's not so bad in the end."

"You're sounding like a Marine again," my mother said.

"She means that as a compliment," Ethan added.

"I'll take it that way."

Suddenly Ethan leapt to his feet, and we all jumped. His eyes were wide open and he was staring and pointing out the window. I couldn't see anything except bushes, and grass, and trees—and then two zebras trotted across the frame of the picture window!

"You get out of my garden!" Chris yelled as she got to her feet. She ran to the door, grabbing a broom on the way.

My mother and brother were right on her heels. I hesitated for a second, then grabbed the remaining piece of cheese and went after them. To my shock, there weren't just two zebras, but four of them—plus a llama and an ostrich!

"You leave my garden alone!" Chris yelled.

She ran after them, swinging the broom. The zebras ran away, kicking and bucking, and the llama ran after them. For a split second it looked as though the ostrich was going to argue, until Chris smacked it on the side. Then it practically took flight, jumping and flapping its puny little wings and rushing off to join the others.

She turned back to us. "I told you there were other surprise guests. I think the zebras are cute when they're not eating my shrubs, but I must admit I hate that ostrich. I've never liked them. They look like a snake attached to a bird!"

Almost on cue the ostrich reappeared. Or at least its neck and head did. It looked over the tall hedges that separated Chris's cottage from her neighbor's. It did look like a snake. It turned its head and stared at us with one big eye and—there was the sound of a gunshot, followed by a second and a third.

11

At the sound of the gun, the ostrich took off. We stood staring at each other until my mother said, "That's rifle fire."

I knew that too. You grow up on a military base with a firing range and you quickly learn the difference between the sounds a pistol and a rifle make. At least it was single-shot action and not an automatic weapon.

"Which direction did it come from?" Chris asked.

There was another shot, and then another. I pointed in one direction and my brother another. My mother had another opinion: she pointed south, away from the direction we'd come from.

"You three stay here and I'll go and investigate," she said.

"No, we're going with you," I snapped.

Before my mother could respond, Chris did. "We're all going with you. If it's safe for you, it's safe for us."

Mom nodded. "Just stay back. Give me a couple of dozen paces' lead."

She started off along the little path and we followed. She was holding her gun in both hands while keeping it pointed to the ground. People stood on their porches or looked over the fences as we passed. Some asked what was going on, but Chris just shrugged her shoulders. There was another shot and I involuntarily bent down. Wouldn't it have been a smart idea to run in the other direction?

Three kids on bicycles were coming up behind us. One of them started to ring his bell to warn us they were about to pass.

"Stop!" I yelled as I stood up and blocked the path, and they skidded to a halt.

"You can't go this way. You have to go back!"

"We just want to go and see what's happening," one of them protested.

"What's happening is somebody is firing a gun. What's happening is that somebody could get shot, and you shouldn't go there!" I yelled at them.

"She's right. You need to go home. Let your parents know that you're fine," Chris said.

They turned their bikes and started pedaling away.

We turned back around, and by this time my mother had moved quite a bit farther up the path. We hurried after her, while instinctively staying low, moving slightly bent over.

"I don't think people here fully understand," Chris said as we caught up to my mother.

"Gunshots aren't real until somebody is shooting at you," she answered.

As we came to the last cottage we stopped and took shelter, peeking around the corner. Well into the distance we could see across an open baseball field, where a long bridge crossed over some water.

Huddled at the near end of the bridge, hidden behind its pillars, were three men. I could see rifles in the hands of at least two of them. I had to assume they were guards but I wasn't sure. On the other side of the bridge, in the forest, I could see dozens of people spread out among the trees. I couldn't see exactly how many, or if they were armed.

As we waited, a group of men crowded in behind us and asked what was happening.

"I'm assuming those people on the other side of the bridge tried to cross over and our guards stopped them," Chris answered.

"What do you think they want?" one of the men asked.

"Food, shelter, the things everybody wants," my mother answered. "Does that bridge connect to Main Island?"

"It's the only link between Ward's Island and Main Island. That's why we have it guarded."

"It needs to be better guarded, or barricaded," my mother said.

"Is that Sam out there?" Ethan asked.

"I think so. I'll check." Chris stood up, waved, and called out, "Sammy!" That didn't seem like such a smart thing to do. He turned and waved back, but didn't get up.

"I'm going to go out and talk to them," said my mother. "Chris, can you please stay here with my kids? I'd like three of you men to go out too, but wait here until I signal."

She moved quickly across the open field, gun still in hand, closing the gap until she slid down beside Sam, sharing the pillar he was hiding behind. I felt a sense of relief when she had reached shelter. She waved, signaling the men beside us to approach. Two men left right away, but none of the others volunteered to be the third.

"Joshua, please go as well," Chris said to one of the remaining men. He nodded and then ran fast to catch the others, getting there at the same time as they all tried to hide behind the same pillar as my mother.

They huddled together for a while, and then my mother and Sam got up and started over the bridge, while two men from behind the other pillar joined them. The other three started running back toward us.

"What are they all doing?" Ethan asked.

The three men skidded to a stop in front of a picnic table. Together they picked it up and started carrying it back toward the bridge. Now it made sense. They were going to build the barricade my mother had mentioned.

My mother and the others stopped at the very middle of the bridge, the place where the arch flattened out. The men with the rifles dropped to the ground, flattening themselves out and taking aim. My mother and Sam, one on each side, using the wall of the bridge as partial cover, stayed on their feet.

"You will not be allowed to cross the bridge!" announced my mother, yelling out to the people on the other side so loudly that we could hear her words. "This is not your property! We will defend this place with force if necessary!"

The three men got to the top of the bridge with the picnic table. They turned it on its side and my mother sheltered behind it. They ran back—I hoped to get another.

More people had gathered behind us, and Chris directed another four men to gather tables as well. I was impressed—not only because she knew everybody and was able to make decisions, but because people listened to her.

Picnic table by picnic table, the barricade was being constructed. The people who were eating picnic meals or sitting watching soccer games just a couple of weeks ago could never have predicted their use now—stopping people and potentially stopping bullets.

"You need to leave!" my mother yelled out. "You will not be allowed to cross the bridge!"

A woman just behind me spoke. "Who is that woman?"

I almost said "My mother," but Chris spoke first. "She is a friend of mine, a guest."

"A guest shouldn't be speaking for us," the woman said.

I turned to face her. "Do you want to go out there where they're firing guns and be the spokesperson?" I asked—this time not able to stop myself.

She looked taken aback.

"I'm sure my mother would be willing to let you talk. Why don't you go out there? Maybe you could even stroll over to the woods and talk to them face to face."

She shook her head. "I'm not the leader . . . I shouldn't be out there."

Chris put a hand on my arm, and said to the woman, "We have to decide who is going to speak for us."

"We need a community meeting to make that decision," one of the remaining men said, and there was a mumbling of agreement and nodding of heads. Strange how one of the people without enough guts to go and bring picnic tables was speaking so strongly.

The barricade continued to be built until ten tables formed what looked like a solid wall across the top of the bridge. Nobody was going to be crossing over that easily. It was harder to see, but the people on the other side of the channel seemed to be taking my mother's advice, as there were fewer heads poking out and I could make out movement down the path going away.

Finally, my mother, along with Sam and the men who had been moving the tables, started away. The two men with rifles remained on the top of the bridge, behind the barricade. I was so glad when she returned. I wanted to give her a big hug—something Ethan had no problem doing.

"Thank you," Chris said to my mother.

"You should be thanking Sam. He's the one who repelled them."

"It was a little scary," he said. "There were at least fifty of them. We tried to talk to them, persuade them not to come," Sam said.

"And did they fire at you?" Chris asked.

"That was our gunfire, when words weren't working," Sam said.

"You shot at them?" a man gasped.

"We shot into the air, well over their heads. We didn't want to hurt anybody," Sam said.

"But they didn't fire at you, right?" another one of the men asked.

"They didn't have guns, as far as we know."

"I guess we were lucky they didn't have weapons," the woman said.

"I said they didn't have guns, but they did have weapons. They had clubs, baseball bats, and a couple of them were carrying knives."

"But why would they have weapons?" she asked.

"Why do you think they had weapons?" Sam asked. He sounded annoyed.

"Um . . . perhaps they were afraid and they wanted to defend themselves."

"Yeah, and I guess I should have asked them that question," Sam replied. I could hear the sarcasm in his voice. I liked that.

"You should have tried to talk to them," she persisted.

"I tried asking them not to cross the bridge. That didn't work, until we fired the guns to scatter them."

"You shouldn't have fired," my mother said.

Everybody turned to her. "We shouldn't have?" Sam asked.

"You used a lot of ammunition," she said. "One or even two shots would have worked. How much ammunition do you have?"

"I have close to fifty rounds for my pistol, and I think there's about the same for the rifles," he answered.

"You might need that ammunition. The next group might have guns," my mother said.

"You think they're going to come back?" Chris asked.

"If it's not them, then it's going to be somebody else."

"You can't know that," the woman said.

"Nobody can know anything, and it's really not my business to even say anything," my mother said.

"No, it isn't," the woman said, clearly feeling bold. "Nobody might come, and if they did we could probably talk to them, reason with them."

Sam snorted. He looked like he was going to say something, but his grandmother silenced him with a look before he could start.

"I think we have to meet and discuss what we're going to do in the future," Chris said. "Wouldn't everybody agree with that?"

How could anybody disagree?

"We'd better get going," my mother said.

"We appreciate what you did," Chris said.

"Yes, we really do," Sam said.

"I was just following my training," my mom said.

"She's a Marine," Ethan said proudly.

Some people looked impressed. Others—that angry woman included—looked even less pleased.

"I'll walk you back to your canoe," Chris said. "But first, can we make one stop at my cottage?"

12

The rain kept coming down. The first night, the sound of rain against canvas was gentle, and it lulled me to sleep. Now, after three days of steady rain, it was just driving me crazy. My mother had rigged a tarp to three trees to make a roof so that we had a place to stand and a place to cook. It was drier, but not dry. As soon as the wind came up it blew spray underneath. Thank goodness there was rain gear in with our camping gear. It didn't keep you completely dry, but damp was better than wet.

I put my book aside. I'd read it three times. It wasn't even a good book, but it was the only one I had. I'd noticed a wall of bookshelves at Chris's cottage. I'd have to ask her if I could borrow a book or two. I was sure she'd lend them to me. After all, she had already given us some cheese, a big container sloshing with goat's milk, and four big packages of seeds.

My mother had taken advantage of a break in the rain to use our camping shovel to plant the seeds. She'd chosen a spot in the middle of the island, surrounded by bushes but open enough to get sunlight—assuming the sun was ever going to shine again. It was important to plant the seeds in a place where nobody else could see them, since there was no point in growing food that somebody else was going to harvest and eat.

I didn't expect the seeds to shoot up but I checked on them each day, just because what else was there to do? So far there was nothing to see but tilled black earth. At least it looked like good soil. How long would it take for them to grow? Would we really still be out here by then? Was it possible this—whatever it was—was going to last that long? And what if it lasted longer? It wasn't like we could live in a tent through the winter . . . could we? I tried to put that thought out of my mind. Winter was still seven months away, and there was enough to worry about today without worrying about the future.

I crawled out of the tent and found my mother and brother sitting on flat rocks at the edge of the fire. There were a couple of shoes strategically hung above the fire to dry out.

"We're almost out of dry wood," my mother noted.

"We've used up most of the windfall on the entire island. We're going to either have to go off the island to gather more or think about breaking or cutting branches," I said.

"Emma, we're not cutting much with our little hatchet," she said.

It was the companion to our camping shovel and it was small. At least it was sharp. Mom had shown us how to sharpen the edge on a rock, and Ethan had been good about doing that.

"Maybe Chris could lend us an ax," I suggested. "And maybe some books. I'd like some books."

"I don't care about books," Ethan said. "I'd like to be dry. We could get out of the rain there."

"I was thinking we could drop in for a visit, but not today."

"So we're just going to sit here in the rain today?"

"We're not in the rain. We're under a tarp," she said.

I sat down on the third of the rocks that surrounded the little fire. The warmth felt good. As I sat down, Ethan got up. I could understand him wanting a little space. Living in a tent with your mother and sister wasn't anybody's idea of fun.

"I think it's almost stopped raining," he said. He was standing at the edge of the tarp, his hand out. "Maybe I should go fishing."

"I'm not sure how we'd be getting along without you," my mother said. "But be careful."

"I'm bigger than all the fish I might catch," he said as he grabbed his rod.

"You know what I mean. Stay alert, and get out of sight and into the bushes if anybody comes."

He nodded and started off.

"Ethan!" I called out, and he turned around. "You really are making a difference, you know, you're helping us a lot."

He smirked. "Now I'm worried. Things must be really bad when you start being nice to me."

"Then I'll stop. I hope you fall in the lagoon."

"That's better." He turned and was gone.

I was happy it was just me and my mom for a while. I had things to ask her that I didn't think I should ask when he was around.

"I've been wondering. You asked Sam how much ammunition he has. How much do we have?"

"I have four clips."

"So you have sixty bullets," I said.

She looked surprised that I knew that.

"I'm a Marine kid. I know the Beretta M9 holds fifteen bullets per magazine."

"That's a lot of bullets," she said.

Or not nearly enough, I thought but didn't say.

"Have you given any thought to us going to Ward's Island? I mean to live there?" I asked.

"I've thought about it, but nobody has invited us."

"We could ask them if we could join. You did help them," I said.

"Judging from the looks I got from some of those people, they didn't appreciate my help, or even understand that anything was wrong."

"How could they not know there was a problem?"

"People have a powerful ability to deny what they don't want to deal with. Let me give you an example. During one of my last shifts in the ER, a woman came in with her daughter, who was about your age. They told the triage nurse that her daughter had abdominal pain."

"Yeah?"

"Well, it was pretty clear to everybody that the daughter was pregnant, and the abdominal pain was probably the beginning of labor."

"But what's obvious to a nurse may not be to other people. I don't know if I'd know somebody was in labor," I said.

"But you would know she was pregnant just by looking at her. Neither the mother or the daughter seemed to know."

"Come on, they had to know."

"They claimed they didn't, and judging from the reaction of the mother when I told her that her daughter was fine and that she was going to be a grandmother, I'm positive she didn't know," my mother said. "And strangest of all, that was the third time in my nursing career I've had the same thing happen."

"That's almost impossible to believe."

"People don't see what they don't want to see. It's part of human nature."

"So you're saying that the people on Ward's Island don't know they're pregnant, right?"

She laughed. "In a roundabout way. I think some of those people will deny that anything might happen because they're afraid of what *could* happen."

"But ignoring or denying it won't stop it from happening," I said.

"In fact, it makes it more likely to happen. Have you ever heard that timing is everything?"

"Of course."

"I think we're going to have to wait until something happens before we ask them, or they ask us, to be part of things. We just have to hope it isn't too bad."

I was going to answer when we heard my brother scream.

13

My mother jumped to her feet and raced off in the direction of the scream. I hesitated for a split second and then spun around and grabbed my bow and quiver of arrows, which I'd hung on one of the trees supporting the tarp. I ran after her as he let out another scream.

I skidded to a stop just at the edge of the beach. Just past my mother I could see two men, and one of them was holding my brother around the neck, a knife in one hand.

"Stay back!" the man yelled.

My mother had the pistol in her hand, but she didn't move or respond.

"Look, all we want is the fishing rod and the canoe!" the second man yelled out. "We don't want to hurt anybody."

"But we will if we have to!" the first yelled. The knife was now not just in his hand but held close to my brother's throat.

"Look, you've brought a knife to a gunfight," my mother said. Her voice was calm and quiet and almost reassuring. "You can just leave and nothing will happen."

"I may only have a knife, but I have it to a throat. Put down the gun or I'm going to use it."

"No, you're not," she said. "Because if you do harm him I'm going to kill both of you."

"Not before I can kill him. Just back off. Let us take what we want and we're gone. I'll let the kid off on the other side of the channel."

My mother didn't answer. Was she thinking or stalling? Either way, I had to do something. I moved to my right through the bush. I didn't think they'd seen me, so maybe I could surprise them. I moved as quickly and quietly as I could until I was certain that I was past the bend in the beach. I came out into the open, and I was right. I couldn't see them but I could still hear them.

I pulled an arrow out of the quiver and slipped it onto the string. The sand of the beach softened my footfalls. I rounded the bend and the first thing I saw was the bright red of our canoe. Beside it was a small, weathered, beaten up little rowboat. That must have been how they'd got here. They'd come ashore and somehow seen our canoe and were going to steal it. It was now pulled out of the bushes where we'd hidden it and it was halfway in the water. They must have been ready to leave when Ethan saw them.

I continued to move forward and could now see the men still holding Ethan. Their backs were partly to me and their attention was fully on my mother. I crept on, positioning myself so that I was between them and the canoe and their little boat, blocking their escape route.

I was positive that my mother could see me now. She continued to talk, keeping their attention. Nobody was moving, and she had calmed them down. They were still yelling but it wasn't as loud, or as rambling, and the man holding Ethan had lowered the knife slightly so it was away from my brother's throat.

"It's time for you to put the knife down completely," my mother said to them. "You are now surrounded."

They looked around and I could see their surprise to see me. I dropped to one knee, pulled the arrow back, and aimed. The man holding Ethan brought the knife up higher again. That was not what I'd hoped for.

"Emma," my mother called out. "If he doesn't drop the weapon I plan to shoot the one holding the knife. I'd like you to kill the other one. Put the arrow right through his chest, all right?"

I adjusted slightly so he was right in my sights. "I can do that."

"We'll kill him!" the man yelled. He slouched down, trying to use Ethan as a shield.

"No, you won't. I'll shoot you in the head, and you'll simply release the knife as you drop to the ground dead. This is your last chance to put the knife down and leave."

My mother brought her weapon up and aimed, and I did the same, targeting the very center of the other man's chest. And then I realized that while this might all be a bluff, it might not be. If my mother was going to shoot the man in the head then I was ready to let my arrow fly. That thought should have terrified me, but it didn't. I was ready.

"Put down the knife!" the second man yelled. "It isn't worth it for a canoe!"

There was a slight hesitation, and then the man dropped the knife and released my brother. I felt a wave of relief rushing over me. Ethan, to my complete surprise, bent down and scooped the knife up before running to our mother.

She lowered her pistol, and I did the same with my bow

but kept the tension in place. I could pull it back up and fire in an instant.

"Both of you get to your boat," my mother said.

I eased off toward the side so that I offered them a free path to get away. They started backing away, stumbling, trying to move without taking their eyes off my mother. She advanced toward them and toward me. By the time they'd got to their boat she was at my side.

They started to push the boat back into the water. "We didn't mean to harm anybody," one of them said.

"You had a knife to my son's throat!"

"I wouldn't have done anything," he said.

"I guess that's where we're different. I would have shot you in the head," she said. "And if you ever come back here, I'm going to do it. If I see either of you again I'll simply kill you on sight."

There was such a calm tone in her voice. I didn't know if they believed her, but I did.

They both jumped in their boat and began to row away. They were digging in with the oars, trying to move quickly, but watching, as if they thought a bullet or arrow might still be coming their way.

"Are you all right?" my mother asked Ethan.

"Yeah, sure, I'm good I guess."

I could tell he was trying to hold back tears, and I smiled at him. "Thanks for saving our canoe. You were very brave."

We walked along the shore so that we could keep them in sight as they moved out of the lagoon and toward the lake. They stopped rowing and one of them stood up in the boat. He began gesturing and yelling at us. I could just barely make out the words—the threats. They finally grew tired of yelling and began rowing again. We watched as they grew smaller and smaller until they disappeared around the tip of the big island.

"Mom, would you really have shot them?" Ethan asked.

"If I had to."

"And you?" he asked me. "Would you have done it, shot them?"

"I would have tried, although I might have hit you instead by mistake. The important thing is that they're gone." I turned to our mother. "They are gone, right?"

"They are, but that doesn't mean they won't come back."

I hadn't thought about that. And now I realized it might be all I would be able to think about from now on.

After that incident, we decided that we had better explore more of the little islands around us. We wanted to see if any offered more protection. We didn't want to chance a repeat visit from those two guys—or anybody they might have told about what they'd seen—and we also needed to do something for Ethan. He was clearly shaken by what had happened, and he needed to not just sit around. It couldn't have been easy to have had a knife held to his throat. I was impressed he wasn't bothered even more, although my mother said that people in shock often show nothing on the surface.

We paddled around and ignored those islands that were too little. We needed a place that would be big enough to give us room to live and hide. Ideally, it wouldn't be too far from our present island—not just because it would be easier to move, but also because we'd be going back to water the garden we'd planted. It wasn't like we could un-plant the seeds and take them with us. So, we focused on the nearby islands that were as big as, or bigger than, our little home.

Over the past two weeks there'd been more activity around our island. We'd been hearing more voices, some from people passing in canoes or kayaks or little rowboats, some in motorboats. It was the same with the boats as with the cars: if it was old enough, it seemed to work. A couple of times there had been multiple boats, like a little convoy. One of them had four boats and twenty people. Hiding in the bushes, I'd seen that they also had weapons, including a couple of rifles. Knowing how many other people were possibly lurking around made me feel very exposed out here on the open water.

"Do you hear that?" Ethan asked.

I heard something but I wasn't sure what it was.

"Is it an animal?" Ethan asked.

"It's a baby," our mother said. "It's a baby crying."

The sound was getting louder and seemed to be coming from the little island to the left. Our mother steered us toward a small beach, and we picked the canoe up and walked it up and along a little path that led into the middle of the island before putting it down. I reached inside for my bow and arrow. The jackknife was in my pocket. Ethan had the knife that the men had dropped, which he had immediately claimed as his own weapon. And, of course, my mother had her pistol out.

The baby kept crying, and we followed the sound.

"Voices," my mother whispered.

I tilted my head to the side. I could hear them as well. Male and female—more than just two or three.

"Maybe we should go back," I whispered.

"We need to know who our neighbors are," she replied. "We'll stay quiet."

She continued forward along the path and we followed. The crying was now so loud that we had to be close. We were almost there, and suddenly a woman rounded the corner, holding the crying baby. She screamed in shock.

"Please don't shoot! Please don't hurt us!" she yelled.

My mother lowered the pistol, and at that same instant three men appeared, skidding around the corner of the path, surrounding the woman. One of them was holding a rifle. He pulled it up so it was aiming right at us.

"Drop your weapons," he yelled out, "or I'll shoot!"

I felt a rush of complete fear fill my entire body as I stared at the rifle—wait, something looked wrong.

"I think you'd better put that down," my mother said, "before I decide to fire my gun."

He didn't move. Nobody moved.

"Please," she said. "I have a real gun that fires real bullets, and you have a pellet rifle that fires BBs."

That was what was wrong. It was a pellet gun, basically a toy—the barrel and muzzle were just too small to fire real bullets.

"Look, I don't want to hurt anybody. We heard a baby crying. I'm a nurse and I thought—"

"You're a nurse!" the woman exclaimed. "She's not well. Please, could you help her, please?" The woman rushed forward so quickly that my mother hardly had time to holster her gun.

"Let's find a place where I can examine the baby."

We all sat around at three picnic tables surrounding a little fire. There were seven of them—Ian and Jess and their three-month-old baby Olivia, another younger couple, Jim and Paula, and two older men, Julian and Ken, who looked like they were also a couple. It had been the baby's father, Ian, who had threatened us with the pellet gun. He'd apologized half a dozen times and thanked my mother another half a dozen times for looking at Olivia.

My mother had used a towel and a pot of hot water to help get steam into the baby's sinuses. The baby had stopped crying. Everybody was grateful, but nobody more than the parents.

"It's not much more than a bad cold," my mother said as she handed her back to her mother. "Just give her steam a few times a day to help clear the congestion."

"Thank you. With all this rain, it's just been hard to keep her dry, to keep anything dry," Ian said.

"Where are you staying?" my mother asked.

"Here, right here," Ken explained.

"Here, where?" I asked. I didn't see tents or any kind of shelter.

"Under the tables. The plastic tablecloths have been our only protection from the rain. We have one table for each couple, and the baby with her parents," Ken explained.

"And it's not much protection at that, but it's better than being back there in the city," his partner Julian added.

"You came out from the city?" my mother asked.

"We had to. It's a nightmare," Jim said. "We had a man with a boat take us out to Main Island."

"We all paid somebody," Ian added. "We figured it would have to be better here. We tried to get the people over on Ward's to take us in."

"But they barricaded the bridge and took shots at us," Jim added.

I turned to Ethan to silence him in case he started to tell them who had been leading that charge.

"Really, they were firing into the air," Jess said. "But still, they didn't want any part of us."

"Did any of you know each other before this started?" my mother asked.

"No, we just sort of connected for protection once we were out here," Ian said. "Some of the other people out here are forming groups too."

"He means gangs," Ken said. "Or packs, like wolves. Everybody is getting desperate. People have been turning on each other. We thought it would be safer to be away from everybody else, and this little island looked like our best choice."

"And how did you get out here to this island?" I asked.

"Paddleboats. We borrowed—I guess stole, really—some paddleboats from the amusement park. And these tables were in the picnic area on the big island. We floated them out."

"Do you have any weapons other than the pellet gun?" my mother asked.

"We have a couple of knives, and a hammer, and a few

other things that could be used as weapons. I brought along my toolbox," Julian said. "Ken and I run a home renovation business."

"Where did you three come from?" Paula asked.

"We left the city the day it all happened," my mother said. "We've been living out on one of the neighboring islands."

"So you don't know anything about the city at all," she said.

"We've been back. We've watched the fires, and we've heard from other people how widespread it all is," our mother answered.

"We've heard that it could be our entire country," Ian said.

"I have no question it's the entire country," my mother said.

"How can you know that?" Jim asked.

"If it was only part of our country then the federal government would have intervened and helped. Nobody is coming to offer us assistance. We're on our own to survive."

"I don't even like to think about that," Jess said.

"But maybe we don't have to be so alone," my mother said. "We don't have much, but we have more than you have here. Why don't you join us?"

"You're going to help us?" Jess said.

"Yes. And you're going to help us. I think we're stronger together."

14

The smell was better than anything I had ever smelled in my entire life. A big goose was suspended on a spit and roasting over the fire. Ian had not only killed it—that pellet gun was apparently good for something—he had plucked and cleaned it, and now he was cooking it. Having something other than fish was going to be a real treat. Not that there was anything wrong with fish.

My brother remained the king of fishing, but Paula had become his sidekick. Over the last week and a half they'd caught so many fish that we were able to dry and store what we didn't need for food right away. They had also taken two volleyball nets from a court on Main Island and put them together, which made the holes small enough to trap fish. Ken had built a drying rack for the extra fish out of pieces of driftwood.

We had taken three dozen tables from the picnic area and floated them out to our island. That was maybe the strangest sight, because we were using two of the paddleboats from the amusement park—the ones that looked like gigantic swans. They weren't fast or powerful but they did the job.

Once on our island, the picnic tables were disassembled and we used the planks to build four small buildings—sleeping quarters—plus an open-air shelter that was now the cooking area. With a combination of mud, tarps, and plastic table-cloths the shelters had been made waterproof. They weren't much bigger than our tent, but they were more solid, and while you couldn't stand up all the way inside, they provided the best shelter. We'd given our new friends our three extra blankets, too, since we still had our sleeping bags.

The smoke from the fire and the aroma of roasting goose floated up and out through the open sides of the cooking shelter. The roof wasn't much but it kept the area dry enough to cook, even when the rains were strong.

Ian walked over and gave the goose a little spin on the spit to cook another chunk.

"It smells amazing," I said. "This is going to be the most delicious dinner. And we have you to thank!"

"Well, I don't know what we would have done without the three of you joining up with us," he said. "Believe me, we're very grateful for your help."

"We're all helping each other. We couldn't have made this shelter without you guys."

"Who would have thought that any of us would be so grateful for a wooden shelter and a blanket?"

"And a goose," I added.

"And a goose. Still, four weeks ago this would have been the dream of nobody but a homeless man."

"Four weeks seems like forever ago. And I guess that's what we are now, a bunch of homeless people."

"I don't like to think about it that way. You know, for years I used to look across the harbor and think about how amazing it would be to have a little place out here on the island."

I couldn't help but laugh. "I guess you should be careful what you wish for."

Jess, holding Olivia, came out of their shelter. "Are you talking about marrying me?"

"That wasn't just a wish. That was a dream," Ian answered.

The two of them kissed, and then he took the baby from his wife and held her close. It made me smile. They really loved each other. They were a couple . . . a family. And that was what we used to be, that was what we used to have. Would it all end for them someday, just like it ended for us?

"So, where is everybody?" Jess asked.

"Paula and Ethan—"

"Are obviously fishing," Jess said.

"Of course. Ellen and Ken and Julian are on Main Island scavenging, and Jim is on watch on the far point," Ian said.

"Speaking of which," I said, "I think it's time for me to relieve him."

I grabbed my bow and arrows to take with me. I continued to practice every day. I was getting better, and that made me feel better.

"You're not planning on eating that without me, are you?" I asked.

"You have my word, although I'm going to continue to smell more than my fair share," Ian said.

I wasn't worried. I trusted him. I trusted all of them.

We'd decided not to leave our little island after all, and I, for one, was happy to stay. We'd become a tight little group, and together we'd made things better for everybody. My mother had been right about that. While we didn't really have a leader, she was sort of the leader. She was the only one with military training, so she gave all the directions about security, about keeping us safe. Other people had different skills and abilities to contribute, but even those ideas all seemed to run through her. Safety was the most important thing on everybody's mind. And I knew that I was feeling safer these days.

During the day there was always somebody watching the perimeter of the island, patrolling along a clearly marked path that was not visible from the water. At night the perimeter path was unmanned, but somebody was on watch at the camp. It made it easier to sleep, knowing that somebody was always watching over us.

It also felt safer to have wooden walls instead of the nylon of the tent. We slept on a little platform that got us off the ground, so it was warmer, and the dampness of the ground didn't penetrate our sleeping bags. I'd started to wonder, though, what would have to be added—what could be added—to make the shelters adequate for sleeping during the winter. What worked in June wasn't going to work in January. Really, though, the old pioneers didn't have much more than this. There wasn't much difference between a log cabin and a plank cabin, was there?

I knew Jim would be walking clockwise so I walked counter-clockwise, and it wasn't long before we met. He had the binoculars around his neck and a baseball bat on his shoulder, like a guard with a rifle. I wished it were a rifle.

"I can smell that goose on every circuit," he said.

"It's even better up close. Have you seen anything?"

"A surprising number of boats out on the lake, but nothing came near. People are putting older boats back into service. It would be nice to have a motorboat."

"It would be nice to have a paddleboat that didn't look like a swan," I suggested, and he laughed.

One of the swan boats was hidden close to the camp and the second, along with the canoe, was with my mother and Ken and Julian on their scavenging trip to Main Island. There was something so funny about getting around on a swan-shaped paddleboat; it always made me smile. Here we were, camping out on a little island, thrown back in time, living off the land, and fearful of everything around us. And yet we got around in a couple of swan paddleboats.

Jim turned over the binoculars to me and headed back to camp while I took up watch. The island was now my world, and I knew it better than I had known any chunk of land in my entire life. This wasn't home and it wasn't much, but it was what we had.

I stopped walking as the towers of the downtown came into view. The city struck me as almost as strange as the swan paddleboat. There it was, across the harbor, so near and so far. We could see it but we were separate and safe. No, not safe, but safer.

During the day everything looked pretty much the same as it would have before. From this distance you wouldn't have been able to see the cars or the people. It was only after the sun went down that everything was different. The city, instead of standing out in a blaze of lights, disappeared into darkness. The towers were still visible—darker shades against the darkness—but the only lights were from the occasional vehicle on the mainland, or the running lights of an old boat moving across the harbor.

Our new friends had been in the city more recently than

us, but even their reports on what was going on there—and in the larger world—were already dated. I thought the people at Ward's Island might know more, but my mother was still reluctant to go over there. She said we couldn't go there as "beggars"; we needed to wait until we could go with an offer of strength, because lots of people were going to be showing up at their borders asking for things. We knew that for certain because our new friends had been there to ask for something, and we'd been part of turning them away. That little secret remained with the three of us.

As I walked and looked out over the water, my eye caught some movement well out in the harbor. I pulled the binoculars up. It was a boat, but it wasn't that small. It was hard to tell from this distance, but I figured it to be twenty or even thirty feet in length. There was a deck, and a flying bridge. I saw a couple of outlines on the bridge and brought that into focus. There were three figures . . . and two of them had rifles.

Quickly I started scanning the entire boat. I counted another dozen people, and many of them seemed to be carrying weapons. Of course from this distance I couldn't tell a rifle from a pellet gun from a baseball bat. I tried to count the people aboard. There were at least a dozen. I couldn't tell how many might be below deck. All I knew for sure was that they were coming in our direction.

I turned and ran toward the camp. I was alarmed to see a thin trail of smoke from our fire rising up into the air and marking exactly where the camp was located. If I could see it, wouldn't they be able to see it from out there on the water? I ran faster, skidding to a stop by the fire.

"There are people coming!" I yelled.

They all jumped to their feet.

"Where, how many?" Ian asked.

"Lots, on the water, and they've got guns." Then I remembered. "We have to put out the fire! It's visible."

Jim grabbed a tub of water and was about to pour it when Jess stopped him.

"No, that will create smoke and steam—that will make it even more visible." She started picking up dirt and throwing it on the edge of the fire to smother it.

"Be careful of the goose!" Ian exclaimed.

"Dirt on the goose is the least of our problems," Jess said.

"I've got to get Ethan and Paula," I said. "They've got to get away from the shore."

"I'll get them," Jim said. "I'll bring them back—no, I'll bring them to the meeting spot."

We had a prearranged place to go on the far side of the island where we had a much bigger version of one of our hidey-holes. It was a hole about four feet deep, topped by wooden beams that were covered with dirt and grass to blend in and hide what was beneath. The wooden door was also hidden in the bushes. It wasn't big, but we could all crowd inside to hide. My mother had insisted that we needed it, and Ken and Julian had designed and created it. At the time it had seemed like a lot of work to me, and the end result reminded me of an underground parking garage. Or worse—a mass grave. I couldn't stop myself from thinking that while we were excavating it. Were we digging our own grave?

The fire was out and the smoke trail had vanished. They would have nothing to follow now, and even if they'd already seen it, for all they could tell it might have been coming from anywhere on the big island.

"Jess, take Olivia and go to the hiding place," Ian said.

"Aren't you coming with us?" she asked.

"I'll join you there, but first, I need to see them." He turned to me. "Emma, do you want to go with me or with Jess?"

"I'd rather stay above ground as long as possible."

Ian gave Jess a long hug goodbye and then kissed Olivia on the forehead. I had a flashback to my father hugging us and giving my mother a kiss goodbye as he was leaving on a tour of duty. I wished he was here, with us. It would all be so different.

I turned away. There was no time for this. I rushed along the path and Ian fell in beside me.

"I wish my mother and the guys were here," I said.

"I wish the pistol and the pellet gun were here," Ian replied.

"I don't think that's much of a match for a bunch of guys with guns," I said.

"It's a better match than me with a knife and you like Katniss with a bow and arrows."

"Actually, Katniss would have been a match for them."

I was surprised to hear Ian laugh. "Sorry," he said, "but doesn't this all seem more like a movie than reality?"

"I was thinking more like a bad dream."

We stopped at the end of the cover at the edge of the island, and I heard voices. A shiver went up my spine. Had they already landed? Were they on the island? No, they'd been too far away, and anyway I could still hear the sound of a chugging engine.

Ian moved forward, bent over to be better hidden, and I followed suit. Slowly, trying to be quiet, we poked our heads into and through the last row of bushes. The boat was close, but it had moved slightly past us. It was far enough away for me to feel safe looking, but close enough for me to see what I was looking at.

It was an older boat—its paint was peeling and the engine was loud and trailing a cloud of bluish smoke. On board were lots and lots of men. There had to be thirty—so many more than a boat that size should have held—and they were carrying weapons. I could clearly make out that there were rifles; at least a dozen barrels were showing. Others had bats and clubs, and I thought I caught the glint of light off a blade. It was clear that there was no way we could ever be a match for them.

"Where do you think they're going?" I asked Ian quietly.

"All I care about is not here. And it's clear now that they're not stopping to visit us!"

The voices and engine noises faded away to silence as we watched them continue away from us.

"They're going toward the marina and the community at Ward's Island," I said.

"I don't know about the marina, but those people at Ward's can handle a fight. They have weapons."

"Not that many," I said.

Ian gave me a questioning look. I'd said too much, but now I had to say more.

"We've been there."

"And they didn't shoot at you?" he asked.

"Not then, but things have changed. We know somebody

there. She gave us the seeds we planted, and some food," I explained, making sure to leave out some other parts.

"Do you think they'd give us more, or even let us live there?"

"My mother doesn't think the time is right yet to ask them for anything. Our friend gave us those things secretly, and some of the other people really didn't seem too happy that we were even there."

"Well, if they didn't shoot at you then you got a nicer reception than we did. Maybe I should talk to your mother about them."

"I'm sure that would be fine." I wanted to change the subject. "We should get back and let people know we're safe."

Whatever danger those men meant was past us . . . and heading straight toward Ward's Island.

It wasn't long before my mother returned with Ken and Julian from their scavenging trip. We told her everything we knew about the boat, and about where it seemed to be headed. She calmly listened but didn't react, except to ask Ken to go and get the others from our hiding spot. There was no point in hiding any longer, and even less point in wasting the dinner.

"This is really good," Ethan said as he took another bite of the roasted goose. "This is even better than McDonald's."

"The words that all chefs long to hear," Ian joked.

"It's the best thing I've ever tasted," Jess said. "And this is coming from a vegetarian."

"The protein is good for you. Any food is good for you while you're nursing," Ian said.

"He's right, and that's a medical opinion," my mother added.

Eight of us—and Olivia in Jess's arms—sat around a picnic table having our meal. Jim had agreed to stay on watch. Ian had set the picnic table with the fine dishes and silverware that my mother and the guys had scavenged from a little restaurant on Main Island. Unfortunately, with the exception of some spices and a few tins of tomato soup that had been hidden in the back of a cupboard, all the other food had already been taken before they got there. In the middle of the table was a large, formal, silver candle-holder with six candles. They weren't lit—they were too valuable to waste for show—but it certainly looked nice. And surreal. It was like denying a pregnancy: we were sitting here eating a feast when we'd just dodged danger and maybe death.

"Did you hear that?" Paula asked.

We all stopped talking and listened.

"It sounded like thunder, or—"

My mother shushed us and the sound came again. I knew what it was.

"Gunfire," Ethan said.

My mother got up from the table and started off toward the shore. I reached back and grabbed the small remaining piece of goose meat from my plate and followed, as did everyone else except Jess and the baby.

Reaching the edge of the island, we could still hear the gunfire and now we could also see where it was probably coming from. In the distance were thick, black pillars of smoke rising into the sky.

"That's Ward's Island over that way, isn't it?" Ethan said.

"Yes," my mother said. "I think they're under attack."

That was what we'd feared was going to happen, but there was nothing we could have done except worry about Chris and Sam and the others. We couldn't have warned them, and even if we had, what good would it have done?

The gunfire was soft and muted but steady.

"What should we do?" Jim asked.

"There's nothing we can do," Paula answered.

"She's right," my mother agreed. "Just like there was no way to warn them." She paused. "Tomorrow, at first light, I'll go out on a recon."

"Recon?" Ian asked.

"Sorry, Marine talk. A reconnaissance mission. I'm going to go and look around."

"I should go with you," I said.

"I was thinking I should go alone."

"Nobody should ever be alone anywhere now," I argued. "An extra set of eyes can only help."

"I'm not going to be able to convince you differently, am I?" she asked.

"Probably not."

"We'll watch Ethan while you're gone," Jess offered.

"Then I guess it's decided," my mother said. "Let's get back and finish our meal."

15

"Emma, it's time to get up," my mother whispered.

I opened one eye. It was almost as dark as if it was closed. "What time is it?"

"Around four-thirty. You don't have to come if you don't want to."

I thought about my warm bed and about the rain that had sounded against the shelter for most of the night. I couldn't hear it now. "Has it stopped raining?"

"It's stopped for now."

She crawled toward the door and out. Ethan was still asleep. I grabbed my bow and my quiver and crawled out after her. There was no need to put on clothes or shoes because I always left them on these nights.

Ken was on watch, and he and my mother were talking in low voices by the fire. There were still a few embers glowing, and other than the stars there was no other light. The sun wasn't even a rumor yet.

Single file, the three of us moved along the path toward the place where the canoe and swan boats were hidden. We all knew the path so well that we didn't need to see it. The canoe was well up from the shore and hidden beneath some branches.

Wordlessly we picked it up and carried it to the water's edge. I went to get in the front and my mother stopped me.

"I'm taking the front. You should go in the middle," she said.

"Ken, are you coming with us?"

"Only as far as the other shore," he said. "I'm going to bring the canoe back here where it'll be safe, and I'll come back to get you later. Any idea how long this is going to take?"

"I'm not sure. It could be two hours or ten depending on what we find. Don't worry if it's longer. That might even be better news."

"I'll make sure the perimeter guard keeps an eye open for you," Ken said.

Silently we glided across the water. I'd stopped thinking about this little opening between islands as a gap and had started thinking about it as a moat. It was protection for the castle of little wooden crates that we called home.

Once on Main Island, we got out and pushed the canoe back out.

"And Ken, could you watch over everything while I'm gone?" she asked.

"Don't worry about anything."

He paddled off and we started walking. The plan was to approach the community from the side facing Main Island. That meant we'd pass close to the marina to get there. My mother had assured me that we'd try to stay in the bushes and under cover as much as possible, but there were going to be some open spots, and that was why she wanted the darkness to provide cover.

I felt more than a little nervous. I knew people were living here the same way we were on our island. I often heard or saw them, either on the island or on the water in the lagoon.

As well, my mother had told me stories. She and the others would come across people while they were scavenging. Most, she said, were friendly, but they were scared and disorganized, and that made them potentially dangerous. It wasn't going to be too long before there was almost no food left on the island that wasn't already caught or dug up, and most people didn't even have the skills or tools to get those things. Who would have thought that our fishing rods would end up being so crucial to our survival?

I tried to move as silently as my mother was moving. So far so good. We hadn't seen anyone yet. My mother stopped and I almost bumped into her.

"Do you smell fire?"

"Is it a campfire?" I whispered.

She shook her head and continued moving. We were on the edge of a row of trees that lined the path leading toward the ferry docks and the marina in one direction and Ward's Island in the other—the way we were heading. My mother darted across the path and I followed. It wasn't nearly as dark now, and suddenly I felt exposed for the few seconds it took to get across. The sun still hadn't risen but it wouldn't be long now. Maybe we should have left even earlier.

Up ahead was the white outline of the bridge that crossed the channel separating Main Island from Ward's Island. That was the bridge my mother had ordered to be barricaded, the only way across, and we couldn't possibly know if somebody was up there, armed and waiting for us to approach.

"How do we get across?" I asked.

"We don't. It's too dangerous to try. Before they just shot

into the air—now they might be shooting at people. Everything could be much worse now."

"Do you think those men from the boat are there?"

"What I think doesn't matter. We came here to get information."

"But how do we get that information if we can't cross the bridge?"

"We take a position on this island and watch. It's amazing what you can find out just by watching."

We moved toward the shore of the channel separating the two islands but away from the bridge itself. I tried to picture what was on the opposite shore. I thought we were close to where the baseball diamond sat. We settled into a little thicket of bushes that was right by the channel.

"If we'd canoed all the way we could have landed where we did before," I said.

"We're better here. On the water there's no place to hide and no place to run."

It was starting to get light. The outlines of buildings across the way were the first things to emerge, backlit by the rays of the rising sun. Next to appear, over to the right, was the backstop of the baseball diamond, which was right across the way. Everything was quiet and still.

Then as the sun continued to rise I could make out more detail. There was smoke rising from one of the cottages and its front was a blackened skeleton. Behind the façade of other houses there were two more pillars of smoke rising into the sky. Were other cottages on fire?

Suddenly there was motion as goats and sheep came running around the side of one of the buildings. Among them were two zebras and an ostrich. I watched, amazed, as they ran onto the baseball field and—I saw something out on the field.

"Are those people lying on the field?" I asked.

"They were people," my mother said.

I felt a chill go up my spine.

"There are also bodies on the path leading to the bridge," she added. She was looking through the binoculars.

I looked toward the bridge. I saw another bump and a second and a third. The picnic table barricades had been pushed aside and the bridge was deserted.

"There's nobody on the bridge. Is there anybody in the houses? Are they all gone?"

"I only know what I can see, and I can't see anybody," she said. "Just the animals and nothing—"

She stopped at the sound that we both heard. Our heads swiveled in that direction, toward the bridge, but on our side, on Main Island. A group of people had appeared on the path. They were huddled together so it was hard to tell but there had to be a dozen . . . no, definitely more. I felt a rush of fear. Was it those men? No. I could make out a couple of smaller figures. There were children and people in dresses. There were also rifles visible in the hands of two of them.

"I think it's people from the Ward's community," my mother said.

I looked harder, trying to pick out Chris or her grandson or anybody I knew by sight. We continued to watch as more people gathered. They were materializing out of the under-brush and the trees.

"I'm going to approach them," my mother said. "I want you to stay here."

"No," I said. "We need to go together."

She looked as though she was going to argue, but she didn't. "Okay, we'll go together. Follow my lead. We move slowly. Be prepared to duck and run if we need to."

We stood up and walked away from our hiding spot. We left the cover behind, but instead of walking directly toward the people we headed toward the path.

My mother undid the flap on her holster but didn't remove the pistol.

"Should I get an arrow out and put it on the string?"

She shook her head. "No. I want to be ready but not threatening. Just remember, calm and slow."

There was a sudden movement off to the side, and I jumped. My mother's hand went to her holster. There in the bushes were two figures—two children—a boy and a girl. They couldn't have been any older than six or seven. They were clinging to each other and they were wide-eyed, their faces dirty. They looked terrified.

"It's all right," my mother said. "We're not going to hurt you. Are you alone?"

The boy, who looked to be slightly older, nodded.

"Didn't I see you riding your bike over on Ward's Island?" I asked.

He nodded again.

"We're going there now. Do you want to come with us?"

By way of an answer they both came out of the bushes. They were holding hands, and then the little girl threw an arm around me and buried her face in my side.

"Don't worry," I said. "You're safe."

Strangely, saying those words—even if it was just a reassuring lie—made me feel less afraid. It was like I had to be brave for them. I guess I'd already had practice doing that for Ethan's sake.

We started back along the path with me holding the hands of the two children. My mother was slightly in front of us.

"My name's Emma. What are yours?" I asked.

"I'm Liam, and my sister is Allegra," the boy said.

"Can you tell us what happened?" I asked.

"Men came with guns. They were shooting. We had to run. Everybody had to run."

"And your parents?" I asked without thinking.

"It's just our mom," Allegra explained.

"She ran with us, but it was dark, and there were people running, and then she wasn't with us anymore."

"We'll help you find her," I said. "I'm sure she's fine but I bet she's worried about you two." Was that another reassuring lie? How could I know how or where she was or whether she was fine?

I turned and realized there was a couple with a small child between them on the path behind us. We must have passed them hidden in the bushes. I didn't see any visible weapons. They didn't look dangerous, just scared. I gave a small wave and they weakly waved back.

"Mom, there are people behind us," I called out.

She turned slightly around. "I saw them as they came out."

We rounded a turn in the path and the mass of people were there a couple of dozen yards in front of us. It was a larger group now, and more were still coming out of the trees as we approached.

"Mommy!" Allegra yelled out.

The children let go of my hands and ran toward the crowd. A woman broke free and ran out to meet them. Liam and Allegra jumped into her arms, practically knocking her off her feet.

A group of people came out of the crowd toward us and I felt panic—then I saw Chris and Sam among them. Chris waved to us, and then she wrapped her arms around the mother and two children. Sam motioned for us to come forward.

We stopped beside the family. "Thank you, thank you so much!" the woman said between sobs.

People were gathering together now all around us. The couple and child behind us rushed to join with others, and there were more hugs and tears as happy reunions took place.

"What happened?" my mother asked.

Sam started to talk and others added excited words. It all came out in a rush, and it was pretty much what we'd expected to hear.

The Ward's Island community had been attacked by a group of men who came in off the beach. They had weapons and started breaking into houses, taking food and whatever else they wanted, setting fires and shooting anybody who tried to stop them. Those were some of the bodies we'd seen on the field. Some people managed to escape by running out the back doors and through the narrow lanes. It was the people of Ward's Island who had broken through the barricade on the bridge to get away to safety. Once over here they'd hidden in the forest waiting for daylight.

"Have they gone, or are they still over on Ward's?" my mother asked.

"We don't know," a man said, and others nodded.

"Until you know, you need to get everybody into the forest and under cover," my mother said.

"Do you think we're in danger here?" Chris asked.

"If you're in rifle range you could be in danger."

Chris nodded. "Sam, can you move people away?"

"Sure thing, Grammy." Sam and another man quickly started moving the crowd into the trees. Allegra, still holding onto her mother with one hand, grabbed one of my hands and pulled me along. My mother followed closely behind. We stopped when we came to a small clearing in the middle of the forest that had some benches and a volleyball court. The nets were gone, and I wondered if somebody else had figured they could be used as fishing nets.

Many of the children were dressed in pyjamas and many of the people were shoeless. Some were limping, and others had scratches and cuts on their faces. One woman was being carried and her top was blood-stained. Had she been shot? I pointed her out to my mother and she nodded. Maybe she could help.

Chris approached my mother. "Could we talk?"

She walked away, and we followed behind as she went through the crowd asking a number of people to join us. Satisfied, she led the group—there were five other people, including Sam—and we walked out of the clearing.

"We need to make a decision," Chris said. "What do we do now?"

"We can't just stay here in the forest," a man said.

"He's right," another man jumped in. "We need to get people home, we need to check on the people we left behind, and we need to get food and water and care for the injured."

I wanted to ask a question but kept my mouth shut as Chris asked it instead.

"And if the men with the weapons are still there, what happens?" she asked.

"We didn't see anybody," a second man said.

"Not seeing anybody from across the channel doesn't mean that there's not anybody there," Sam replied. "They could be hiding in the houses and we'd never know until we were close enough to get ourselves shot as well."

"Then do we just wait?" the woman asked.

"I could go over and check," Sam offered.

"Not by yourself," Chris replied. She turned directly to my mother. "Would you go with him? Would you be part of a group that goes over?"

Everybody was looking at my mother. She shook her head. I was shocked.

"I won't be *part* of a group, but I will *lead* a group," she said.

I almost laughed out loud. That was so like my mother.

"I'm a Marine. I've been trained. And everybody in the group has to do exactly what I tell them to do."

"I'll agree to that," Sam said.

Chris nodded. "We'll all agree. I'll make sure of it."

16

We divided into two groups. The two people in the first group had guns and were going to take up a position at the bottom of the bridge. They weren't to cross until they were given a sign. The second group included my mother, Sam, and one of the big, bearded men we'd originally met at the beach weeks before, Garth. I was the fourth person, because I refused to stay back, and my mother reluctantly let me join. It seemed a lifetime ago that I didn't want to even be around her; now I didn't want to be away from her.

We headed to a spot where we were under cover and the channel was the narrowest. The goats and sheep were grazing on the baseball field but nothing else was moving. Behind them the community was clearly visible in the morning light. It was almost nine and the sun was bright, making everything—including us—very visible. One cottage had been completely burned down. All that remained were blackened posts. Behind that first row of cottages, two thin pillars of smoke continued to rise into the blue sky. I assumed they marked two more cottages that were still smoldering.

My mother motioned for Sam and Garth to go forward. The two men went to the edge of the channel and took up positions crouched behind a log, their rifles trained across the way. My mother moved to their side and then past them, silently easing into the water. I knew her gun was in its holster. I also knew it was completely waterproof. She swam across without making a splash, reached the far side, and pulled herself out and onto the shore, where she moved across open territory and took shelter behind a park bench. She signaled for me.

Crouching over I covered the distance to the channel. I slipped in and gasped when the cold water hit me. Holding my bow in one hand, with the quiver on my back, I dog-paddled across the opening. In the water, with the banks rising up, I couldn't see anybody or anything on either side.

I reached the shore but hesitated as a shiver went through my entire body. I think it had less to do with the cold and more to do with the fear of what might be ahead. The thought occurred to me that maybe convincing my mother to take me along wasn't such a great idea after all. But now I had no choice. I pulled myself out of the water, onto the bank, and in sopping wet clothes crossed the gap of open land. At last I reached the bench and slumped down beside my mother. Her gun was drawn so I pulled out an arrow and set it on the string. Part of me realized this was almost ridiculous, but the bow was in many ways more an emotional shield than an actual weapon. It was all I had to hide behind, except this bench.

My mother gave a signal and Sam slipped into the river. His rifle, which wasn't waterproof, was placed on a small wooden float. He pushed the little float ahead of him as he swam. He reached the shore and took up a position at the edge of the bank, lying flat and aiming his rifle at unseen dangers in the community.

Garth quickly followed. Now all four of us were on this side of the channel. My mother gave a signal to the other two men, and they quickly responded by moving up and over the bridge. They jogged along the path until they came to the edge of the baseball outfield and took cover behind a couple of garbage cans.

Leading with her pistol, my mother moved across the open grass. I looked left to Garth and right to Sam. They both had their rifles aimed forward, sweeping back and forth. I wanted to say something to them but my mother had insisted that we remain as silent as possible.

In a matter of seconds we reached the fence surrounding the first cottage. My mother motioned for me to stop there and she continued up the walk and onto the porch. The front door was open. She flattened herself against the wall and first peeked in and then headed inside, disappearing from my sight. I held my breath and—she reappeared and motioned for me to come with her. I raced forward, crossing the porch in one step, into the safety of the house.

"I'm glad nobody was—" I stopped myself as I saw the body lying in the corner.

"Don't look," she said.

"Is she . . . is she . . . ?"

"Yes."

The wooden floor beside the body was stained dark red with blood.

There was a thumping on the porch, and before I could react Sam and Garth came in through the door.

"Damn," Sam said. "That's Mrs. Fraser. She's a good friend of my grandmother's." He bent down beside her. "Who would want to shoot an innocent old woman?"

He took a tablecloth from the table and gently covered her with it. I was grateful.

"Did she live here by herself?" my mother asked.

"Yes. She was always here, my entire life, and now she's gone."

Sam looked shaken. Garth didn't look much better. My mother looked calm and in control. Thank goodness for her.

"Sam, I want you to signal for the other two to move up to this position. Garth and Emma, I need you to come with me as I move to the next house."

Neither Sam nor Garth moved. They were both staring at the covered body. For me it was an old dead woman but for them it was a person—Mrs. Fraser.

"Gentlemen!" my mother snapped. "I need you to do as you're ordered."

They both jumped to it. Sam ran out the door, and we followed my mother as she headed through the kitchen, pausing at the back door before proceeding out. Garth and I bumped into each other as we went through the door and we both apologized. We took cover behind a barbecue on the back deck and watched as my mother disappeared inside the back door of another cottage.

"I'm glad your mother is here," Garth said. "She really knows how to take charge."

"It's her specialty."

She reappeared and gestured for us to come forward. We crossed the opening, hopped over a small fence, and then skidded into the kitchen of the house. The cupboards were all open and canned food was scattered on the counter and had spilled onto the floor.

"Do you know who lives here?" my mother asked.

"I know who lives in every house. This is the Saunders' place. Noah and Suzette, and they have a son, Jaxson."

"Did they get out?" my mother asked. "Were they over with you on Main Island?"

"I don't think I saw them, but that doesn't mean much. They could still be over there hiding someplace."

"I understand. It's just that I thought I heard something," she said, her voice barely a whisper. "I want you to call out their names, so if they're here they'll know it's you."

"You think they might be here someplace hiding?" Garth asked.

"Possibly."

Garth walked into the living room. "Noah . . . Suzette, it's Garth! It's safe to come out!" he called out in his deep baritone voice. "It's me, it's Garth!"

There was noise from above. We looked up to a sleeping loft and suddenly a panel slid open from the rafters and a man looked down—I assumed it was Noah.

"Garth, it's so good to see you!"

He lowered himself down and then helped a boy and then a woman. They clambered down a wooden ladder and all three threw their arms around Garth. They all looked terrified, and the woman looked as though she'd been crying. They went on to explain that they'd seen men on the street and on the path behind their house. They'd seen them shoot at people and smash in the front door of the house beside theirs. When they realized they couldn't flee, they hid, getting into the attic just before their front door was kicked in.

Then they explained that they hid in the rafters while the men tore apart their house. After the men left they could hear them moving around the neighborhood until sometime in the middle of the night.

"I want the three of you to go over the bridge to Main Island," my mother said.

"Aren't we safe here now?" Suzette asked.

"We won't know until we clear all the houses," my mother answered.

"Sorry, I don't mean to be rude, but who are you?" Noah asked.

"She's a friend," Garth answered before she could. "A friend who's helping us."

"Go out through the kitchen and over to the bridge," my mother directed. "There are people waiting for you there."

"Sure, and thank you. I didn't mean any offense when I asked who you are," he said.

"No offense taken. Being careful is what needs to be done. I'm just glad you're all fine."

They disappeared at almost the same instant Sam came into the house.

"Are you three ready for the next house?"

"As ready as we're going to be," Sam said. Garth and I both nodded.

"I'm a little shaky," Garth admitted.

"If it's only a little, you're doing well. That's two down and a whole lot more to go."

I sat in the corner of the meeting room at the community center, trying to blend into the background. My mother—along with Chris, Sam, Garth, and another dozen people—sat at a large table. My mother had been almost completely silent, unless she was asked something directly. I figured she had her reasons.

I sat and listened as they described what had happened.

They hadn't seen the attack coming. The attackers had been ashore and on the streets so quickly that even their defenders with guns were caught by surprise, unsure how to react. The invaders set fire to six of the cottages. Three burned to the ground. They went from cottage to cottage looting what they could and shooting whoever they found—even if they weren't fighting back or were simply trying to run away. In the end they counted thirty-four people killed, over thirty wounded or injured, and another dozen who still hadn't been accounted for. My mother had stabilized the injured as much as she could, but with two it was probably just a matter of time before they died and added to the death count.

At my mother's direction the bodies had all been collected and were in the big room adjacent to the meeting room. They had been laid on the floor side by side, covered by sheets. A room that had once been used for yoga and kids' gym classes was now a morgue. I couldn't stop thinking about them in there. I thought that I could even smell the bodies.

Those bodies were the only part of this that seemed real to me. What I heard was only numbers. What I saw in the reactions of the people out there and around this table reminded me that these numbers represented real people. I hadn't known these people when they were anything except bodies. This wasn't a dream, or a nightmare, or even a bad movie I was watching— this was real. Those were real people. No, those used to be real people.

So much of what had happened over the past weeks seemed unreal. We were living in a makeshift camp on an island, scavenging for food, hiding from people with guns, while civilization ground to a halt.

"So what do we do now?" Chris asked.

There was silence around the table.

"Ellen, what do you think should happen now?" Chris asked my mother.

"It's not my place to say anything."

"I understand your reluctance," Chris said.

"And we all appreciate what you've done for us," another woman added.

"I guess what we're asking is probably something not you or anybody else can even answer. Will they come back?" Chris questioned.

"Oh, no, I can answer that," my mother said. "They will be back. That's a guarantee."

"You can't know that for sure," a man argued.

"Yes, I can," my mother said. There was that certainty in her voice—calm, sure, and confident. "If it's not them, it will be somebody else who will do the same thing."

That sent a visible chill around the table.

"Here you have resources that they need, and you've shown no ability to protect those resources. They took some, the things that would fit in their boat. They know there are more valuable items here so they will be back. The only questions are when, how many more people will they bring the next time, and how many more of you are going to die."

"Are you saying we should leave?" Chris asked.

"You have to make your decisions. I'm not part of your community," she said.

"But if it were you, if you were part of us, would you recommend we leave?" Sam asked.

"Leave for where?" she asked. "You have no other place to go."

"So you're saying we can't stay and we can't go," one of the other women said.

"I'm suggesting that you have to take measures to defend your community," she said.

"And how would we do that?" Garth asked.

"I've already spoken more than I have a right to." She got to her feet and I got to mine. "We have to go."

"Wait!" Chris exclaimed as she got to her feet. "Could you two please wait outside? It will just be a minute, I promise."

My mother and I stepped out and waited outside the community center. There was still daylight, but the sun was starting to go down.

"Can we get home before dark?" I asked.

"If we leave soon we'll be all right."

"You're sure those men are coming back, aren't you?"

"Why wouldn't they come back? I'm more surprised they left. This place is full of resources, and none of these people have the faintest idea how to defend it."

"Could you tell them how to do it?"

"I have some ideas, but ideas aren't enough. They need resources and weapons and, maybe most important, a will to fight. And I'm not certain if this place is even defensible."

"But if they ask you, will you tell them?"

"I'll offer them what—"

The door opened and Sam poked his head out. "Could you come back in for a minute, please?"

We went inside and my mother retook her seat at the table. I stood behind her chair.

"I've been authorized to speak for the group," Chris said. "And I want to start by once again thanking you for assisting us. We appreciate your help."

"Neighbors help neighbors, and I guess, in a way, we're neighbors," my mother replied.

"That's actually what I'd like to talk to you about. We've discussed it, and we want to offer you and your children an invitation to join our community."

That was exactly what I had been hoping for. I reached down to touch my mother on the arm.

"You have certain skills that we're lacking," a man added.

"That presents a problem," my mother said. "There are not three of us. There are six others, as well as a baby."

"A baby?" Chris asked.

"She's four months old," I said. "She's a good baby."

"We've come together to help each other. They're all good people," my mother said.

"With skills that could help," I added. "They know how to build and fish and do things."

"We couldn't consider anything without them being included," my mother said.

"I guess we could talk about the others coming," Chris said. Others nodded or said something to support that.

"I also have to speak to them to ask if they'd be willing to come," my mother said.

"Talk to them and see if they're interested, and we'll continue our conversation here," Chris said.

"Thank you, I will talk to them. But you have to understand, I'm not sure I can recommend to them that we do come here."

I was shocked. They all looked as surprised as I felt.

"But . . . aren't you just living in tents?" Chris asked.

"We've built more solid shelters now."

"Certainly not more solid than these cottages and homes," the man said.

"Not more solid, but safer," my mother explained. "We haven't been attacked by anybody."

"And if that group had attacked you could have resisted them?" the man asked.

"Oh, no, not a chance," my mother said. "But the difference is that we're hidden. Nobody knows we're there. We can only come if we feel that we'd be safer here than where we are, and at this point, this place isn't safe."

"But that's why we want you to join us," the man said. "To help make it safer."

"That can be done, can't it?" Chris asked.

My mother didn't answer right away, and the air felt thick with tension. "It's possible," she said, and the tension seemed to dissolve a little. "But it's only possible if people listen to what I have to suggest and do what I tell them to do."

"You want us to put you in charge of everybody?" the man questioned.

"We can't do that!" another added.

"I don't want to be in charge of everybody or anybody," my mother said. "But I would need to be in charge of security, or at the least have a big say in it. If you won't take steps necessary to safeguard the people of your community, then I don't want to live here to begin with."

"And if we did put you in charge, could you guarantee that we could withstand an attack?" Chris asked.

"If you want guarantees I can give you two of them. First, no place is secure from an attack with enough weapons. And second, without significant changes you're all going to be forced to live someplace else. That is, assuming you're still alive." My mother got back to her feet. "Thanks for the offer, but we have to get going." We got as far as the door.

"And if we gave you total charge of security, would you come?" Chris asked.

"Is that the offer you're making?"

They all started talking at once until Chris silenced them.

"That's the offer," she said.

"We'll let you know by noon tomorrow," my mother said. She turned and walked out the door. I hurried to catch up to her.

17

My brother clicked the light on and off and on and off again.

"Stop playing with that."

In answer he turned it on and off again.

"You know it's daytime and you don't need a light."

"I know the time of day."

"Then why are you doing it?" I asked.

"Because I *can*. I can turn on a light. I can sleep in a real bed. I can even play old-school video games on an old TV."

I did understand. It did feel good, like a little miracle.

"Turn the light off so we can use it when we need it tonight," I said. "Okay?"

He nodded.

The power was coming from a solar panel on our roof. In a world without electricity we had a little tiny bit of it, and it was pretty amazing.

It had been nine days since the Ward's Island people had invited us to join their community. Four days since my mother and all the others had agreed. And now, three days since we'd moved into this house. Really, it wasn't much more than a cottage. It was much smaller than our old house—even smaller than the condo—but we had beds: one for my brother and a second, bigger one that I shared with my mother. It had rained last night but we didn't have to worry because we were inside and we were dry and warm. It felt so good to hear the rain falling against the roof and the windows. It felt so good just to have a roof and windows. And since yesterday we had a door that closed and opened and even locked. Ken and Julian had rehung the door that had been kicked off its hinges during the attack.

My brother was lucky because he hadn't been in the house—Mrs. Fraser's house—until after it was cleaned up, and Mrs. Fraser's body had been removed, and the blood stain scrubbed from the floor. I didn't know her when she was alive but I certainly knew her in death. I couldn't help but see her lying there on the floor, by the window, first with blood pooled around her and then with the sheet draped over her.

We were there when they buried Mrs. Fraser—when they buried all of them. It was a mass funeral, the graves dug in a spot over by where the old school had been years before. There were nineteen graves for the thirty-nine bodies, with some of the graves shared by members of the same family. I'd never been to a funeral before, and I certainly had never even imagined a mass funeral. That many people dying at once was beyond anything I'd ever imagined. At least before all of this. Somehow I had expected more tears. Instead it was like everybody was in shock. I guess that made sense, because that was the way I felt and I didn't even know any of these people.

Three houses down the path from us, Ken and Julian were sharing a larger house with Jim and Paula. Jess and Ian and Olivia had their own place, a cute little cottage on the far side of the community. We were living in the homes of the murdered. We had been invited to live here only because people had been murdered and they needed my mother to help prevent more people from getting killed.

My mother seemed to be working twenty-four hours a day. She was helping the community decide what to do, where to build, how to defend, and how to survive if we came under attack again. With each passing day she was helping to make the little village more secure. People seemed to be feeling more confident. My mother wasn't so sure that was a good thing, though. As she explained it to me, it was important for people to feel insecure because the sense of danger would motivate them to listen, to work, to take precautions. Feeling safer could end up making people less safe.

My mother knew we were still in danger here, so she'd also set up an escape plan for us and the other people who'd come with us. If the place was attacked and about to fall we were to get out, get back to our island. We'd left behind lots of things we hadn't told them we even had. There were tools—the ax and camp shovel—some knives and clubs, one of the fishing rods and some tackle, the tent, sleeping bags and blankets, and all our camping equipment. It had all been buried in the hidey-holes.

Of course we'd also left behind the small vegetable patch that we'd planted. The little shoots had broken through the soil and the garden was really growing. The rains would keep them watered, and we'd weeded the bed before we left. They were fine for now, and we planned to continue to water and weed and keep the veggies growing. Chris had given us the seeds but hadn't mentioned anything about it—maybe she'd forgotten. Nobody knew about it except for those of us who had lived there. That garden, along with the shelters and the tools, was our backup plan. If something happened—if, in my mother's words, everything "went south" here—we would meet at a designated spot on the other side of the channel, and if all else failed we were to go straight to our little island. It felt good to know we had a place to go.

Part of me felt guilty for thinking like that, for planning like that. It felt selfish to plot our escape when we couldn't bring any of the others with us. The people of Ward's Island had welcomed us, given us houses, food—and yet we had a secret plan to abandon them. On the other hand, they had only taken us in because they needed us. Well, they needed my mother and what she could do.

I knew that we weren't as safe here as some people were trying to pretend. I was wearing a pair of shoes that used to belong to a woman who was murdered. I was in a dead woman's shoes—my two pairs were soggy and muddy. I wiggled my toes. They were a nice fit, and while not what I'd normally choose to wear—they were sort of old-fashioned sneakers—they were better than anything else I could find. It wasn't like I could go to the mall and buy something nicer or newer or trendier.

I'd looked through all her clothes. Again, not my style, but what did I expect from a seventy-five-year-old woman? I'd taken a few sweaters, and there was a pair of jeans that didn't fit too badly. My mother took some of the other things. At one point it actually crossed my mind that if somebody younger had been killed I could have got a better collection of outfits. That thought made me sick and uneasy for days.

The thing was that we hadn't just been given a place to live, we had really been welcomed. People were so friendly. Despite everything they still smiled, shook hands, and hugged each other—not only those people who had known each other for a long time, but even the new people, like us. I certainly felt a lot more welcome than I ever had in the city, even before all of this started.

I'd talked to my mother about all of this cheerfulness. She thought it was their way of denying what had happened and what might still happen. It was sort of like whistling as you walked through a cemetery, or people laughing at a funeral. But there was more to it than that. So many of them were artists or actors or writers, and they seemed to see the world in an unusual way.

This place was very different from the military bases where we'd lived. The people were different from our parents, and from the families who were our friends in the Marines. Marines were all business, and that business was about discipline and about killing the bad people. These people were nice and friendly and a little bit . . . quirky.

I used to think that the Marines could use a little softening, but now I found myself thinking that these people could use a little toughening up. I couldn't help but wish that there were a couple of dozen Marines living here. For starters, a Marine would certainly have offered better protection than a sculptor, a painter, a yoga instructor, or an author or illustrator of children's books.

I had to give them credit for other things, though. For instance, they knew a lot about finding food in nature. I took a sip of my tea, which was some blend of natural teas that they'd gathered from the surrounding forest. It was sweetened by honey from their beehives, and I'd added some goat's milk, from the local herd.

There was a knock on the door and I was so startled I spilled my tea. I could tell my brother was just as jumpy, but we both pretended not to notice. There was another knock on the door and I could see through the little window that it was the kid, Liam, from three doors down, the boy we'd walked back to his mother the day after the attack.

Ethan opened the door and Liam invited him for a bike ride.

"Can I go out?" Ethan asked me.

"I'd be glad to get rid of you," I said, and then realized it was bad luck to even joke about things like that. "Sure, but remember, okay?"

"I remember," he said.

There was no need for me to say anything more. Our mother had made us go over the plan a dozen times, repeating from memory exactly what would happen. It all involved what he had to do if something bad started to happen. He had to come back here if he could. That's where we'd meet. Not just us but Ken and Julian, Jim and Paula, Ian and Jess and the baby, and my mother. Our house was picked because it was the closest one to the bridge and to the channel—our two escape routes.

Ethan went out and I watched as he and Liam ran down the path to where two other guys around Ethan's age were waiting. They greeted each other like long-lost friends and vanished.

Ethan had always been good at making friends. I guess with all the moves we'd had he'd learned that skill. He'd quickly made friends at each base we'd lived on. I envied him the ability to do that. He just threw himself head first into relationships, and within a week or so it was like he'd always lived there, like these were lifelong friends. He'd done it in the city, too—well, before we'd had to flee.

I never found it so easy. There were some girls in this community who were close in age to me. One was a little older, two were a little younger, and one was almost exactly my age. Her name was Graine. What a stupid name, but there were lots of stupid names around here. There was Raine and Rainbow, Tulip, Dusk, and Dagmar. They had seemed friendly enough at first, but then I'd heard one of them say something sarcastic about my bow and arrow, and I knew that I would always be the outsider here.

I didn't care what they said—I continued to carry my bow with me wherever I went. In these circumstances it was just smart. A few more weapons in the right hands might have made a difference the last time, and if those girls weren't smart enough to know that, then they weren't smart enough to be my friends.

There was also a guy named Willow. Again, what a stupid name, especially for a guy. That was actually too bad. He was sort of cute in a hair-too-long, clothes-too-baggy way. It was funny, but most of my friends had always been boys. Girls always seemed too "girly," and the guys didn't talk as much about each other or go behind each other's backs. Guys just punched each other in the face and that was the end of it. Although I suspected a guy named Willow was more used to getting punched than punching somebody else.

There were other reasons for me keeping my distance. I was just so tired of making friends and leaving them behind each time we moved. This was no different than any of the bases we'd been posted on—how long would it last? That was how it always was, you made friends and then they moved, or you moved. Or in this case, they died. Or you died. Okay, I couldn't allow myself to go down that road. I needed to get my head someplace else. I'd go and see if my mother needed help.

I grabbed my bow and slung the quiver on my shoulder. I didn't care what anybody thought or said. I was going to head for the beach. I figured that was where my mother would be.

Walking along the path, I passed people working in their yards, sitting on their porches, or out walking and biking. Almost always they would say hello or at least nod their heads to greet me. The friendliness was part of what made them all seem so odd. I guess it might have been normal if you were living in some small town someplace, which in a way they kind of were. But there was no way it was normal to see all these super-friendly people now carrying weapons. A couple of men had clubs with them and greeted me warmly as they passed. A woman pushed a baby carriage along and smiled, and then I caught a flash of light and realized she had a knife strapped to her waist. And while I couldn't see anybody with a gun, I knew that all the weapons would be out at the borders of the community. I only wished we had more weapons. A lot more weapons.

Growing up on military bases, you got used to having weapons around. It wasn't just officers with side arms, or soldiers marching in formation with rifles on their shoulders, but armaments of all types. Seeing a tank or a rocket-propelled grenade launcher, or a half-track, or an artillery piece driving by was all part of life. What I wouldn't have given for a tank and a crew that knew how to use it. Let those guys in the boat come back any time and they'd be blown out of the water before they came anywhere near the beach! Some guys coming at us with rifles would have been as effective against a tank as a yoga mat would be against a gun. And it was too bad yoga mats didn't make effective shields because we sure had plenty of them.

Each morning people would gather in the park and do a yoga class. I couldn't help but think that being "centered," relaxed, and limber wasn't going to be much protection if those men came back. There was also a group of seniors who met by the beach and practiced tai chi. It was fascinating to watch. It was sort of a combination of dance and really, really slow martial arts movement.

The night before, the local theatre company had put on a play in the little clearing behind the houses. It was Shakespeare, A Midsummer Night's Dream. Lots of actors lived here. I couldn't believe they were doing that, but my mother explained it was just their way of trying to forget. I had to admit it was a pretty good play, and everyone seemed to enjoy themselves. I had fun, and for the first time in ages it felt like I'd even forgotten what was going on for a few minutes. Maybe putting on the play was a good thing for everybody.

Before I got to the beach I could hear the sound of hammering and the high-pitched buzz of power tools. I rounded the corner to a beehive of motion, and I quickly picked out my mother in the middle of it.

This was where the attackers had landed—the same place where we'd put in with our canoe when we'd first paddled over. A large part of the island was surrounded by big slippery rocks or a high cliff, but here there was a sandy bottom; all you had to do was come in close to the shallows and then wade to shore. Now they were building a barrier to make it harder to do that.

I stood there and watched. The shoreline was now mostly blocked by a fence that stood almost ten feet tall. It stretched out more than twenty yards, from one side, where there was a cliff, to the other side, where there were rocks and boulders too big and slippery to scale. They were building using materials that they had stripped and salvaged from fences and from the remains of the burned out houses.

Ken and Julian were leading the building efforts. They were being aided by a number of people with carpentry skills. And it was going up pretty quickly with all those hands helping.

My mother saw me, gave a wave, and wandered in my direction.

"It looks good," I said, gesturing toward the construction.

"It's a beautiful fence, but it's not much of an obstacle to a group of armed men. It will slow them down but not stop them."

"Isn't that where the armed guards come into play?"

"Well, we don't have that many weapons, only about sixteen guns and limited supplies of ammunition."

That wasn't what I wanted to hear.

She looked all around to make sure we weren't being overheard. "There are many ways to attack this community. Off this beach, up off the rocks, over the bridge, or simply coming in across the channel."

"But you have a plan for all of them, right?"

"We're going to try our best, but the problem isn't just the lack of arms, it's the lack of people willing to use those arms." She let out a big sigh. "I shouldn't really be telling you all this, but there's only one person here that I really trust."

"Who's that?"

She smiled and gave me a one-armed hug. "Well, you, of course."

I hadn't expected that, but it didn't really surprise me, either. Somehow as the world was getting more hostile, the relationship between us had become friendlier.

Mom sighed as she looked around at the beach. "Those two men on the shore that night, do you know what they did when the attack happened? They ran away and hid without even firing a shot."

"What can you expect?" I asked. "It's not like they're Marines."

"They're the farthest thing from Marines. Maybe I have to remember that and not be so hard on them . . . so hard on everybody."

From her, that was as close to an apology as I'd ever heard.

"Sometimes you have to be hard to survive," I said. "Maybe those guys ran because they figured they just couldn't stop them."

"They couldn't, but they could have slowed them down, or at least fired at them and warned people. Do you think if they were Marines they would have turned and run?" she asked.

I moved in closer. "But *we're* planning on leaving if it gets bad."

"It's important to always have a backup plan."

"And how is that any different?" I asked.

"Running away and making a tactical retreat are two very different things. We're going to try to make it work. I'll do what I can do."

"But you don't think it can work, do you?"

She shook her head.

"Then shouldn't everybody have a backup plan?"

"I can't be responsible for all of them," she said.

"But what about Sam, and maybe Garth? What about Chris?"

"I've thought about that. We just have to be careful about who and how. This has to be kept a secret, and there are already ten of us who know."

"I don't think we have to worry much about Olivia saying anything."

"After you, she's the one I trust the most to keep it secret." She paused. "It would be hard to take Chris with us. This is her community and she's not going to leave them behind. That's what would make getting Sam to go so difficult. You'll have to trust me to find the right time to ask . . . if we're going to ask them at all."

She was quiet for a minute, then she said, "These people, they just don't get it."

"They're helping you build the defenses."

"Some of them are. Others are too busy putting on plays."

"It was a good play."

"It was a bad move. Aside from draining the batteries, think about the danger of having those stage lights on at night out in the open like that."

I hadn't thought of that.

"We shouldn't be drawing such attention to ourselves. There shouldn't even be lights on in people's houses without blackout screens to block the light."

"Have you talked to Chris about that?" I asked.

"I've talked to her and she's talked to people, but like I said, some of them just don't get it. It's like they didn't see the bodies, weren't there for the funerals."

"I guess they're just scared."

"They should be scared enough to try to do the things that they need to do to survive." She realized her voice had gotten louder and some people were looking at us. "Look," she said quietly, "in the meantime, we'll do our best here to prepare them. For now we'll think hard, work harder, and keep our eyes open for anything that might make the survival of this community possible."

I nodded in agreement, although I didn't know what I could really do.

My mother gave me a long hug and then turned and went back to work.

I thought about what she'd said about trusting me more than anybody else. It made me feel good to know that was how she felt. But was it really reassuring to think that my bow and arrows and I were the next best thing to the Marines right now?

18

As I walked back to the house, lost in thought, two ostriches appeared on the path just ahead of me. They stopped and stared at me the same way I stared at them. The difference was that they didn't look afraid of me. They stood there, turning their skinny heads, aiming those beady little black eyes directly at me.

"Shoo!" I called out.

They didn't move away.

"Go away!" I yelled, and stomped my feet.

They didn't run away but instead took a couple of steps toward me. Almost instinctively I went to take an arrow out of my quiver, but I stopped myself. Did I think I needed to shoot them? I just had to find a way around them. The path wasn't wide and bushes hemmed me in on both sides. I'd turned to start back when I realized the whole scene was being witnessed.

It was Willow, the boy in the baggy clothes. "I don't like them either," he said.

He walked right up beside me and the two of us stared at the big birds.

"I read that an ostrich can kill a lion with a kick," he said.

"Something about them just unnerves me," I admitted. "Chris says they remind her of a snake attached to a bird."

Just then three little boys rode up from behind us on their bikes. Before I could even think to stop them they shot past us and raced straight toward the ostriches. They screamed and yelled and the two ostriches jumped and ran away, disappearing through the hedges.

I couldn't help but laugh. "I guess little boys are scarier than lions."

"I thought for a second you were going to take a shot at the ostriches with your bow and arrow," Willow said.

"I wasn't," I lied. "But if I had I would have hit one of them dead on."

"I believe you. I've seen you practice out by the abandoned house."

"You've watched me practice?" I'd deliberately gone to a spot where there was nobody. Not just because I didn't want to accidentally hit somebody but because I didn't want to be observed.

"Don't get me wrong, I didn't watch you for long, and I wasn't stalking you. That would be creepy."

"That would be," I agreed.

He looked embarrassed.

"I guess there are no secrets around here," I said, trying to ease the awkwardness.

"Not many." He smiled. "It looks like a nice compound bow."

"Thanks . . . wait . . . you know it's a compound bow?"

"I know a little bit about bows. And you're pretty accurate with it. Of course, it's not nearly as effective as a crossbow."

"A crossbow?"

"It's a medieval weapon that—"

"I know what a crossbow is, I just didn't expect you to mention it."

"Did you know that crossbows revolutionized warfare? They're more accurate, have a longer range, and can be taught to people with less training and with less skill. It takes a long time to get as good as you are with a bow and arrow."

"Thanks, I guess. And just how and why do you know all of this?"

"Unavoidable. My father is sort of a medieval geek."

"I'm not even sure what that means."

"It's almost embarrassing to say, but he and my mother go to medieval fairs. They're into LARPing."

"Okay, now I'm lost."

"LARP stands for Live-Action Role Playing. They dress like they're in that time period, use imitation weapons, and act out things like battles."

I stared at him and tried unsuccessfully to hold back a laugh.

He grinned. "Yeah, I know, it does sound strange and funny."

"Well, my parents sort of did that too."

"They did?"

"They dressed like Marines and went to places with real weapons and killed real people."

"That's very different. Trust me, it's hard enough to be named Willow without having parents who do things like make-believe sword-fighting."

"I guess it is a different sort of name."

"If they were going to name me after a tree, couldn't they have gone with Oak or something more, you know, masculine?"

"I don't think of trees as being male or female," I said.

"You would if you were called Willow." He paused. "Now I'm even more embarrassed to tell you that when I was little they used to bring me along. And obviously, I was a prince," he said, and laughed.

"Believe me, all parents make us do things we don't want to do. But wouldn't it be great right now if your family actually had a crossbow to go along with your costumes?"

"We do have a crossbow."

"A real crossbow?"

"Yeah. Would you like to see it?"

The crossbow was surprisingly heavy, made of dark wood, and it had a really powerful feel.

"It's beautiful," I said as I hefted it in my hands and admired the decorative engravings in the wood.

"I really appreciate you saying that, Emma," Willow's father said. "Not many people appreciate the beauty of a crossbow."

We were gathered in the living room of Willow's house, which was two streets over from the one I was staying in. It was made with stucco over wooden slats and it even looked like a medieval cottage.

"And you have the arrows—I mean the bolts—that go with it, right?" I asked.

"At least a hundred."

"I think more," Willow said.

"Many, many more," his mother added.

He shrugged. "What good is a crossbow without bolts? From medium to close range it's as deadly as a gun."

I thought I'd rather have a gun.

"To be honest, I've always liked the elegance of a sword. I'm much better with a sword. I'm a bit of a swordsman," his father said.

"He is," his wife agreed. "He's won more than his fair share of tournaments."

I looked at Willow and he answered my glance with a subtle snicker, unseen by his parents.

"Some people think we're a bit odd for having this as a hobby," his father said. "They can't understand all the pretend, but there's nothing pretend about the trophies I've won or the sword I used to win them. Would you like to see my sword?" he asked.

"Sure."

He led me through the kitchen and out to the backyard. Willow came with us. The yard was filled with lots of strange metal sculptures. Some looked new and others were rusting away. He opened a sliding door to a garage and flicked on a light. Inside the door was a mannequin wearing a full suit of armor. It practically glittered in the light.

"Welcome to the Middle Ages," he said as he shepherded us into the garage.

On the wall were a couple of shields, a big long pole that I recognized from movies as something that knights used to knock each other off horses, a big mace thing with spiky balls attached, and a sword. Along another wall were all sorts of books, and pictures of knights on horses, and castles. There were also models of castles on a shelf, some of them very large and intricate. At the far end of the garage was some machinery, like big power tools. They seemed strangely out of place in the medieval setting.

"This . . . this is amazing," I stammered. "This is what you do for a living?"

"This is my passion and obsession, but not my occupation."

"My father is a professional magician," Willow said.

Somehow, I wasn't surprised—here on the island that was a normal-sounding job.

"And I am his lovely assistant," Willow's mother said as she gave a little bow.

Willow avoided my eye.

His father took down a large sword from the wall. "This is Caliburn, or as you might more commonly know it, Excalibur. Do you know the story of the sword in the stone?"

"Didn't King Arthur pull a sword out of stone, and that meant he was the real king?"

"There's a little more to the story than that, but that is the essence of the legend. You realize if we were in medieval times none of this would have happened."

"None of what?" I asked.

"What we're going through. It's our reliance on modern technology that has left us so vulnerable to its sudden loss. Great kingdoms lived and died without computers, or telephones, or electricity. Back in the day all a man needed was a suit of armor, a sharp sword, and his steed."

He'd started speaking in an English accent, which made

the whole thing seem more bizarre, and Willow looked even more embarrassed. But after all, embarrassing kids was what parents did best.

"I don't know about steeds, but there are a couple of zebras around you could ride," Willow said. "Do you want me to try to saddle one up for you?"

"Making fun of your old man again? That wouldn't have happened back then either, but alas, we are all fated to live in the times we are born in, and this is my fate."

I was still holding the crossbow. Forget the rest of the stuff he was rambling on about. This weapon was real, and it could be used.

"It's too bad we don't have more of these," I said, holding it up.

"They're not difficult to make. This one took me less than two weeks."

"You made this?"

"I made all my weapons and my suit of armor. I used this equipment—this is my workshop," he said, gesturing to the machines at the far end. "I'm better with metal so the wood, especially the carvings, always takes much longer."

"Could you make more and forget about the carvings?"

He nodded. "I could do that."

"I'd like to have my mother talk to you," I said. "Would that be all right?"

"Certainly. And please, tell her, my skills as a swordsman and as a maker of weapons are at her disposal. My sword is hers."

He went down on one knee, bowed his head, and offered me the hilt of Excalibur.

"Dad, get up, you're not asking her to marry you," Willow said.

This was getting stranger all the time.

19

The audience cheered as the actors came out for a final bow. This was the opening night of their new performance. After doing A Midsummer Night's Dream for a week they'd rehearsed and were now performing a play called A Streetcar Named Desire. I had to give them credit: they'd managed to create a set that looked like a beat-up old apartment right in the middle of a clearing.

Chris walked onto the stage and asked the audience to give one more round of applause to the actors. I clapped, but I really didn't like the guy who played Stanley. I wished that the Stella actress had just slugged him. I guess that meant he was either a bad guy in real life or he was a really good actor. All things considered, I liked the Shakespeare play better.

"I'd like you all to stay for a while," Chris asked. "I have a few things I'd like to say."

Those who had started to get up sat back at Chris's request. Almost everyone in the community was there, sitting on the grass or on folding lawn chairs, with kids sleeping in little wagons. Everyone who wasn't out on guard duty, of course.

"Could we turn off the stage lights, please?" Chris asked.

The big beams, which shone their light toward the stage, were turned off. It took a few seconds for my eyes to adjust to the darkness. There were still a few lights, just sufficient to see each other and find our way out, but it was nothing compared to the bright stage lights. I noted that this play had been moved to a more wooded space so the light would be less visible from outside the community.

Moving just beyond the crowd were sheep and goats and a couple of grazing zebra. I'd noticed that they scattered whenever that Stanley guy started yelling "Stella! Stella!" Apparently they didn't like him any more than I did.

"Do you think this is going to work?" Willow quietly asked me.

"I'm not sure." Willow, his parents, Chris, and a few others were the only ones who knew what was about to be said.

"It's wonderful to be here tonight for the play," Chris said. "It was all so absorbing, so wonderful, that I forgot what was going on around us, outside the emerging walls of our community. I have to apologize for taking away the magic now but I need to talk about reality once again. Ellen, could you please join me up here?"

The audience fell completely silent as my mother joined her.

"We've all seen the transformation in our community over the past few weeks," Chris said. And she went on to talk about those changes. The fence now effectively blocked the beach, and the barricade over the bridge had been replaced and made much stronger. A wire fence topped with a couple of strands of barbed wire had been strung all along the water's edge where we were separated from Main Island by the channel. A schedule had been established for regular guard duty.

It all sounded impressive. But I knew better because my mother knew better. We'd built a shell, but eggs had shells and they could be easily cracked. With that in mind, our smaller group had continued to make plans for what would happen if this place fell. We'd taken more tools and supplies out to our little island and hidden them there. We'd watered and tended our secret garden, which was thriving. I wondered what the people here would think if they knew what we were doing.

I felt guilty about not telling Chris or Sam or even Willow and his parents about our secret plan. I felt particularly bad about Willow not knowing. He had become my friend—my first friend since we'd moved. Not telling him felt wrong, but going against my mother's orders and telling him would have been worse, a betrayal. My mother and I had talked about bringing them along if things didn't work out here. This just wasn't the right time to talk to any of them about it.

"We know that none of this could have happened without Ellen. Could we give her a round of applause before I ask her to speak?" Chris said.

The audience reacted as requested, although some were much more enthusiastic and some were only being polite. I knew how people felt. Some were glad she had been invited in. Others were indifferent or even angry. A lot of people still wanted to live in denial and didn't realize that without my mother's help they might not be living at all.

"Thank you, Chris. All of these changes were done with the help of a lot of people," my mother said. "I want to thank all of you for all your work. You've done everything I've asked." She paused. "We now need to talk about what more still needs to be done if we want to survive."

There was a rumble from the crowd.

"It's worked so far!" somebody else called out.

"It's been almost two weeks since the attack," another yelled.

"Thirteen days. Do you think we could withstand those men if they returned?" Chris asked the audience.

Nobody had anything to say to that.

"We cannot forget about those bodies we had to bury," my mother said.

"They weren't bodies, they were people!" somebody yelled out angrily.

"They were people," my mother said. "They became bodies, and there will be more if we don't all agree to do more."

Yet again, Chris held up her hands and the audience was silenced. "Please let her speak."

I knew how important it was to have Chris standing at her side. There was a lot of resentment directed toward my mother. They didn't like some "soldier," some "outsider" telling people what to do and preparing the place like it was some kind of "fort."

"We don't have enough weapons to protect us," my mother said. "We don't have the training and we don't have the resources to turn this community into a garrison. This is the farthest thing imaginable from a military base. And that might be what saves us."

I could tell by the confused looks and the noise level that nobody understood what she meant. I knew what she was going to say—after all, I'd basically thought of it in the first place—but was any of it really possible?

"First off, I think I owe many of you an apology," my mother said.

I hadn't expected that. She had many strengths, but apologizing certainly wasn't one of them.

"I wanted you all to be soldiers when you weren't. Instead, we need you to be who you are. We need actors, and potters, weavers, artists, and craftsmen to make our new plan work."

"How can an actor help?" the man who played Stanley asked.

"Or a potter?" asked a woman potter.

"Tonight is not the time for specifics," Chris said, stepping forward. "For tonight, we just want you all to know that we have a new plan, one that we believe you will all be happy to play a part in. Go home, get some sleep, and tomorrow we'll meet with each of you individually or as groups and put forward what we want from you."

"And if we don't want to come to the meeting?" somebody asked.

"Or we don't want to do what you ask us to do?" another questioned.

"Then Tom, and Scott," Chris said, "you do not need to come or comply. You can feel completely free not to hear how you could be part of saving the lives of your family, friends, and neighbors."

I hadn't expected her to be that blunt, and then she got blunter.

"But our chances to survive increase with the involvement of everybody in this community. Without the help of all, I am certain that we will be facing the death of us all. Go home, go to sleep, and tomorrow we'll talk."

In complete silence the crowd got to their feet and started to shuffle away. Willow came along with me as we walked to my mother and Chris.

The remaining lights went off and we were thrown into almost complete darkness.

"Do you think they're even going to come to meet with you?" I asked.

"They're nothing if not a curious lot. They'll come to hear what we have to say," Chris said.

"And will you be able to convince them to do what you're going to ask them to do?" I asked.

"I believe the plan needs to come from somebody other than your mother or me," Chris said.

"Who else is there?" Willow asked.

She pointed first at me and then at Willow.

"Us?" Willow gasped.

"Why do you think they'd listen to us?"

"First off, you two came up with this plan, so I believe it is fitting that it should be presented by its creators," Chris said. "And second, you've already convinced the two of us, and Willow's parents, so you'll be able to convince others."

I looked to my mother for direction. "She's right," my mom said. "I think it will be more powerful coming from the two of you."

Willow and I exchanged a worried glance. What if we couldn't convince them?

20

_____

The next morning, Willow and I found ourselves sitting at the front of the meeting room in the community center, with my mother and Chris standing at the back. The room was filled with the actors, the set designer, the costume designer, the director, the stage manager, and the stagehands from the play. They were loud, and there was a lot of laughter and joking going on.

I looked at my watch. "We'd better get started," I said to Willow. We had a tight schedule for the day.

I stood up. They didn't seem to notice. I cleared my throat. They didn't seem to notice that either.

"Excuse me!" Willow said loudly, and they stopped talking.

Now that we had their attention I had to begin.

"Thanks for coming today," I said.

"It's not like we had any place better to go," one of the stagehands, Luke, said.

"This is awfully early though," the actor who had played Stanley said. He didn't look nearly as intimidating in the daylight but he did look tired.

"You could have scheduled us for the afternoon," another actor said. She had played Blanche.

"Late afternoon," another added, and they all chuckled.

"We wanted you first because of how important you are to the survival of this community," I said.

"You're about the most important," Willow added.

"If we're the most important, I'm worried," the actor who played Stanley said. Again there was laughter.

"He's right, if you're counting on this motley crew to protect us we're all going to get much worse than bad reviews," the play's director said.

"That's where you're wrong," I said.

"We need all of you to help," Willow added.

"We need you more than almost anybody else," I continued. "That's why we wanted to get your cooperation before we talked to the others."

"Look, guys, we're mostly just actors," someone said.

"Very good actors," I said, and everybody looked pleased.

"And that's what we need. We need you to act brave and strong," Willow told them.

"Last night, you had us all convinced you were a very tough, desperate guy that nobody would want to mess with," I said to the actor who played Stanley. "And you set designers transformed a field into a tenement apartment in New Orleans."

"It felt like we were right there," Willow added.

"Thank you," Luke said. "We could have done better in a real theatre, with more resources."

"But you did it anyway. And now, we need your help—all of you—to transform this island into a fortress," I said.

"But we just do illusion," the set designer said.

"Exactly! We need to create an illusion to fool people. If they see this place as a fortress then they'll be less likely to attack," I explained.

"So . . . smoke and mirrors," the set designer said.

"Sometimes illusion is enough," I said.

"And my father is going to help with suggestions, based on his expertise, about how to make it more than just illusion. For example, we can utilize many of the features of a real castle," Willow explained.

"Things like a barbican by the bridge, towers, arrow loops. We already have a moat," I pointed out.

"So you want us to help build a castle, is that correct?" Luke asked.

I nodded. "Basically the façade of a castle."

"What about the people who make costumes, how can we help?" a woman asked.

"We need you to produce uniforms that will make it look as if there are a hundred Marines manning our walls," Willow said.

"That would take a lot of fabric," she said.

"We'll get you what you need," Chris called from the back. "Would old clothes do, things that people were getting ready to give away?"

"Yes. If you can round up enough, we can dye the fabric and reuse it. I can make you enough uniforms to dress the entire community!" she exclaimed.

"Excellent." I paused. "So, will we have your help?"

There were a few seconds of silence and I held my breath.

"It would be hard to turn down a starring role in a production this big," the Stanley actor said. "Of course, we'll need a director."

At this point the director stood up. "What am I, chopped liver?" Everyone laughed.

"And Captain Ellen, U.S. Marine Corps, will be your technical consultant," Chris said.

"Then count on us. The show must go on!" Luke yelled, and the others applauded. "We'll make this place look like a castle crossed with a military base manned by a hundred or so deadly-looking Marines, if that's what you think will work!"

The applause got even louder. I felt a little embarrassed . . . and a lot relieved.

———————

We'd gone from meeting to meeting all day. With each successful meeting, I'd gained confidence that we could really convince people. This was our second-to-last group. In addition to the theatre folks we'd met with magicians, weavers, and woodworkers, and with writers and illustrators. This group was made up of sculptors and potters, and we asked them to make replica weapons to look like assault rifles. At first they just seemed confused, but then, like every group we met with, they agreed. They left with a lot of positive words, leaving the last group to be ushered into the room. This was going to be the hardest group to convince, and that was why we'd left them until the last.

They were the yoga teachers, the tai chi instructors, the pacifists, and the Buddhists in the community. They were people who didn't believe in violence, or weapons, or us needing to defend the community. They were the most vocal opponents to what had been happening.

They took seats at the table. They were quiet, calm, almost serene.

My mother came up beside me and bent over. "Emma, I'm going to leave."

I understood. She was the Marine, the one with the weapon strapped to her side.

"We'll try our best."

"It might not work. Try to get them as neutral as possible, even if they won't help."

She slipped out of the room. I was pleased that Chris had stayed. She was sitting at the back of the room. This had been a long day for all of us and she was a lot older. I could only hope I was that energized at her age. Heck, I just had to hope that someday I'd live to see my eighties—or to be eighteen.

I whispered in Willow's ear. "You know these people, so maybe you should take the lead." He nodded and then cleared his throat.

"Thank you all for coming. It's been a long day and—"

"Actually, we'd like to make an opening statement," one of them said, cutting him off.

"Um, sure," Willow said.

"Thank you. We wish to say that we are people of peace. We cannot and will not participate in taking the life of another human being. We came to this meeting only out of respect for you and the other members of the community," Zoe said. She was a yoga instructor, a Buddhist, and a sculptor.

Chris spoke up now. "And you are respecting them by refusing to take part in defending them?"

"We do not believe in—"

"Staying alive?" Chris asked. "You have to know that if we can't make this community stronger then we are all going to die. Everybody, including yourselves, including the children, including your children. Everybody. That's a very strange way to show respect."

"That's not fair," another one said.

"Perhaps you could do me a favor. Could you all please take a minute and close your eyes."

"What?" one of them asked.

"I want people to close their eyes while I speak," Chris said. "Think of it as a visualization technique."

I kept my eyes open while, one by one, they all closed theirs.

"I want you to picture the bodies that we took from the streets after the attack. I want you to picture those people being brutally killed. I want you to picture the people you love and care for, your friends and your neighbors, being next. I want you to—"

"That's not fair," one of them said. Eyes were opening around the table.

"Not fair? Well then maybe you should keep your eyes open as you picture your own painful death. I want you to see—"

Willow jumped in now. "I know we're all tired and worried, but I think you might be getting the wrong idea here about what we're asking from you."

"We need your help," I added. "And we won't ask you to betray your own values."

There was silence. Were they going to respond at all?

"I could teach self-defense," Fred, the tai chi teacher, said.

"That would be wonderful." Willow turned to Chris. "I think karate would be very beneficial for people. And Fred has his fourth-degree black belt."

"But what about the rest of us?" one of the women asked.

"We need you to tend the crops, make meals, look after the children, and we'd like those of you with first aid experience to receive additional training," I explained.

"What sort of additional training?" a woman asked. She seemed hesitant.

"There are going to be people hurt," I said. "They'll need to be cared for. You know my mother is a nurse. She will offer first aid training, specifically around gunshot wounds."

One woman got to her feet. "I will help save lives in any way I can."

A second and third also rose and offered the same commitment. One by one they rose until they all were standing. We'd done it. We'd got everybody to buy into the plan. Now we just had to pray that we were offering them more than just false hope.

21

The church bell rang out to signal a possible attack, and I awoke from a deep sleep and jumped to my feet. By the time I got to the ladder leading down from the loft my brother was already standing at the bottom. He was in his PJs and he looked scared. I worked hard not to have that same look.

"Is Mom here?" he asked.

"She left before I went to bed to check on the sentries," I said.

She did that every night, walking around, checking, talking, answering questions, and reassuring people. Some nights I went with her. Tonight I'd gone to bed early. Sleep and reading books were my two big escapes from reality. Sleep was sometimes hard to come by, but Mrs. Fraser's house had more books than most libraries.

I came down the ladder. I was already dressed and was wearing my shoes.

"You get next door," I said.

According to our emergency plans, some people would head to the walls for defense while others stayed to care for children.

He started for the door. "Ethan," I called out, and he turned around.

"Yeah, yeah, I know the plan if things go wrong. I know where to go if we have to go." He hesitated. "Do you think we'll have to go tonight?"

I forced myself to smile at him. "This is probably nothing. But if it's a real emergency, we've done a lot to get ourselves ready to defend the community. I'm not worried."

He turned back to the door, then spun around again and threw his arms around me.

"Please be careful," he said. "I only have one sister and I don't want to lose her."

I hugged him back tightly, then tried to lighten the mood. "You're not going to kiss me, are you?"

"Nope. I wouldn't want to make Willow jealous."

Before I could even react he slipped out the door. Willow was just my friend, and Ethan knew it, but deep down, I had to admit to myself that I wondered if he might become more than just a friend.

The bell tolled again, sounding even louder somehow, and I pushed thoughts of Willow away. I looked around the house, then grabbed my helmet and crossbow before leaving. I still had the bow and arrow but I'd also been one of two dozen people trained to use the crossbow. It was deadly accurate at close range and still effective up to fifty yards—well, at least for me. It was an easy weapon to use, but some of us were better at it than others. I figured all the work I'd done training with the bow and arrow had translated to the crossbow.

People were coming out of many of the houses and cottages I passed on my way to the wall by the beach. I caught glimpses of light as doors opened, and there were small lines around windows where the black-out curtains didn't quite fit completely. Although the bell ringing in the dark was scary-sounding, people weren't panicked. They moved quickly and deliberately, speaking to each other in calm, low voices. We'd practiced, just like fire drills at school, so that we were all well rehearsed.

I arrived at the beach and found a lot of people already stationed along the wall, holding real rifles, fake rifles, and real crossbows. Most of the people were wearing helmets—crafted by Willow's father—and almost all were dressed in their "costume," the uniform of a U.S. Marine. In the dark and in the distance they all looked real.

I walked along the line until I located my mother. She was moving from person to person, talking, encouraging, offering a calming voice. I would have liked to have seen Sam or even Garth, but I knew neither of them would be here. They had quickly become my mother's lieutenants. Sam was watching the bridge and Garth was by the channel. Those were the two most likely places, along with the beach, where trouble could be brewing. But the fact that my mother was here meant that this was where things were happening.

I took a spot on the wall and peered out one of the slots. I didn't see much of anything except darkness, and all I could hear was the sound of waves and the murmur of voices from along the wall.

"What is it?" I asked my mother.

"There are reports of boats. They were spotted as they came close to shore."

"I don't see them," I said.

"I don't see them either. It might be a false alarm."

A false alarm would be nice. We'd had a few of those over

the last two weeks. It was annoying to be woken out of a deep sleep for nothing, but nothing was better than something. At least the false alarms during the day didn't wake anybody. It was often because of a boat that just came too close, or a sighting of a group of men in the bushes or trees on the other side of the channel, or somebody approaching too close to the bridge.

All at once lights shone out over the water. The big stage lights had been repurposed as searchlights. They swept back and forth across the water. I followed along as one of them made wide passes and—there it was! The light caught a boat with at least a dozen men on board, and it looked as though all of them had some sort of weapon. The men held up their hands to try to shield their eyes from the light, which must have been blinding.

A second light hit the boat from another angle, and the boat was caught between the beams. It felt as if it was held in place by the power of the two lights.

"Attention, boat! Attention, boat!" an amplified voice called out. I recognized the voice—it was "Stanley" from the play, whose real name was Joshua. "You are in our waters. You must leave immediately or we will take action!"

His voice was firm and clear and deep and sounded very confident. He was a good actor.

"This is your only warning!" Joshua called out. "If you do not leave we will be forced to take action and destroy you!"

I leaned close to my mother. "Destroy them?"

"Sometime an idle threat is better than no threat," she said.

Suddenly I saw flashes of light from the boat and instantly gunfire rang out. Somebody from our line gave a little shriek!

"Everybody down!" my mother called out, and it was repeated down the line.

The gunfire from the boat stopped but the boat itself continued to dance around, trying unsuccessfully to get free of the lights. As it bobbed about, it came close to another boat, which was revealed in the light; there were armed men on it as well.

My mother pulled up the walkie-talkie. "Do you think you can put a shot toward them?"

"We can try to put a shot *into* them," came the voice in reply.

It was Willow's dad. He was in charge of the catapults. With his help they'd used old telephone poles, leather, and wire to construct three medieval catapults. They were certainly impressive-looking, and I'd seen them practicing. I knew they could fire that far, but could they actually hit something that was that small bobbing and moving on the water?

There was a whooshing sound and then a gigantic splash over the starboard side of the closer boat! Water shot into the air. They hadn't missed by much at all.

I heard a second launch and almost felt it going over my head, followed by a big splash. This one missed by a mile, and the splash was caught by a few flickering rays from the searchlights.

I had to guess that the first one had just been lucky. There was a third whoosh, and the boat in the light exploded! Chunks of wood flew up in the air, and the whole deck seemed to collapse as the boat dipped and swayed, shoved off to the side by the impact.

There was a collective gasp as people along the wall saw what had happened, the boat still bathed in light. People were either thrown over the side or jumped into the water as the boat started to tilt and dip. The cinder block that had been thrown by the catapult must have gone through the deck and then right through the keel. It was sinking right before our eyes and everybody was abandoning ship, but where would they go? Would the other boat pick them up?

I looked around, finding the second boat well off to the side, still caught in one of the other searchlights. It zigged and zagged along, trying to get free. Did it even know that the other boat had been hit and that there were men in the water needing to be rescued?

I turned back to the damaged boat just in time to see the tip of the stern rise up into the air as the rest of the boat sliced into the water. And then it was gone! It had all happened in less than a minute.

Still visible were people in the water, struggling to swim in their wet clothes. Most of them were still holding onto their rifles. There were a few pieces of debris on the surface—chunks of wood—and some tried to hold onto or clamber up on them. There were bodies on the surface as well, unmoving, injured or unconscious or even dead. Others were starting to swim. They were coming toward the island. There was still time for them to be rescued.

What they didn't know on that other boat was that there was no more ammunition loaded in the catapults. Three catapults and three cinder blocks was it. It would take at least four or five minutes to reload and then reposition them to aim in that direction. They had plenty of time to get those men out of the water and get away before they were in danger again.

The second boat was still in the light but it was moving away quickly, seemingly unconcerned about those in the water. They were just leaving them to drown or come ashore. Wait, what were we going to do when they did come ashore?

Our wall was up from the lake at the edge of the beach. Below was a strip of sand that was anywhere between five and twenty-five yards wide. All logs and large rocks had been removed by our work crews. It was open, and there was no cover to hide behind. Those men could make the shallows and then the shore, but they'd be on an open beach, exposed, with no place to hide. If they came ashore they'd have no choice but to surrender. If they tried to fire at us we would fire back. We had guns and crossbows. I could easily hit a target from this distance. But they weren't targets. They were living, breathing people. If I hit one of them, it would cause a terrible wound. It could kill them. Could I really do that? Could any of our people do that?

All three of the searchlights were scanning the surface, trying to keep the bobbing, swimming men in view. I could only see two in one light, another in the second, and two more in the third. Were they the only ones left?

"Hold your fire!" my mother called out.

I heard the message being passed down the line.

She got back on the walkie-talkie. "How much power do we have left for the lights?"

The searchlights were powered by batteries that were charged by the solar panels. It had been a sunny day, but the supply was limited, and those lights drew tremendous amounts of power.

"We're good," came the reply. "We have at least twenty more minutes. Do you want us to go to two lights?"

"Negative. I want two lights to follow the men in the water and the third to scan the lake for other boats."

Almost instantly one of the beams started to make sweeping search patterns across the lake. If there was anything more out there it wasn't being found. The second boat had turned tail and chugged away.

My attention went back to the other lights on the men in the water. They were trapped in the beams, their struggles caught for everybody to see. We were watching a life-and-death event happening before our eyes. There in the water were five men fighting for their lives . . . I did a quick count. I could only see four now. One man was either moving faster or slower or had simply slipped under the water and was gone.

I heard a murmur of conversation from around me. Somebody said something like "Shouldn't we save them?" I couldn't help feeling the same way. After all, we were just standing there doing nothing. But I thought about how these were people with guns, people who had been coming here to shoot at us, and then I felt like telling them to feel free to jump the wall and swim out if they wanted to save them. There was really nothing we could do but watch.

The first two men sloshed through the shallows and then dragged themselves up onto the beach, collapsing onto the sand. One had a rifle strapped to his back and the other had something in his hand, maybe a pistol. Two more joined them. I waited for the fifth. He didn't appear. He probably never would. They were caught in the brilliant, blinding lights, sprawled on the sand. They were so close that I could see their expressions as they tried to shield their eyes from the light.

"Get to your feet, and hands above your head!" Joshua thundered over the bullhorn.

They didn't respond. Were they too stunned, or too scared, or just in shock from what had just happened?

"I repeat! Get to your feet and put your hands in the air immediately or we will open fire!"

Still they didn't respond. Were they too exhausted to stand?

"Okay, everybody!" my mother yelled out. "Stand up and aim your weapons."

All at once, all along the line, everybody, including me, stood straight up so that our heads and helmets and weapons, real and pretend, were visible. At the same time the mannequins were activated. A dozen mannequins in four sets of three, wearing uniforms and holding assault rifles that were as fake as they were, were shifted upward so that we had what looked like another dozen Marines ready to fight and fire. They were the work of an island woman who was a puppeteer.

I could only imagine how terrifying it would have been to be standing out there, completely exposed, with sixty or so Marines training weapons on me.

"This is your last warning before we fire!" Joshua thundered. "Do as you are told or die!"

The four men struggled to their feet and put their hands into the air. One of them had to be helped by another to get up.

"Drop your weapons!" Joshua ordered.

One man dropped a pistol. A second took the rifle off his back and dropped it to the sand. A third pulled a pistol out of a holster and did the same. The fourth man, the injured man, did nothing. They all put their hands back up into the air without being asked.

"Everybody hold your fire," Joshua called out.

My mother looked over at me. "Time for the next part of the performance," she said. She was gone before I could even ask her what she meant.

Down the way, a hidden panel in the wall opened and five people emerged, with my mother taking the lead. The four men with her were all dressed as Marines, with helmets and replica weapons in their hands. I recognized them as members of our acting troupe. I figured the only real weapon they had was my mother's pistol, which she was holding. Our real weapons weren't nearly as fierce-looking as the fake assault rifles.

I pulled up my crossbow and placed it against the support at the lower edge of the arrow slot, aiming at the chest of one of the men on the beach. I was ready to fire if necessary.

My mom and the others came up to the men. Their arms were still in the air and they didn't look like a threat. One of our men bent down and picked up the pistols and the rifle from the sand and moved them safely away. All four men were frisked for other weapons.

I felt that I could relax and I removed the crossbow, putting the safety back in place and lowering it. Now I was just curious. I moved down the wall to the place closest to where the action was taking place. I got there to the opening just as a small rowboat appeared, carried by four men.

"What's the boat for?" I asked.

"I'm not really sure but we were told by your mother to go and get a rowboat," one of the men replied.

Were they going to search the water for the fifth man? No, that couldn't be it. None of these guys had weapons—even fake weapons—and there was no way they'd send people out into the dark and the unknown. That other boat may have driven away, but it could still come back.

There was only one way to find out what this was about. I leaned my crossbow against the wall and then took up a place at the back of the boat. I was going out. Nobody seemed to object. I ducked down as I headed through the opening. We marched down the sand toward where our men, my mother, and the prisoners stood.

My mother's hand went up to stop us well short. We set the boat down on the sand. Standing there, bathed in the searchlight's glare I felt even more exposed. Was there somebody out there on the water, hidden from view, aiming a rifle at us right now? That thought made me want to take cover behind the boat itself, but we all stood stock-still and straight. My mother gave me a look—direct eye contact—that made me want to take cover behind the boat even more. It was obvious in that quick glance that she wasn't pleased I was out here. She turned back toward the men.

"Put your hands down," she ordered, and they did.

"I need to know about your group. Number of men, weapons, and where you're stationed."

"And then you'll kill us?" one of them asked.

"And then we'll release you. That's why I had the rowboat brought down."

"You're just going to let us go?" another asked. He sounded as though he didn't believe her.

"We don't want prisoners, and we don't want to simply

shoot you," she said. "That isn't the way the Marines trained us."

"You're Marines?" one questioned.

"Do you think these are costumes?" my mother asked.

That question shocked me, then I realized it was a good ploy—making it sound silly that we would be wearing costumes.

"Look at the wall," she continued.

They all gazed up at the people peeking over the wall, and I did the same. We were standing in front of what looked like a couple of companies of heavily armed Marines. It was an impressive sight and I found myself intimidated, even though I knew the truth.

"So how many men do you have?" my mother demanded.

Nobody answered.

"I told you we don't want to shoot you," she said. "But believe me, we will if you don't cooperate." She pointed her pistol directly at the head of the closest man. "I'll kill you first."

He reacted instantly. He told us there were twelve in his boat and fifteen in the other. I had to assume that the eight others in his group had been killed. They were from the city. They had a place they stayed in by the lake, an old warehouse. There were another seventy-five people living there, a dozen more armed people and the rest were wives and kids. They'd created their own little armed camp, the same way we had. In fact, as she asked questions and they answered, it was obvious that they really weren't that much better armed than we were.

"Our boat," one of them said. "What did you hit us with? It just exploded."

"We're not out here to answer your questions," my mother snapped. "We could have sunk the other boat just as easily but we left it alone because we wanted to give them the opportunity to pluck you out of the water."

The men looked at each other. They obviously weren't pleased that they'd been left to drown or be captured. The injured man just looked dazed, as if he was about to fall down. It was then that I noticed he had a large bump on the far side of his head. He'd probably been struck by something when the boat shattered into pieces.

My mother asked them more questions about what it was like in the city. They told stories about the city emptying out, about fires being set, people being attacked, and how everybody was just scrambling to survive. Groups had formed for protection and survival, and now these groups were preying on each other and on anybody unfortunate enough to be alone.

"Look, we didn't mean any harm," one of the men said.

"Sure you did, and that's why you came back," my mother said.

"We've never been here before," he answered.

"Never?" she asked.

"We've been on the island, the middle part, scavenging for food, but never here," he said. He looked as though he was telling the truth, but people could be pretty good liars.

"Is there any police or military presence in the city?" my mother asked.

"There are some cops who have come together, the way the rest of us have, to try to survive."

"And I heard some talk about a military group," another said. "They call themselves The Division."

"They're a division?" my mother asked.

I knew that a division was made up of ten thousand or more men. We could only hope that this was wrong.

"That's what they call themselves. I think there's five or six hundred of them."

"And have you seen them?" she asked.

"We've seen enough of what they do to know we don't want to see them," he said. "They're big, with lots of weapons, and they're ruthless, and they just kill whoever gets in their way."

"We kill people too if we have to," my mother said. "But we're not ruthless. We're letting you go, but you have to know, you have to tell your people, that if you come back we will not hesitate to end your lives. We will sink your boats on sight and shoot any survivors who manage to make the shore. This is our warning. You are our messengers."

"Look, we're not bad people," one of them said.

"Anybody who comes here looking to take what we have is bad. And will become dead. Nobody should think they can mess with this many Marines and end up anything but a corpse floating in the water."

I knew this was all just part of the act, but I knew that if we really had this many Marines we'd be a force nobody would want to mess with.

"We understand. It's just, if we did come back with our families . . . would you think about maybe letting us in? We could help defend the place," he said.

"Do we look like we need your help to defend ourselves?" she asked. She turned to us. "You five, put the boat at the water's edge and then get back inside the walls."

We picked up the boat and carried it over to the lake,

dropped it onto the sand, and followed orders as we trotted back to the opening. I stopped at the gate and watched as two men jumped into the rowboat and the other two pushed it into the shallows. They moved it into waist-deep waters and then they jumped in as well and started rowing. Their journey was followed by a single searchlight.

My mother led the men back to the opening. There were smiles on their faces and they were talking—not loudly, but you could hear the satisfaction in their voices. They went inside and my mother stopped beside me.

"You shouldn't have come out here," she said, quietly.

"I just wanted to know what was going on."

"I would have told you."

"I guess I just couldn't wait. It wasn't that dangerous."

"That's where you're very wrong. It was dangerous to the entire community."

"What?"

"Would a military operation, a *Marine* operation, need to have a young girl come out into the open like that?"

"I . . . I hadn't thought of that."

"We're trying to survive on illusion, and we can't afford to let that illusion be shattered."

"I'm sorry. I just didn't think about it."

"Emma, I need better than that from you."

I felt like I was about to cry.

My mother gave me a small smile. "It's not fair, I know that. I shouldn't be asking so much from you . . . and you've been so good . . . so brave, but I need more."

I let out a big halting sigh, trying to drive back tears. I nodded my head. "I'm sorry, and I'll try harder."

"I know you will. For now we can only hope that those men were so dazed by the attack and blinded by the searchlights that they didn't notice you or make sense of you being there."

We turned around and watched as the rowboat got farther and farther away until it was barely visible. The searchlight stopped. Either we'd run out of power or they'd decided to turn it off.

"So, how did that all sound?" she asked. "Do you think they bought what we were selling?"

"I know the truth and you almost had me convinced and scared. You wouldn't have really shot them, right?"

"I would have if they'd resisted, but we won't be shooting surrendering prisoners with their hands up. Not on my watch. The problem is that prisoners are work to guard, take resources to feed, and we don't want them inside to see this is all just smoke and mirrors."

"Not all just smoke and mirrors," I said. "We did sink that boat."

"A lucky shot. Sending them back also sends a message to them and to others out there. We want the rumor to spread that we're a fortified base filled with armed Marines. That we can sink ships at will, that we will shoot prisoners, that we're ruthless."

"Like that Division he mentioned?" I asked.

"They might be no different from us—some military people coming together to protect themselves and their families. They could be running the same sort of bluff that we are."

"Maybe we should try to meet them."

"At this time we can't trust anybody enough to meet with them," she said. "But if we do have a meeting, I know who we should meet with first."

"Who?"

She smiled. "Curiosity will have to wait until the time is right."

22

The sun was high in the sky, and it felt good as I lay on a towel on the beach. Around me others were taking in the sun or splashing in the water. There was a lifeguard posted to watch the swimmers. But behind us on the wall were the armed guards posted to watch us in a different way. Occasionally a boat would pass by out on the lake, but unless it came close we could just ignore it. About an hour before a boat had ventured too near and we'd been herded inside the walls until it was gone.

It was strange how it had all become so normal so quickly. Less than two weeks earlier I had been here at night when those prisoners swam to shore and were held at gunpoint. Then the day after that two bodies had washed up onto the beach. The day after that another appeared. I didn't see any of them. They were taken and disposed of— buried on Main Island so that even the bodies didn't invade our outpost.

Now, here, today, it was the middle of the summer, and the only bodies were those lying on towels catching rays. July was my favorite month. The world was bright and beautiful and warm and all seemed well. If it hadn't been for the guards on the walls and the crossbow on the towel beside me, this would have been any beach on a sunny summer day before this all happened.

And we still didn't really know what had happened, what had caused all the power to go out. It was a constant subject of conversation. Nobody seemed to know, and I guess in some ways it didn't matter. For me, it wasn't how it had happened that was important but what we were doing to survive it until it was all fixed again. Maybe that was me just being optimistic. Some people figured it would never get fixed again, that somehow everything had collapsed and it was what we "deserved" for thinking we were above nature. There was a pretty strong anti-progress, anti-technology group living out here, and in a strange way they almost seemed pleased about all of it.

I looked at my watch. I'd been here for over two hours. Willow had been with me for an hour before he'd headed back home. He had become a good friend. I liked spending time with him, and I felt like we could really talk about things. It was good to have a friend like that. Of course, it only made me feel worse about not sharing everything I knew with him.

Ethan was now always teasing me about my "boyfriend," but Willow and I hadn't done anything but hang out, and right now that was all I could handle. I needed a friend more than I needed a boyfriend. I couldn't risk losing one to try to gain the other.

I sat up and looked around. In the shallows there were small children and their parents paddling around. Farther out were more serious swimmers. Ethan was out there with his friends. He was a good swimmer, and the island kids were even more serious swimmers. They all watched out for each other so there was nothing for me to be worried about. Still, worry was something I was good at.

Beyond the swimmers, farther out, were three boats with a dozen people fishing and another half dozen who acted as guards. The lake was our source of water, our protective moat, and a major source of food. There were always people out in boats or casting lines from the shore. Fish formed a big part of our diet, and with the exception of some goats and sheep that had been slaughtered, and the goat's milk and the cheese and yogurt it made, fish was our major source of protein.

Across the water I could see our condo tower. Twenty-five stories almost lost among the taller buildings. We hadn't been there long—we'd now lived on the islands longer—but it was still our home. It still had my bed and clothing and our things. Well, if there was anything left after all the looting. Part of me wanted to know. Another part just wanted to imagine it as it was.

The sun was high in the sky and I was getting really hot. I got up, picked up my towel and my crossbow, and was ready to go. I walked across the beach and went through the gate in the protective wall. I felt my body relax. I hadn't realized that even lying in the sun, out there on the beach, I'd felt exposed. I was now safe. Okay, the illusion of safe.

Walking down the path, heading back to our home, I was surrounded by people doing different tasks. They were working hard to keep us alive and to keep the illusion of normal alive. When we were attacked or threatened it was all about the guards and the walls. The rest of the time it was about what was inside the walls, and the activities and people who were working for survival. All these people were caring for the crops, milking the goats, making cheese or candles, or keeping the solar panels clean and functioning to keep the electricity flowing. There were teams for everything.

So far nobody seemed to be going without food. That was because of the stocks of canned and packaged goods that everybody seemed to have had in abundance, combined with the livestock and what was being farmed, fished, or foraged. Thank goodness for the petting zoo stock that had become so important to our survival.

Almost every day, foraging teams, accompanied by guards, set out to Main Island to look for food. Everything from pine needles to dandelions to assorted berries was edible. And of course there were apple and pear trees growing right in our community. For now there was enough for everybody, although the supply of coffee and sugar was reportedly running very low. Apparently sugar could be made from some plants that could be locally grown, but there was no coffee growing within a thousand miles. When our supply was gone it was gone.

A lot of what was happening was almost organic in nature; people just did things cooperatively and worked together. But Chris and some of the long-term residents had come together to form a committee. They were unelected but were well respected in the community. Most were older—they called themselves the "elders"—but some weren't that old at all.

Technically the committee was in charge of everything, including security, but they basically left that to my mother to run. Without the other things they were all doing we couldn't have survived. Without the security that my mother was in charge of we couldn't have stayed alive to have those other things. That was a fact that was pretty well accepted by everybody. If we didn't have a way to protect ourselves, somebody would sweep over this place and that would be the end of everything—and everybody.

I turned at the sound of metallic banging and three zebras ran across the path, followed by a woman hitting a wooden spoon against a pot.

"Get away, get away!" she yelled. She stopped, looked at me, and smiled. "They keep getting into my garden."

"You have to protect the food we need," I agreed.

The zebras and other animals were able to forage through the trees and the weeds by the shore, but there wasn't nearly as much open grass for grazing because the soccer pitch and the baseball field had been plowed under and planted. The starts of little vines of zucchini and cucumber were already working their way up the backstop and the outfield fences. Each home was free to plant vegetables that they could use or share or trade. Most people were growing vegetables but some still had flowers, or little patches of grass, or gravel-covered Zen gardens.

I got to the house and was surprised that my mother was there. She was so busy being everywhere that it almost seemed like she was no place.

"Cookie?" she asked, gesturing to a plate on the table.

"You've been baking?"

"They were a present from Zoe."

"But Zoe doesn't like you," I said.

"I think she likes me a lot better than she did before the attack."

Our successful defense of our territory had had a very strong impact and effect on the entire community. Before, there had been doubts—was the plan going to work, and would anything we tried help to protect us? But people had now seen with their own eyes that if we worked together we could succeed, and knowing that made them work even harder. Those taking crossbow lessons were more dedicated. There were many people in self-defense classes learning karate. As fences between properties were taken out to allow more crops to be grown, those boards were being repurposed to reinforce our walls around the perimeter.

"These people here are sort of odd, but they really are nice," I said, munching on a cookie.

"Odd seems to be working in our favor, but nice might still be too much of a problem to overcome."

"We've made a lot of progress," I pointed out.

"I don't think we're moving forward as fast as the rest of the world is moving backwards."

"Are you going to explain that one to me?"

My mom reached over and brushed some crumbs off the table. "Each day we are making this place a little bit stronger, a little bit better at taking care of itself," she said. "But I'm afraid that things out there are getting more dangerous faster than we can make them safer here."

"But that's their problem, the people out there."

"That problem will end up here. Desperate people are more willing to do desperate things." She popped a last bite of her cookie into her mouth, then stood up. "I'd better get going. I'm leaving Ward's."

"To go to our little island?"

"Not today. Later this week I'll head over. Do you want to come with me today?"

I hardly saw my mother these days, so I jumped at the chance. "Yes, definitely. Where are you going?"

"I'm leading a security detail to take some people to Main Island to harvest edible plants," she explained. "Where's your brother?"

"He's down on the beach with his friends. How about if I just leave him a note? He'll be fine for a while."

"It would be nice to have you and your crossbow along."

"Who else is going?" I asked.

"Sam and Garth."

I was glad. I didn't want my crossbow to be the biggest part of my mother's backup.

23

The heavy barricade was pushed to the side to allow us to go over the bridge and to Main Island. There were eleven people in our party. While everybody had a weapon of one sort or another, the only four with guns were my mother, Sam, Garth, and a woman named Eleanor. She was a fashion designer by trade and had helped make the Marine uniforms. She was trusted with one of our few and precious guns because she'd been raised on a farm and had previous experience with a rifle. The four of them, dressed in Marine uniforms, were the guards, while the other six, plus me, were going out to gather food.

Along with the fake uniforms, to protect the illusion Sam and Garth were clean-shaven and had cut their hair in a brush cut to look more like Marines; Eleanor had her hair tucked into her helmet to look regulation. Lots of people were doing that to try to look more authentic. They were also receiving basic training, being taught to act and think more like soldiers and less like civilians. It was about drills and following orders, but for the actors in the group this wasn't training, this was "Method acting" so they could better portray their characters.

We walked through the trees on a dirt trail that paralleled

the main cobblestoned path and led toward the ferry docks and the marina. We were going to cut off in the direction of our little island. There was a thick stand of trees over there that our scavengers believed would have mushrooms, some wild onions, and leaves that could be made into tea. There was also a chance we could swing close enough to our former camp to at least see if there was anybody living out there. They probably wouldn't be able to find our buried stash of tools and supplies, but our secret garden wouldn't be so secret to anybody who went out there.

We came out of the trees and my level of anxiety rose. We now had to travel across the open section, where a path of interlocking bricks ran through what had once been mani-cured grass and tended flower beds. Now the grass was long and the flowers were overwhelmed by the weeds that tow-ered over them.

My mother ordered Eleanor to drop back and Sam to go out wide on the left, Garth on the right. Mom kept walking and I fell in right behind her, holding the crossbow at my side. I'd already loaded in a bolt, the safety was off, and my finger was on the trigger. I could swing it up and fire in the blink of an eye.

Between me and Eleanor were the three women and three men who were going to do the gathering. They were all carrying knives or shovels—which could technically be used as weapons, but it was unlikely that any of them would use them that way. They were all part of our "pacifist" group. They weren't stationed at the walls and certainly couldn't be counted on to defend the community, or themselves, in any significant way, but they were doing their part to keep us all alive. As my mother had said, nurses and doctors were needed in the front lines but nobody expected them to shoot anybody. Of course, my mother, the Marine nurse, seemed just as capable of taking a life as she did of saving one.

Off to one side there was a tent town huddled in the shadow of the forest. There were two dozen or more tents of different sizes and colors. In different circumstances it might even have been pretty. Now it was just a worry, although they hadn't been threatening to us in the past. There were a few people visible, and as we continued walking I noticed that more people had come out of the tents to watch us. Watching us was fine as long as they didn't try to approach us. Most likely they were more afraid of us than we were of them. That was what we were counting on.

Up ahead was the marina. The way the island narrowed, there was no option but to get close to it. I thought back to that mob trying to get off the island in the first days. They were desperate to get back to the city. Now, from what I'd heard, everybody wanted to get away from the city. Was it possible that that was just slightly more than two months ago?

"Everybody tighten up!" my mother called out.

The sentries came in close until nobody was farther than a couple of arms' lengths apart. As we closed in we could see a few people moving along the docks, laundry hanging from the masts of a couple of the boats, and two men posted at the gate—where Sam had once stood guard. They had rifles.

"Eyes wide open," my mother said. "Remember. You're Marines."

Their guards eyed us and we watched them. They'd obviously sent out word of our appearance, and more people emerged. We were now outnumbered and possibly outgunned.

"Hey, Sammy!" somebody yelled out. "Is that you?" A man came out through the gate, along with two others.

"Who is that?" my mother asked quietly.

"That's Jimmie and Johnny," Garth answered.

"You met them that day trying to charge people for a boat ride back to the city," Sam said.

I recognized them now—as well as the third man. He was the one my mother had forced to throw away his pistol. This wasn't good.

"Hey Sam, Garth—and is that you, Eleanor?" Jimmie asked.

"It's me," she said.

The two exchanged greetings with everybody.

"Well, this explains a lot, you three dressed up like Marines," Johnny said. "I heard there were dozens of Marines stationed in the community and—"

"There are dozens of Marines," my mother said, stepping forward. "As well as some others being trained to act as guards and security."

"And you are?" Jimmie asked.

"Captain Williams, U.S. Marines."

He laughed. "Sure you are. Do you think I believe your uniform any more than I believe theirs?"

He reached out to touch my mother's uniform and in a flash she grabbed his wrist and flipped him to the ground, sending his rifle flying off his back. She sank her knee into his chest as she pulled out her pistol! Everybody gasped and seemed to be frozen in place, except Jimmie, who yelled out in pain. I was the first to react. I swung up my crossbow and aimed it dead center at Johnny's chest.

"You two drop your weapons, now!" my mother ordered. She was aiming her pistol at them. Jimmie was no threat pinned beneath her knee.

They hesitated, but then took the rifles off their backs and placed them on the ground. She stood, and Jimmie scrambled to his feet and joined the other two.

"You think you can get away with this?" Jimmie demanded.

"I think we just did," Sam said. He went over and picked up the three rifles. "You never were too smart."

"I'm smart enough to have half a dozen armed men over there watching what you're doing. Do you think they're going to just stand by and do nothing?"

I looked over. The two guards at the gate had retreated inside the gate and were taking shelter behind a wooden barricade.

"They're just getting ready to open fire," Johnny said.

"You'd better hope they don't, because those bullets come through you three before they come to us. It's more likely they're going to hit one of you than any of us."

Their eyes got wide, and then Jimmie spun around and started yelling, "Hold your fire! Hold your fire!" He turned back around but still didn't look anything other than scared.

"That voice," the third man said to my mother. "I know you." And then he pointed at me. "And you too. I thought you looked familiar. You're the ones who made me toss my gun into the lake!"

"I see you got another one," my mother said.

Both Johnny and Jimmie chuckled. I was surprised, and judging from his expression so was the man.

"So what happens now?" Jimmie asked.

"The choice is yours. You can be our friends or our ene-mies," my mother said.

"You two could even come and live in the community," another one of the women offered.

"Yeah, I don't think that's going to happen," Sam said.

"Sammy, you've hated my guts ever since I stole your girl-friend in grade ten," Jimmie said.

"You've stolen a lot of things, but never one of my girl-friends. But decisions about who comes to the community are made by a committee, and they only take people who can offer something of value," Sam said.

"Nobody says we want to live there," Johnny said.

"Yeah, we're doing good out here," Jimmie said. "And I'd much rather be in charge out here than getting ordered around over there."

"So, do we get our guns back or are you planning on throwing them in the lake?" Johnny asked.

My mother made a gesture for him to be quiet. She took the walkie-talkie from her belt and held it up. "Hold fire, I repeat, hold fire. Do not, I repeat, do not fire on the marina."

All three looked shocked and concerned. What was she talking about?

"I needed to call off the mortar attack," she said.

"You have mortars?" the third man asked. He sounded completely astonished. I knew the feeling.

"Is that how you sank that boat?" Jimmie asked.

"How do you know about that?" Sam asked.

"We saw it go down," he said. "We were on shore when it happened. It was hard to miss under those spotlights. Was it a mortar that sank it?"

"It had to be," Johnny said. "Those guys who fired that shot, they're good."

"That's what Marines do. They're good enough to hit a moving target bobbing on the lake. They could take out any of the ships in the marina, or the men guarding the gate, at any time," my mother said. "Nobody should ever think to mess with the Marines. Now, why don't you pick up your guns and we'll lower ours."

She lowered her pistol to her side. She may have lowered it but I noticed her finger was still on the trigger. Everybody else on our side lowered their guns, and slowly the three men retrieved their weapons. They strapped the rifles onto their backs again.

"We can always use allies and trading partners," my mother said.

"That might work," Jimmie said. "How about if we come over later today and—"

"Nobody comes in," my mother said. "If you're interested, we'll send a party over to discuss things further."

"It sounds like you're the one in charge over there," Johnny said.

She laughed. "Why don't you tell the colonel that he's not in charge any longer? I'm just a captain. Do you want to hold talks or not?"

"We could do that," Jimmie said. "Some things we have a lot of. Others, well we could use some greens, some veggies."

"I'll arrange for a party to come out over to discuss things," my mother said. "Can you tell me what you're hearing about what's happening over in the city?"

"Bad things," Johnny said. "Last time we were over there was about two weeks ago."

"We almost got ourselves killed," Jimmie added. "Everybody over there seems to have a weapon now, and they're not afraid to use it."

"Not that we aren't well armed," Johnny said. "We gave better than we got. We took care of them."

"You killed them?" Sam asked.

"Don't sound so surprised," Johnny replied. "Didn't you kill those men on the boat? Wouldn't you have killed us if we'd tried to harm you?"

Sam smiled. "In a second."

"Big talk," Jimmie said.

"Big talk and big action. If you want, me and you, we can go right now," Sam said.

I expected my mother to step in to settle things down, but to my surprise she didn't.

"Well, just say the word, you and me walk away into the trees and we'll see who comes back," Sam said.

"Maybe another time," Jimmie said. "So, what are you all doing out here to begin with?"

"The same thing you should be doing," one of our party of scavengers said. "Gathering greens, things that we can eat to supplement the crops we're growing."

"It's funny, I never really did like salads, but now I'd kill for one. Wait, I probably shouldn't say that. People *have* been killing for a salad," Jimmie said.

There was a chill that went through the conversation. Those words just hung out there and nobody seemed to know what to say next.

"We'll let you get back and we'll return to our mission," my mother said. "Sorry for having to throw you to the ground."

"I've had worse dates," he said. "No worries."

They hurried off back to the marina and we went back along our route. My mother and Sam both kept an eye looking back on them as we moved, until we rounded a small stand of trees and the marina was no longer visible.

"Back into formation," my mother ordered.

Sam, Garth, and Eleanor spread out. I stayed by my mother's side, glancing at her profile as we walked along. This Marine sternness was a side to my mother that was becoming more natural as the days went on.

"Can you show me how to do that, throw somebody to the ground?" I asked.

"Yes, I can show you. But first things first. Sam!" she called out, and he trotted to our side.

"Do you trust those two?" she asked.

"About as far as I can throw them—and by the way, that was a nice toss."

"Thank you."

"Actually I've thrown both of them before, as well as popped one of them in the face."

"You've had a fight with both of them?" I asked.

"I've fought them both at once. It was still a pretty fair fight. They're a couple of weasels."

"And now they're weasels who are in charge of the marina community," my mother said.

"Weasels are pretty smart animals," Sam said. "Part of the reason I don't trust them is because they're a lot smarter than they sound."

"So we shouldn't underestimate them," my mother said. "But can we count on them?"

"You can count on them to lie, steal, cheat, and try to screw us over. I can't imagine that they've changed."

"Neither can I. There's safety and assurance in predictability, even if the prediction is that they're going to—"

My mother stopped mid-sentence. We could all hear a dull roar. It sounded like an engine, and it was getting louder. We looked around for a car or a truck as the noise increased, and all at once a small plane shot over top of our heads, so low that I involuntarily ducked. I turned and tracked it. It was single-engine, moving fast, a big star on the wings and fuselage. Wait.

"That's a military plane. It's a U.S. military plane!" I yelled.

"It's a P-51 Mustang," my mother explained. "That's the plane our military flew in World War Two."

That made sense. If old cars could still drive, and old boats could still motor, then old planes could certainly still fly. We watched as it got lower and lower and was blocked by the trees in the distance.

"Why is it flying so low?" Eleanor questioned.

"I have to assume that it just landed at the island airport," Sam said.

"Do you think there are military people there?" I asked.

"I only know they have a flying, functional war plane. That, and we need to find out more about them," my mother said.

24

Our boat chugged along. We'd passed the marina and all of Main Island to get to the western island that was home to the airport. There were eight of us on board, including my mother, me, and the guys from our original group—Jim, Ian, Ken, and Julian—along with Sam and Chris. We were heading to the island airport, where we thought the plane had landed. Chris was along because she was most likely to know somebody at the airport, and Sam, well, he'd become the person my mother trusted the most—after me, at least. Sam was at the controls of the boat. He was a good captain, which was another advantage to having him along.

We'd borrowed the boat from the marina. Over the past two weeks the people there had become more or less our allies, but we weren't entirely comfortable as partners. We'd given them some vegetables, and my mother had looked at and treated a couple of minor injuries they'd sustained. We were friendly, but we still weren't letting any of them into the community. We had too many secrets we needed to keep, about who we were and what weapons we had available. We wanted them to believe our stories, false facts about our strength and weapons, and even spread them around.

As we'd cruised along the shore we had seen evidence of people everywhere on Main Island. There were glimpses of red and blue tents through trees, small chimneys of smoke rising into the air, and sightings of people on shore. We were far from alone, and our passing seemed to attract attention.

On the water there were sailboats and old motorboats, but none came close to us.

We had two flags fluttering from the back of our boat. One was the Stars and Stripes and the second was the Marine Corps flag. The U.S. flag was real, while the Marine Corps flag had been made by one of our costume designers. It wasn't perfect but it had basically the right colors and the right parts in the right places. From a distance nobody could tell.

We also had three more flags, not displayed but on board and ready for use. Two of them were simple pieces of material—a red triangular top over a yellow triangular bottom—mounted on short poles. These were semaphore flags, used in military situations to communicate in radio silence—or in this case when there was no radio communication possible. The third flag was a simple white flag. To most people this meant surrender. To military people, though, it meant a truce or cease-fire, or a request to negotiate or communicate. If the airport people were military, then they would not only be able to read the semaphores, they'd understand the meaning behind the white flag. If they weren't, we would still be keeping enough distance to probably avoid any fire they might aim at us.

The airport grounds came into view and I was instantly struck by the changes to the shoreline. The fence we'd seen back in the early days when we'd come past in our canoe was now more like a wall topped by fencing and strands of barbed wire.

My mother was looking at it through our binoculars.

"What do you see?" I asked.

"They've built quite the fortification," she said. "Barbed wire, slots for observation or to fire, higher walls."

"Can you see anybody?" Chris asked.

"Negative, but there's no doubt they see us."

The airport was on a thin peninsula of land, surrounded on three sides by water and on the fourth by a narrow strip of land, a causeway that had been built to connect it to Main Island.

"How much closer do you want me to bring us?" Sam called down from the flying bridge.

"This might be close enough. Position the bow out and I'll signal from the stern."

She hadn't said why, but I knew the reason. She wanted the ship to have a narrow profile and to be aimed away, ready to race off if necessary. My mother went to the back of the boat and picked up the two semaphore flags. She pulled the binoculars off her neck and handed them to me and gave Julian the white flag, which he draped from the aerial of the flying bridge.

"I want you to stay low and keep scanning the shore. If you see anything out of sorts you let me know right away."

"What am I looking for?"

"Anything."

"Are you sure this is such a good idea?"

"We need to know who's sharing these islands with us," she explained. "Especially if they have a working plane."

I slouched down so I was mostly hidden by the gunwale of the boat. She began to signal a message. Each movement was a specific letter or number. I knew the basic message. She was asking for a meeting.

I used the gunwale of the boat to steady the binoculars as I scanned the shore. Beyond the wall I caught sight of the control tower. I assumed there were people behind the dark glass looking at us.

I went back to watching the wall. I stopped at a spot where there was a dock extending out. Behind it was a set of stairs leading up to the wall—was that a gate right there?

"Does anybody see anything?" my mother asked.

There was a chorus of "Nothing."

"Do you want me to go in closer?" Sam asked.

"Negative. They can see us and the flags from here. I'll run through the signals one more time."

I watched her out of the corner of my eye. She was standing so strong, so straight, and she was so visible. It wasn't just the flags that could be seen. I thought about how she could be targeted by a marksman with a sniper rifle.

"There!" I yelled. "There, there's movement! Somebody is coming out to the dock!"

"I see him."

He was carrying something. Was it a weapon or—no—it was semaphore flags! He walked to the end of the dock and started signaling.

He continued to signal, then stopped, and my mother began to signal back.

"What did he say? What are you saying?"

"He invited us to come to shore and I'm agreeing. Sam, take us to the dock."

Sam gunned the engine and we spun around.

"I want everybody to keep your weapons down and out of sight," my mother called out. "Only two of us are getting off at the dock. As soon as you drop us off, head back out and wait off shore at a safe distance until you're signaled that it's safe to come in."

"What's the signal?" I asked.

My mother thought for a second. "I'll go down to the dock. If I lift one arm, then come in. If I lift two, then you know I'm being forced to try to bring you in and it's not safe. You have to leave."

"We can't just leave you," Chris said.

"You might not have a choice. Have faith that we'll figure it out."

"How do we know that this isn't just a trick and they're not just trying to capture us all right now?" Julian asked.

"I guess we don't." She took her pistol out of the holster and handed it to him. "This is for you."

"But shouldn't you have it with you, just in case?" he asked.

"If there's a problem my pistol isn't going to be the solution." She turned to me. "You should leave your crossbow on the boat as well."

"Yeah, sure . . . am I the person going with you?"

"Of course."

"Shouldn't it be Sam, or at least one of us?" Jim asked.

"It's better that we appear non-threatening, and taking Emma is the best way to accomplish that."

As we got closer, two more men stepped onto the dock to join the man holding the flags. I didn't see any weapons, but that didn't mean they didn't have them. Besides, I was sure there were dozens of weapons on the wall that could potentially all be trained on us.

"Sam, no stopping, and straight back out at full speed," my mother ordered.

"You got it."

She turned to me. "Are you okay with this?"

"We're going into a strange place to meet people we don't know, leaving our weapons behind, and hoping they won't shoot us. Why shouldn't I be fine?"

Her mouth curled into a quick smile. "When did you get so smart?"

We moved to the very front of the boat. We were coming up to the dock and the three men. The gap of open water narrowed to almost nothing and I readied myself to jump. The boat suddenly decelerated and I was thrown forward, my mother grabbing me before I tumbled overboard.

"Jump, now!"

She was still holding me by the hand and we leaped into the air and crashed onto the dock, almost falling off the other side.

As we struggled to regain our footing, I heard the boat engine roar as it backed away to safety.

"That was quite the docking procedure," one of the men stated.

"But welcome ashore and . . . you're a captain," one of the others said.

"Captain Williams."

All three men stood at attention and then, to my shock, saluted.

My mother returned the salute. "At ease. You're all Marines?"

"I am, ma'am. Warrant Officer Gonsalves," the one with the semaphore flags replied.

"U.S. Army, ma'am. Sergeant Miller," a second added.

"Lieutenant Wilson," the third and obviously oldest man said. "Retired member of the greatest fighting force on the planet, the USMC."

Really they hardly needed to answer her question because they all seemed *so* military.

"Ma'am, no offense, but we need to search you, and your um, assistant—"

"My daughter, Emma."

"Yes, ma'am, and your daughter, we need to undertake a search for weapons before allowing you to enter the grounds. With your permission, ma'am," Sergeant Miller explained.

"Certainly. Standard procedure."

My mother held her arms above her head and I did the same. They undid the clasp on her holster and then proceeded to do a pat-down.

"She's clean," Gonsalves said as he finished searching my mother.

"Her too," Sergeant Miller said as he finished his search of me.

"Please follow this way, the colonel is waiting," the warrant officer said.

He led and we followed, with the other two behind us, through the gate. I hesitated for a split second, ducked my head, and went through the opening.

There was something so familiar about the way the three men moved. Military men had a stiffness to their backs, a certain swing of the arms, an exactness in the steps.

Ahead of us stretching into the distance was a long black tarmac. Off to one side was the control tower I'd seen from the lake. It had dark windows that circled the top layer, and it would have had a commanding view of the entire grounds and off into the lake. On the other side of the runway was a series of small buildings, bigger airplane hangars, and perhaps a dozen houses that looked very similar to the ones in our community.

Some of what had once probably been open or grassy areas had been put to cultivation: brown soil, ridges of dirt, and crops growing. I was surprised that not all the grass had been converted to growing food. As well, somehow their crops didn't seem as tall, or as full, or as lush as ours. Was it the soil, or the seed? Or didn't they know how to grow things?

Then I saw the planes—not one, but two Mustangs parked over on a small paved extension to the runway. There were a couple of small private planes peeking out of one of the open hangar doors. Beside them was another, larger passenger plane. It was also old school, with four propellers. I wondered if it was flight-worthy. Something that big could fly a lot of people over a long distance if it was—I could get to my father in that plane.

That thought hit me hard. I still wished he were here, or we were there. Everything had been so busy, so dangerous, so new that there were now days that I went without thinking about him at all, and that thought made me feel even guiltier. I hoped he was doing well. Even more, I just wished he was here with us. Somehow I figured that he could fix all of this, or at least protect us from what he couldn't fix. I felt bad—it was almost disloyal to my mother to have those thoughts.

She'd been here for me and Ethan, for all of us. Maybe it would have been better for my father if he were here to be looked after by her.

Looking back over my shoulder, I saw men with rifles spaced at regular intervals along the wall. They were certainly better armed than we were—unless some of those weapons were as fake as some of ours. I also noticed lots of people who weren't on the walls—men, women, and children, and a lot of them seemed to be standing around, staring at us as we walked past. There were military personnel here, but these were obviously civilians. Were they the families of military people?

We came up to a side door leading into the terminal and were ushered inside. The large waiting room was now filled with beds and bedrolls separated by blankets that were serving as crude walls. There were lots of people, and many of them turned and watched as we were marched by.

"Who are we going to see?" my mother asked.

"The commander of our complex," Sergeant Miller explained.

We entered an office area and Sergeant Miller knocked on a closed door. There was a brief silence and then a deep male voice called out, "Come." The sergeant opened the door and my mother led us in.

An older man with gray hair wearing a Marine uniform was sitting behind the desk. He looked up at us and I saw he had an eagle on his lapel that signified his rank as colonel.

My mother came to attention and saluted. He returned the salute and then offered his hand and they shook.

"I'm Colonel Wayne—Robert Wayne."

"Captain Williams, sir. Ellen."

He started asking her questions about where she had been stationed, and it quickly became clear that they knew some of the same people. He mentioned a base where he had been stationed most recently.

"We lived there," I said.

They both turned to me, and I realized I probably should have remained silent.

"This is my daughter, Emma, sir," she said.

"Hello, Emma. So you're a Marine brat."

"Me and my brother."

"My wife and I raised our boys on bases around the country."

"Are they here?" I asked.

"I wish they were. Both are Marine pilots. They were stationed overseas when all of this happened."

"My husband—my ex-husband—is stationed overseas in Iraq."

"My boys too. They might be on the same base. Maybe I'm just trying to convince myself, but I can't picture any place safer than a military base."

"That's what my mother said, too."

"And that's why we went out and brought their wives and our three grandchildren here. We've brought a lot of family here for safety and security."

I was right about the civilians, then.

"Your uniform?" he asked.

"Yes, sir, it's not Marine issue. We had uniforms made."

"Uniforms? Are there more Marines than just you?" he asked.

My mother looked guilty. "In order to enhance our ability to survive I've allowed a number of people to dress in Marine fatigues."

"Certainly not acceptable in normal situations, but this is far from normal." He paused. "Can I assume that you're from the community on Ward's Island?"

"Yes, sir, I am a representative of that community."

"We were planning on initiating contact with you."

"You were?" my mother asked.

"What you've done over there so far is impressive."

"What do you know about what we've done?" I asked.

"I've sent out recon teams to gather information. We're aware of you, the small group occupying the marina, and half a dozen tent communities spaced out on Main Island. We've also done a number of flybys over your community."

"I didn't know that," I said.

"They have always been at high altitude and not directly over top. Your walls look remarkably solid, your crops are growing well, and you have solar panels and electricity. You need to have better black-out shades."

"My mother's been saying that, but at least we have some shades now."

"We have shades on all windows," he said. "The airport had an emergency generator system that we've been able to utilize. Unfortunately, it's diesel-powered and fuel is at a premium so we can't run it as much as I'd like."

"Our solar panels produce enough power to light the houses and the searchlights on the walls," my mother said.

"We saw those lights in use a few weeks ago and sent up the planes. You were probably too occupied to notice. I was at the controls of one of the Mustangs. I was impressed when you managed to sink that boat."

"You saw that?" I exclaimed.

"Seeing it was the only reason I believed it was possible. If somebody else had told me a ship was sunk by a projectile thrown by a catapult I would have accused them of flying drunk!" he said with a laugh.

"Our crews have been working hard."

"But it was unexpected that you'd be utilizing catapults and crossbows."

My mother seemed surprised, as the colonel smiled. "We've had eyes on you from across the channel as well as from the sky. Basic recon."

"Of course," my mother replied.

"So may I assume that if the uniforms are fake, those assault rifles are also somehow fake?" he asked.

My mother didn't answer.

"I'm sorry. I can understand your reluctance to share information. What I'm going to offer to you is complete disclosure of our compound. I want you to see who we are and what we have. I believe that your community and our community can help each other. There are things we have that you might need, and things you have that we might need. Do you see that as a possibility?"

"Yes, sir. That was why we came here today."

"Excellent. I'll lead you on a tour. We're pretty proud of what we've been able to accomplish."

25

It was still early morning but the heat was already building. Wasn't it supposed to start cooling off as August came close to the end? I walked along the path to Willow's house, trying to stay in the shade as much as possible.

Out ahead, close to the bridge, there were two soldiers from the airport compound who were working with our people to improve the barricade system. There had been a lot of movement back and forth between our community and the airport over the past three weeks. We had sent people over to help them learn how to harvest wild plants, improve their farming techniques, and do things like make candles, put up preserves, and churn butter. We'd also given them ten of our forty-five goats—we really did have too many for the grazing land we had available.

As well, we'd helped them secure two boats—one with a functional engine and the second a larger sailboat—so they could go out onto the lake to fish rather than simply casting from the shore. They'd been able to increase their catch substantially. The boats were from a side trade with Jimmie and Johnny. They had more boats than they could use, and they needed almost everything in the way of food that was on offer. My mother had warned the colonel about Johnny and

Jimmie and he'd appreciated the information. "Forewarned is forearmed," he said.

In return for the things we'd given the colonel and his community they'd helped us with security, given us a few rifles, provided training, and made a promise to come to our aid if we were attacked. That last one meant a lot. We were an illusion, a house made of straw, and the fear was that if somebody blew too hard it would all tumble over.

Despite the increased fortifications, and the extra training, weapons, and support, my mother hadn't abandoned our backup plan. Julian and Jim and I had been out to our little island the week before. We'd watered our crops, which were progressing well, and then stashed away some sealed containers of jam and jelly, and a couple of dozen candles. It felt wrong to take from the community's supplies. I knew it was like stealing, but lots of things that weren't right seemed to be okay now.

The partnership with the airport hadn't been without problems, because of the historical conflict between the people who lived on the island and those who flew out of the airport. As well, there were some members of our community who felt we didn't need any extra help. It was as if they'd been tricked into believing that we really were as strong and safe as we were pretending to be. We weren't. We weren't even close, even with all the changes that were taking place. After a lot of debate, though, Chris had been able to get full agreement to the new alliance.

As I got closer to Willow's house, I could see him on his porch. He got up, his crossbow on his shoulder, and met me on the path. I, of course, had mine with me too.

"Emma, do you know what this is about?" he asked.

"With my brother, I'm hardly *ever* sure what it's about. He just said he wanted to show us something."

"That sounds mysterious, and important."

"Knowing Ethan it could be anything, but important? Probably not."

"I just wish he'd stop calling me names. Elm, Maple, Christmas, Palm, Oak . . . actually, I sort of like Oak."

"I think you should go with Maple. Maple syrup, maple muffins, maple cookies. Anything with maple is always sweet and tasty."

"So you think I'm sweet and tasty?" he asked.

I blushed and looked away. I didn't know what to say to that.

"It's okay, I think you're pretty sweet too."

"Um, thanks, I guess."

My stomach started churning and my hands were sweating. This was stupid. I'd faced armed men, so why was this making me so nervous?

We walked in silence through the cottages and to a path around the woods that stretched out along the east side of the island. I think neither of us knew what to say next.

"I hear we might be cutting down these trees," Willow said.

"That must be painful for you, you know, killing your tree brethren."

"Funny. I see where your brother gets it from."

"My mother said it would open up sight lines, provide some more land for cultivation, and supply firewood for the winter."

"I don't even like thinking that this could last that long," Willow said.

"Do you see it getting any better?"

"From everything we've heard it's only getting worse." He paused. "Ever think about going over there?" He gestured to the city visible past our walls and across the harbor.

"I think it's really dangerous."

"Do you think we're safe here?"

I hesitated before answering. "We're safer, but not safe."

"I know. I just like to pretend. Isn't that a lot of what we're doing, pretending, to make us safer?"

"We're trying to fool the outside world but not ourselves. We can't get caught up in believing the magic is real."

"I guess we should be grateful for the airport people," Willow said. "Some people are pretty upset about the flyovers but I like them. They make me feel better."

A couple of times a day, one or two of their planes made a pass over top of the community. I found it familiar and comforting. Base planes did that all the time as a way to say hello or goodbye to their families below.

With those planes they had the ability to go farther afield and check out things that other communities could only wonder about. I'd been told by the colonel that they'd established contact with three other communities that had airstrips. They hoped that if they could get the big plane into the air, with somebody at the stick who could fly it, they could start trading larger commodities back and forth.

We went along the path that ran just inside the wall. At regular intervals we passed our guards. They were always in pairs, dressed in Marine costumes, one carrying a real weapon and the other a fake assault rifle. Those rifles certainly looked real. Each pair of guards was within sight of the next pair, and if one set saw something they could alert the entire wall. Each guard we passed said hello or nodded. It was getting to the point that I knew most of the people in the community. And even those I didn't know certainly knew me and my mother and brother.

"Do you think you could take me to the airport the next time you go?" Willow asked.

"I can ask my mother."

"It would be great just to get off this island."

"You could go out with one of the fishing boats," I suggested.

"I don't want to fish. I just want to be able to walk somewhere that isn't here."

I'd been over to the airport compound four times as part of our exchange groups. I liked being there. I liked talking to the colonel. He was nice and kind to me, and he was military. He reminded me of my father, and my grandfather, and all the military people and places I'd lived for most of my life. There were times when being a military brat and living on bases had seemed so restrictive that it made me want to run away screaming. Now it just seemed right.

My mother and I had talked about moving to the airport community. The colonel had made it clear that he'd always be willing to open his doors to a Marine and her family. In my mind it was sort of a Plan B to our other Plan B. It was a better backup plan than the one we had.

We came up to the eastern boundary of our community. The wall had been constructed well up from the beach, separated by some scrubland and trees and an open space. It was decided that the shoreline itself—a cliff that was as tall as a house—was the best defense. We followed along the fence until we came up to the northeast corner. There, a small guard tower had been constructed. It looked more like a little tree fort that a couple of kids had built than anything else, but it did give an elevated view. The guards up in the tower waved to us and we waved back.

"So where is he?" Willow asked.

I shrugged. "I'll ask."

We walked over to the base of the tower. "Have you seen my brother and his friends?"

"I'm seeing them right now," he said. He pointed out over the fence.

Willow and I climbed up onto the little observation ledge and looked over the wall. I gasped, and Willow started laughing. My brother and one of his friends were out there—on top of two ostriches. They were riding them! A group of eight or ten boys were off to the side, watching and cheering as Ethan and his friend Justin bounced along, each riding one of the gigantic birds.

"That is hilarious!" Willow exclaimed.

"And dangerous! You wanted to go outside the walls, come on!"

I raced off to the gate leading out of the community, flinging it open, and we ran out. My brother saw me coming and yelled out my name and waved, almost falling off before he grabbed the ostrich around the neck with both hands.

"None of you should be out here," I yelled to the group of boys watching.

They all looked at me without reacting.

"All of you, get back inside the wall!" I ordered.

They all continued to stare at me but didn't move.

"Now!" I yelled, waving my crossbow, and they suddenly jumped and ran toward the gate.

The two boys and their mounts were at the far end of the clearing, moving fast. The birds were kicking up clumps of dirt as they ran. I raced toward them, waving my arms in the air and yelling.

The boys seemed to ignore me, but the two ostriches didn't. Justin's ostrich twisted and turned, and Justin was tossed into the air and landed on the ground with a thud. I gasped, but he instantly bounced back to his feet, raising his hands in the air as if he were waving to the nonexistent crowd.

I turned to look for Ethan and caught sight of him and his bird racing away down the path and into the woods. That path led to the cliff. Was that bird smart enough not to run off the cliff? And if it wasn't, was my brother smart enough to jump off the bird before it did?

I ran across the clearing, past a stunned Justin, and down the path, my feet barely touching the ground.

The ostrich reappeared but without my brother on its back. Was he hurt? Had he been smashed against a tree or tossed over the cliff as the ostrich turned away?

I slowed down but didn't stop moving, scanning the sides of the path as I ran, and then I saw my brother. And two men. One had a rifle and the second was holding my brother by the arm, dragging him along, while Ethan struggled to get away. In one motion, the man pulling him slapped my brother across the face, which would have sent him sprawling if the man hadn't been holding onto him.

"Let him go!" I screamed.

They stopped and turned. They looked surprised. My brother looked terrified. Then, as they saw me, their expressions changed to amusement. I saw blood running down the side of Ethan's face.

"Leave him alone!" I ordered.

The man with the gun chuckled. "You think you're in a position to be giving anybody orders?"

"We have lots of guards. They're coming right now."

His smirk faded and he tried to look past me and down the path. "I don't see nobody." He started walking toward me. "Don't make me go chasing you because that will only get me mad," he said as he continued to close in. "I got no patience, so you just come now before I have to shoot you."

He started to swing the rifle up.

Without thinking, I dropped to one knee, swung up the crossbow, aimed, and pulled the trigger. I heard the bolt fly, and at almost the same second I saw his reaction. His eyes widened, his mouth opened, he gasped, clutched his chest, and fell over backwards.

I now looked past him to where the other man was still holding my brother by the arm. Their stunned looks of disbelief were exactly how I felt. All three of us were frozen like statues. It was like time was standing still. And then I acted.

I dropped my crossbow and jumped to my feet. I raced across the gap between me and the fallen man to where his rifle lay. I got there before the other man even had time to think about fleeing. I scooped up the rifle and brought it up, ready to fire, my finger on the trigger as I aimed it directly at his chest. From this distance there was no way I could miss.

"Let him go," I said.

He released his grip and raised his hands above his head as Ethan ran to my side. I kept the rifle aimed right at him, my eye looking down the sight and right at his chest. My finger was still on the trigger. All I had to do was just squeeze a little bit tighter and he was dead.

I looked up from the sight to his face. He wasn't that much older than me—maybe late teens. He was somebody who could have lived up the street from us, or three floors down in our building. He could have been the older brother of a friend. He could have been the guy fixing the elevator in our building. Or he could be the man I shot dead right here.

I heard movement on the path behind me and took a quick glance. It was Willow and Justin.

"You should go now or I'll kill you," I said.

He didn't move. Willow and Justin got to my side. Willow had his crossbow up and aimed.

"Did you hear me?" I asked through clenched teeth.

He nodded. "Yes . . . thank you."

"Don't ever come back," I snarled.

He shook his head. He slowly lowered his arms and took a couple of steps backwards, still looking at me like he didn't believe I wasn't going to shoot him. He turned and took a few more steps, looking over his shoulder, and then started running. He was visible for only a few seconds before he disappeared behind a curve in the path, moving into the trees.

"Are you all right?" Willow asked as he lowered his weapon. I kept mine aimed into the distance.

"Oh, my goodness, is he dead?" Justin asked.

He was staring down at the man. The bolt was sticking

partway out of his chest, blood seeping out. His eyes were open but vacant, blank. I looked away.

They all stood there, looking down at the body, nobody moving.

Then I walked away, still carrying the rifle, stopping only briefly to pick up my crossbow. The three of them appeared at my side. I didn't know what to say. I just wanted us back inside the wall.

26

"It's beautiful," Colonel Wayne said. "I never thought I'd think a vegetable patch was beautiful, but it is."

We were standing—Chris, Sam, Colonel Wayne, his second-in-command, Lieutenant Wilson, and three of his men, my mother, Ethan, and me—in front of our garden on our little island. There were tomatoes and cucumbers, carrots and radishes. All were ready, or almost ready, for harvest.

"These are the seeds you gave us in the beginning," my mother reminded Chris.

"I remember giving them to you, but I never thought to ask what you'd done with them. You did well."

"We planted them before you invited us to join your community," I said. I was feeling guilty that I was telling her a half-truth. But that was trivial compared to the other guilt I was feeling. It had been a week since it had happened. Since I'd killed that man.

"So this is the island where you used to live?" Chris asked.

"Yes. The ten of us. This was our home," my mother replied.

"I noticed that you never told anybody exactly where it was," she said.

Ethan and I exchanged a side glance, but all three of us stayed silent.

"The garden survived very well, considering that you moved away almost three months ago," Chris said.

"It's had some help," my mother said. "We've come out occasionally to weed, and we even watered it a couple of times when there wasn't much rain."

"But you didn't tell anybody about it."

My mother shook her head.

"I understand," Colonel Wayne said. "I understand completely."

Everybody looked at him.

"A good Marine always has a backup plan for all situations and scenarios. This here is your backup plan."

My mother nodded. I noted that she didn't say that it was only *part* of our backup plan. She had revealed the garden but hadn't told anybody about the tools, supplies, and weapons buried elsewhere on the island. Was she going to reveal those things as well? But really, how could she do that without admitting that we'd been taking things from Ward's Island and spiriting them away to here?

"If you worked so hard to keep this a secret that long, why did you bring us here today?" Chris asked.

I knew the answer already because my mother had talked to me about it at length.

"Most of it is now ready to harvest," my mother said. "But Chris, I need your permission to do what I want with it."

"My permission?"

"This crop is here because of your generosity, your kindness to a stranger and her two children."

"That was only basic human courtesy."

"There's not a lot of that around these days. It was an act of kindness, which made it even harder to keep this from you," my mother said.

"What is it you want to do?" Chris said.

"Give it to Colonel Wayne and his community. They have people going hungry."

Colonel Wayne looked at my mother in surprise. "That's incredibly generous. And believe me, I'm grateful beyond words. But why? Why aren't you taking the crops and just trading them to us for something you need?"

"I am trading it for something we need. We need your community to stay strong. We need that almost as much as you do."

He smiled. "Thank you."

"Chris, do I have your permission?" she asked.

"Of course. But if a good Marine always has a backup plan, then what is your backup plan now?" Chris asked.

My mother took a few seconds before responding. This was the biggest part of why she had brought the colonel and Chris together. I knew what she was going to say because I was the one who'd originally suggested it to her, confirming what she was already thinking.

"I've been thinking about this for a while, but much more over the past week," she began.

"Since the terrible incident with your children," Colonel Wayne said.

I didn't know he knew about it, but again, I wasn't really surprised because everybody seemed to know. Most people just said nothing. Other people said things like "Sorry" or "That had to be hard." Others said stupid things like "I could never kill somebody" or "I'm glad it wasn't me." Even Willow didn't seem to know what to say to me.

"Yes, since that incident."

"And you're both all right?" the colonel asked.

"I am, because of my sister," Ethan said.

They all looked at me. "I'm fine. I was fine then."

"From what I heard you were calm and brave," Colonel Wayne said.

"I just did what I had to do."

That was the line I'd been using since it happened. It was the line that I repeated to myself over and over on the nights when I lay in bed unable to get to sleep.

"Emma, can you tell them what you've been thinking, what we've talked about?"

I hadn't expected to be the one to do the talking. "I can try."

"Things like that do get you thinking," Colonel Wayne said.

I nodded and took a deep breath. "I started to realize that we can't stop people from coming onto our island. If I hadn't stopped them, if they'd really wanted in, if there had been ten of them instead of two, then my brother would be dead. I'd be dead."

"But you aren't," Chris said.

"Not this time," I said. I turned to my mother, suddenly feeling tears coming on. "Could you . . . please?"

She nodded. "Chris, she's right, if there had been three of them, my children would have been dead. If a hundred men had scaled that cliff then we would all have been dead. We tried to build a secure place but we failed."

"I don't see failure. We're stronger, safer, better, and we've survived."

"We're nothing more than an illusion."

"An illusion that's provided food, water, shelter, and security to over eight hundred people," Chris said.

"But we're still an illusion. Nothing we've done can withstand a direct, powerful attack," my mother argued.

"Then we'll continue to make ourselves stronger."

"We can't fix the basic problems. We don't have enough weapons, or people who know how to use them. There are too many places where we can be attacked and not enough ways to defend them."

"But we do have food and water, power, shelter, and—"

"And those are the things that are going to draw people to attack us. It's just a matter of time," my mother said. "As other people have less, then what we have is going to act like a magnet."

"And they're going to keep coming until they take it from us," I said.

"But if we had more armed guards?" Chris asked. She turned to the colonel. "What if we had twenty of your guards?"

Colonel Wayne shook his head slowly. "Chris, we don't have twenty guards that we can afford to give you without jeopardizing our position. I'm sorry."

"The enemy is coming. We don't know when, or how many, but their desperation is going to draw them to us," my mother said.

"Then you're saying we have no future?" Chris asked.

My mother shook her head, and then turned to the colonel. "But neither do you."

He looked surprised. "We certainly are much better defended."

"But you're not better supplied. They won't need to scale your walls. Eventually you'll be starved out. You don't have the resources or skills necessary to feed that many people."

"That's why we're trading with your community," he said.

"And that trading works until our community is destroyed," my mother said. "Our destruction will eventually lead to your destruction. We'll go in the blink of an eye. Your compound's downfall will be slower but no less fatal."

"We're not going to give up without a fight," Colonel Wayne said.

"No disrespect, sir, but it won't be a fight that will end it. It will be the lack of carrots and potatoes."

"Then what is it that you're suggesting?" Chris asked.

My mother looked at me to answer.

"It's time for the two communities to become one," I said.

"We need to move to the airport. Your geographic position is better, your defenses superior, you have the airstrip and a larger parcel of land," my mother explained. "We need to move everything—the people, the solar panels, the resources."

Chris shook her head. "Even if I thought it was best, this isn't a decision that I can make. You know how we work."

"We know, but they listen to you. What do you think?" my mother asked.

She didn't answer right away. Was she trying to find the words to tell us we were wrong—that I was wrong? Then she looked up. "I think Colonel Wayne and I need to talk more before anything else happens," she said.

The colonel nodded. "I agree. Perhaps we could even continue that discussion now. Captain Williams, Ellen, would you join us?"

The three of them walked away, followed at a respectful distance by Sam, Lieutenant Wilson, and the three armed guards from the compound. That left just me and Ethan.

Ethan had been using his fingers to dig into the carrot patch. He'd already pulled up one big orange carrot and now he pulled out a second.

"This is for you," he said, offering me the bigger of the two.

"It's a little on the dirty side."

He rubbed it all around against his pants, dislodging most of the dirt, and then offered it again. It still wasn't completely clean, but I took it and had a big, crunchy bite. It tasted good.

"I like where we live," Ethan said.

"So do I."

"This time it's me who doesn't want to move."

"This time at least you'd get to take your friends with you."

"You too," he said.

"I don't really have friends . . . except for Willow."

"I like Willow," he said. He smiled. "But not the way you do."

I gave him a punch in the arm. "I should have let that guy drag you away."

"You'd miss me. Do you think it's going to happen, the move?"

"What do I know?" I asked.

"You know a lot. I guess I'm glad you're my sister."

"You guess? After what I did you should definitely be glad I'm your sister."

"I am glad. I even gave you a carrot." He looked down. "I know. I could have been dead."

"We don't have to think about that," I said.

"Sometimes I can't think of anything else."

"Me neither."

"I thought it was just me. What was it like? Doing that . . . killing somebody."

"I didn't want to do it, but I had to. I don't want to do it again, but I will if I have to. I'd rather kill than be killed."

"I could kill somebody too," he said. "I could do it to protect you or Mom."

"That's why we have to move, so we don't have to do that again. I just hope they'll listen."

"And all of this was your idea?" he asked.

"Some of it. Most of it. All of it."

"You know, sometimes you're smarter than I give you credit for."

"Thank you. And you know, sometimes you're . . . well you're not as dumb as I give you credit for." I shook my head. "Riding an ostrich?"

"I saw it in a picture once."

"Wouldn't one of the zebras have made more sense?"

"Zebras? Why didn't I think of that? We'll be taking the ostriches and zebras with us, right?"

"We'll be bringing everything we can bring. Assuming people agree to it."

That was a very, very big if, and I knew it.

27

I sat on the porch, reading my book, trying
to put my mind someplace else. It had been a hard two weeks
of discussion, arguments, yelling, tears, accusations, and more
discussion, still without any decision. I really hadn't expected
my idea about moving to the airport community to set off so
many things.

Some people were angry it was even suggested. It was so
odd—some of the same people who hadn't wanted to defend
the place were now arguing that it was well defended. Some
of them had stopped saying hello to me, or even looking in
my direction as we passed. Thank goodness I hadn't been
the only one thinking about this possible move.

There was even talk about how my mother and brother
and I had come here to live but our plan all along had been
to go to the airport. The word "mole" was used. We had "bur-
rowed" in here, pretending to be their friends, when really all
the time we'd been working for the airport community. Of
course, giving the airport compound all of the food we'd
secretly grown on our little island hadn't endeared us to
those people.

As the talks stalled, my mother and I talked about simply
leaving. Sam was part of that discussion. He said that not

only would he understand if we left, but if it weren't for his grandmother he would come with us. We decided then that we wouldn't go anywhere alone. It wasn't just that these people would collapse without my mother—our only chance of ultimately convincing them would have to come from within. The point was that we needed to bring the communities together for their mutual benefit. Ultimately, if the Ward's community tried to stand alone, they would sooner or later be overpowered, but the decision would be fatal to the airport community, too, as they slowly starved. We had a choice: a fast death or a slow one.

"Hey, Emma," Willow said.

I looked up as he sat down beside me. I tried not to notice his leg brushing against mine.

"Seems appropriate," he said, pointing at my book.

It was *The Hunger Games*. "It's one of my favorites. Strange how reading helps me escape from this world by taking me to one that's even more messed up."

"I figure you just identify with the bow and arrow part. You are the closest thing we have to Katniss."

"That's not the first time I've heard that. So, does that make you Peeta or Gale?"

"Probably Peeta. He's always hiding behind Katniss the way I hide behind you."

"Don't be hard on yourself. Beside, you have to admit that Peeta is cute."

"You think I'm cute?" he asked.

"Yeah . . . sort of like a floppy-eared puppy dog."

"I'll take that."

"I'm just glad you, at least, are still talking to me."

"Emma, don't let their stupidity get to you. It's not your fault that you had an idea."

"That's not how some people are seeing it. They think my mother and I are traitors to the community."

"You've kept us alive. Hey, you don't have your crossbow with you?" Willow said.

"It's inside."

"But you always have it with you. Right beside you. Is this because of, well, because of . . . ?"

"Because I killed that man?"

He nodded. Willow looked uneasy, as though he wasn't sure what he should say next, or whether he should even have said that much. "I guess I'm just worried about how you're taking all this."

"I'm okay."

But I wasn't, not really. I was all right if somebody was around, or I was lost in a good book, or when I finally got to sleep. It was getting to sleep that was hard. I could still see his lifeless face in my mind. Open eyes, open mouth, and then the bolt sticking out of his chest. I'd killed that man. A few months ago my biggest problem was that we'd changed cities. Now the entire world had changed, and I had killed a man.

"You know what makes me angry, though? Some people are saying that what I did to protect Ethan is proof that my mother and I are bad people. It really bugs me that anyone here would still mistrust me or my mother or our motives."

"We all have a pretty good idea where we'd be without you." He paused. "Look, you're not planning on leaving and going to live at the airport, are you?"

"We're not doing that."

"That's what I figured. You couldn't leave me behind . . . I have that effect on girls."

I chuckled. "You really are a bit delusional, you know that, right?"

"I live in a world where people I don't know are trying to kill me and everybody I do know. Don't you think a little delusion might be a good thing? Maybe I should start LARPing with my parents again."

"A little delusion doesn't hurt. Besides," I took a deep breath before continuing, "I would miss you . . . a lot."

"Then I have good news. If you did leave, you wouldn't have to leave me behind."

"You'd come with us?"

"Me and my family," he said. He leaned in closer and whispered, "My parents and I have talked about it."

"Really?"

He nodded.

What I wanted to tell him—what I couldn't tell him—was that my mother and I had talked about what would happen if things fell apart here. She'd had confidential discussions with Colonel Wayne and he'd said he would gladly welcome us and any other people we recommended. Willow and his family were on that short list of people we wanted to come along with us. It was just that nobody could know about it.

"And believe me," Willow said, "we're not the only ones."

"Who else?"

"Lots of people think it's the right thing to do."

"Then why don't any of them speak up louder?" I asked.

"They don't want to ruffle feathers."

"So they'd rather die than risk getting people ruffled?"

"Pretty much. Sometimes people just want peace," he said.

"That's the problem with a lot of people here. Peace comes at a price, and sometimes that price is being willing to fight!"

"Hey, you're talking to the wrong person."

"Then you have to tell people. You and your parents and anybody else who believes that we should go."

"I'll talk to my parents about telling other people."

"That would help. People really respect them."

And then we heard the church bell clang. I felt the hair on the back of my neck stand on edge.

"Do you think we're under attack?" Willow asked.

"It's probably nothing at all. How many times have they raised the alarm this week?"

"Four, no, five times."

"And each time it was nothing. It's going to be nothing this time, too. Still, we'd better get to our stations."

A fifth and then a sixth boat joined the ones already stationed off our shore. The first one had shown up almost two hours ago, then one by one the others had appeared. That was when the alarm was sounded. They were coming nearer and then zigzagging back out, staying close enough to present a threat but far enough away that firing on them would have been useless. Even the catapult couldn't chuck a projectile that far.

"What are they doing?" Willow asked.

"Making us really nervous, if nothing else."

"What does your mother think?" he asked.

"Good question. I'll ask her." I took a couple of steps and Willow followed. I stopped. "I think there's a better chance of her talking more openly if it's just me."

"Oh, sure, I understand."

"I'll tell you whatever she tells me. I promise."

He smiled—I liked that smile. He was cute.

I went toward the part of the wall where I knew my mother had gone. I came up quietly and listened in as she was speaking to a group of people. I knew she was trying to calm them down. Everybody was on edge. She finished up and turned to face me.

"How are you doing?" she asked.

"Good. Can we talk?"

"We can talk while we walk," she said.

I fell in beside her. "Most people aren't doing that fine, are they?"

"Not good. I think part of it is my fault," she said.

"Your fault?"

"When I said that I thought we should move and that I had doubts, it planted doubts in their minds as well."

"What do you think those boats are doing out there?" I asked.

"They're getting ready to attack."

"But they've been out there for over two hours. What are they waiting for?"

"Probably for more boats and men to arrive. Or maybe they're waiting until it gets dark. They might be checking out our defenses, or simply trying to make us anxious."

"Shouldn't we at least fire the catapults at them, you know, let them know that we'll fight back?" I asked.

"That would only tell them that we don't have anything more effective to fire. I'm hoping the rumors are still out there that we have mortars."

"I wish we did. Or more guns, or something. Wait, should we send word to Colonel Wayne about what's happening?"

"I already sent Sam."

"Do you think the colonel will send some people?"

"He's offered us support before, so I'm sure he will." She looked at her watch. "It's time for me to go to the back gate and check on the guards there."

My mother had been rotating through all our defensive positions: from here along the wall, over to the place where the ostrich races had taken place, and continuing on to the bridge and the channel. Despite the fact that this was obviously where the danger was, there was no point in assuming it couldn't come from another direction as well.

"Here, take these," she said as she pulled her binoculars from around her neck and handed them to me. "If you see anything that makes you suspicious, send somebody to find me."

She took a few steps and then spun around and came right back to my side.

"You know what to do if . . ."

"I know."

She nodded and was gone.

The "if" was if we were overrun. Our old plan still held: our original group would gather at our house and then move on from there. The big difference was that now we'd be fleeing to the airport instead of our little island.

Soon, Willow and his family and those few others would

be approached and asked to join in with us. It felt so good knowing that soon we'd be able to include them in our plans. Not telling them was the same as lying to them—a lie that could cost them their lives. I cared about Willow—I cared about all of them.

Then I had a terrible thought: What if "soon" was too late? What if today was the day it all fell apart? I couldn't allow that thought to enter my head.

I rejoined Willow on the wall.

"So, what's happening?" he asked.

For a split second I thought he was asking about the plans to escape instead of what was happening here. I put my head back into the right conversation.

"They might be waiting until dark before they attack."

"But we have lights," he said.

"They may not know that."

"Of course they would. We used them during the last big attack, and a couple of times when the alarm was sounded."

Willow was right. "They might just be gathering more people then, or maybe they're just trying to scare us."

"I don't know. People are pretty scared already."

"I guess we'll just have to wait and see," I said.

"Do you think they might just go away?"

"They didn't come out here to do nothing."

"They're probably watching us the way we're watching them, and they'll see the walls and the guns and maybe even the uniforms and decide that it's too risky to attack us," Willow added.

"All we can do is wait and watch and hope."

With that said, I pulled the binoculars up to my eyes.

28

I stretched and yawned as I slowly got to my feet. The darkness was starting to lift. I was cold, and my clothing was damp from the dew that had settled in over-night. All night we'd stayed at our posts, taking turns drifting off into uneasy sleep, waiting. Periodically my mother would materialize out of the darkness, say a few words, and con-tinue on her rounds. If most of us had had little sleep, I was sure that she'd had no sleep.

I looked out to the water. All I could see aside from the dark was a thick fog that hung over the lake. It gave it an even eerier feeling. Those boats were still out there, beyond my view, which made them even more frightening, more powerful, and more dangerous. Before the darkness had set in there had been a total of eight boats. Had another two or four or ten joined them overnight? The unseen, enhanced by my imagination, was an even bigger monster than before.

"Can you see anything?"

I looked over. It was Joshua, the actor, dressed as a Marine captain. He'd recently added that insignia to his uniform and given himself a fake promotion to go with his fake rifle.

"There might not be anything to see," I offered encourag-ingly.

"From your lips to God's ear."

I went back to scanning the water. With each passing second the darkness was lifting and I felt as though I could "not see" more clearly. The fog over the lake was thicker than I had originally thought. I started to wonder if even the full light of dawn would allow me to see through it far enough to where the boats had been stationed.

Then I had another thought. Maybe the fog had driven them away, or at least kept them at bay. In the dark, in the thick fog, it was probably too dangerous to try to come to shore. Maybe the fog was our friend, and I had to hope it didn't get burned off by the morning sun.

As it got lighter there was more activity and noise along the wall as people came back to life. I had to assume that everybody was as damp and tired and hungry as I was, but somehow the voices seemed positive, and there were little bursts of laughter. Were people feeling more optimistic in the morning light?

Eyes glued to the binoculars, I was starting to see through the fog and farther out onto the lake. What I *wasn't* seeing was reassuring—there were no boats. If they were out there they were still far away from shore. Out there—if they were even out there—they could scare us but they couldn't harm us.

I thought I caught a glimpse of something but it was just swirling mist. Was my imagination getting the better of my eyes? I tried to look harder, to see through the fog, and then the bow of a boat appeared and disappeared. My whole body got hot, and that burned away my hope more powerfully than the morning sun burned off the fog. We were not alone. They were still out there—at least one of them. Maybe the rest had gone? I stopped myself. That was nothing more than a dangerous false hope. It wouldn't be just one boat. If one was there, then they would all be there.

Little by little my suspicions were confirmed. A second and third boat were briefly revealed before vanishing again into the fog and the distance. I wanted to convince myself that I was just seeing the same boat again and again, but the location was wrong. It had to be more than one. Then three boats appeared at once. I heard someone else on the wall react: so it wasn't just me.

I lowered the binoculars. I didn't need to see far as much as I needed to see broadly. There were, along the length of the wall, five . . . no, six boats visible. Still far out, but still there. My assumption was that the other two were out there as well, because there was no reason for only some of them to have stayed.

The sun continued to rise. The light felt both welcoming and threatening. It meant we'd lasted the night, but now it was revealing a truth that nobody wanted. Out of the fading darkness, the growing light revealed even worse news. There weren't six boats, or eight, but many, many more. I did a quick count. There were seventeen boats, at least. And there were still patches of fog that could be hiding more.

Then I noticed something else. The entire wall had fallen silent. All the voices, laughter, even coughing had stopped. We were all stunned and scared into silence. I could almost feel the level of fear rise. I looked at the people closest to me, and then to those farther along the wall. There were some who had actually taken a step or two back from the wall, as if they were being pushed away by their fears.

I turned to Willow. "Go and get my mother. She's probably at the bridge."

He jumped to his feet, looking as terrified as I felt. I reached up and grabbed him by the hand and pulled him down slightly so I could speak quietly and privately.

"Willow, I need you to get her fast, but I need you to walk to get her calmly. Do you understand?"

He nodded but his eyes were wide. He looked like a deer caught in the headlights of an oncoming truck.

"Tell her about the ships and that we need her here quickly, soon, but you need to leave here looking almost casual, no panic."

Willow walked away. He glanced over his shoulder at me and I gave him a reassuring smile and nod of the head, and he returned both.

"We're going to be okay," I said.

I realized I'd wanted to think that, not say it, but the words had come out. I looked around to see who had heard me. Those on both sides of me nodded in agreement. It seemed to reassure them.

I got to my feet. "We're all going to be okay," I said again, but this time more loudly and more deliberately, trying to sound confident and calm. Again those who heard seemed to respond well. That was both reassuring and disturbing. Why would my words have an impact on them? It made me realize how much they needed something, and until my mother arrived I was all they had. These people were as fragile and as much an illusion as their fake guns and uniforms.

I walked along the wall, offering a few words to everybody. I realized I was using the same calm, quiet tone that my mother used. That was always her tone, not just here but in her life as an ER nurse, as a Marine, and as a mother.

As I walked I kept scanning the water. The boats hadn't got any closer but a few more had emerged from the fog. I counted twenty-one now. Three were larger but most were fairly small and couldn't have held more than a dozen people. How many people were there out there?

I stopped and rested the binoculars against one of the arrow loops and tried to focus on the nearest boat. Finding a bobbing boat through the lenses always proved difficult for me. I lowered the binoculars, traced a line out, and then retrained the binoculars along that line until the boat came into view. I adjusted the lenses to focus.

Up on the flying bridge of the boat I could see the person at the wheel. With these powerful binoculars I could practically make out his expression. I thought about how if I'd been looking through the scope of a sniper rifle instead of binoculars I could have easily picked him off. Well, not me, but a trained sniper.

I knew Marine snipers. I'd lived on the same base as them, gone to school with their children, been at birthday parties in their houses. They all had some things in common. Even compared to other Marines their hair was a little bit shorter, their uniforms more meticulous. That was what their homes looked like, too. Everything was spotless and in its place. They spoke in precise, clipped tones, with an even voice, as though they were trying to control their heart rate even when they were standing still. They rarely laughed, and I couldn't imagine them ever crying. They were almost emotionally blank.

My mother had said to me that you had to be that way if

you were going to squeeze a trigger, take a life, and not have it register. They could shoot somebody and then take a bite from a sandwich or a sip from their coffee. It was business, and you had to be a certain type to be in that business.

In that moment I wished I was more that type. I wished I could forget what I'd done, or that expression on the man's face, those dead eyes open and staring into space. It was a look of perpetual surprise, sort of like he was thinking, "My goodness, she killed me!" When I looked at myself in the mirror I could still see a little bit of surprise myself—*I'd killed somebody.*

I moved the binoculars to look down on the boat's deck. I couldn't see anybody. Were they below deck, or just sitting so low against the gunwale that they were out of sight? That would have been smart. Staying out of sight meant staying out of sniper sights. If those uniforms had any impact on them they must have been wondering if we had snipers. But really, shouldn't I have been able to see somebody? It wasn't that big a boat, and there weren't many places to hide.

I looked over to find a second boat. There were so many of them that it wasn't hard to find. This boat was one of the bigger ones. The top level was covered, closed in, and I couldn't see through the glass. A few bullets would have shattered those windows, and their confidence, and revealed the captain and the men up there, or even killed somebody.

I scanned the deck. Again, it was empty, but there were more places to hide, and the boat looked big enough to have a compartment below deck.

This all should have been reassuring. Seeing fewer people meant there were fewer people to attack us. Instead it was troubling, disturbing. Why weren't these two boats just overflowing, brimming with people ready to attack? The boats that had attacked here the first time, the ones that had passed by our little island on their way, were filled with armed men. This made no sense . . . unless it made perfect sense.

I quickly switched my gaze to a third boat. It was even smaller than the first. The captain was at the stern and there was another man beside him, rifle in hand, but that was it. Just the two of them. On this boat I could see for sure there was nobody else on board.

This was starting to come together in my head. I moved to a fourth boat, deliberately picking another of the smaller ones. I needed confirmation and I quickly got it. I could see the driver on an otherwise empty boat. I was almost positive I knew what was going on, but still, I wanted one more piece of proof. I needed one more piece of proof.

I heard a commotion and turned around. It was my mother, accompanied by Willow. Thank goodness she was here so I could tell her what I thought was happening. Then I saw that they weren't alone. There were six or seven other people with them. They all had real guns. These were people who had been by the bridge or guarding the channel. She'd pulled them from those posts to come here to guard against an attack . . . oh, my goodness . . . that was exactly the wrong thing to do if what I suspected was true!

I jumped to my feet and started to run until I realized there were dozens of eyes on me. Deliberately I slowed to a walk. By the time I got to her she'd already deployed the seven armed people to spots along the wall. That was the worst thing possible, but at least we now could talk. I just had to get rid of one more person.

"Willow, could you go and check on Ethan and your mother?" I asked.

"Shouldn't I be out here?"

My mother registered that I wanted to talk to her alone. "We don't need you right now. Just go home for a bit."

"Sure." He looked like he was thinking through what I'd asked. "Don't worry, I'll take care of Ethan. I'll keep him safe, no matter what. You have my word . . . both of you have my word."

"Thanks."

He took a few steps and I called out to him, and he stopped and turned. "Stay with him, you and your mother, maybe at your house or our house but no place else, okay?"

He nodded and then was gone.

"I know how hard it is for you not to tell him more. He's a good guy. You know, he reminds me of your father," my mother said.

"My father?" The man who had left her, the man who'd broken her heart and—?

"I mean that in the best way. So, what's happened? What's changed?"

"The boats out there," I said, gesturing toward the lake, "there's nobody on them."

"Nobody?" she questioned.

"Just a captain on each one, and there's another guy on one of them as well."

"You checked out all the boats?" she asked.

"I only had time to look at four of them."

"Then the others could have people, or perhaps you can't see them below deck," she said.

"Some of the boats don't have a below deck." I pulled the binoculars off my neck and handed them to her. "I looked at boats on the north side of the formation. Look at some to the south," I suggested.

She took the binoculars and started scanning the lake. She stopped at one boat.

"I can't see anybody. But then I can't see everywhere on the boat, so there could be people out of sight," she said.

"More likely they're empty because the people who were passengers have been dropped off elsewhere," I said.

"Elsewhere, where?" she asked.

"I only see two choices. Either they're below the cliff, hidden from view of our back gate, or they're on Main Island."

"Or it could be both," she agreed.

"So those boats are just out there to make us think this is where the attack is going to happen, right?" I asked.

"That's the only explanation I can think of."

"How many people do you think they brought?"

"If there were ten men on each boat—"

"Some of them would carry a lot more than ten," I said, cutting her off.

"A few could potentially hold forty or fifty people, but if we say ten per boat then that's a minimum of 210 men, with the potential rising to perhaps double that many," she said.

"But we only have seventeen people with any sort of gun. We could never stop that many armed invaders," I gasped.

She shook her head. "We have to slow them down enough

to make them think it isn't worthwhile, to fool them into thinking they can't win."

"Will the colonel come with some more men?" I asked.

"If the boats dropped off men on Main Island there's no guarantee that Sam even got through to ask for help. He might just be hunkered down out there, safe but unable to move."

"So it's just us," I said.

"I don't think we can count on the cavalry coming. I'm going to pull almost everybody with a rifle off this section. I'll lead half of them to the back gate and fence. The rest I'm going to send to the bridge and channel. I want you to go ahead and let them know at the channel what we think is happening." She paused. "Are you okay?"

I knew I didn't look okay. "No, but I'll do what I have to do."

"I know you will. Here, I want you to take this." She started to undo her holster.

"I have my crossbow," I said.

"I want you to have this as well. I have the rifle." She undid her holster and handed the pistol to me.

Reluctantly I put it around my waist and did up the buckle.

"If things go south, you get to Willow's house, get them and your brother, bring them to our place, and then we'll escape into the woods," she said.

"Not across the channel?"

"Not if that's where the attack is going to happen. Wait for me and the others at the house as long as you can, but if you have to, just get away into the woods. From there, get the canoes and rowboats to the water. Again, wait as long as you can."

"We'll wait until you get there."

"You have to make sure you and your brother are all right."

"We're not going without you."

"Yes you are. You get away and get to the airport. I need to know that you two are safe. The colonel has given me assurances he'll care for you. I can count on you, right?"

I nodded.

"People know they are to rally at our house. You get them moving from there. I'll do whatever I can to meet you, but I have to stay close to the front or our defense will just collapse. You know that."

I did know it, but I knew something else. "We need you more than they do. If it starts to collapse, we need you to get to us."

"I'll move heaven and earth to get there, believe me." She gave me a big hug.

"Do you think I could be wrong?" I asked quietly.

"No, that's the problem. I think you're right."

She released me, turned, and made her way toward the wall to start reassigning people.

I needed to get on with my job as well. An attack was coming. Where and when were the only questions.

29

I made a quick stop at Willow's house, just to lay eyes on Ethan and make sure he was all right. Ethan knew something was wrong. We exchanged a few meaningless words and I was off again. As well, Willow was too smart not to realize how bad things were. I made him promise to go to my house with his mother and Ethan and wait for me no matter what happened. He promised.

Cutting along the path through the houses, I couldn't help but notice how everything seemed so calm, so peaceful, so normal. At the last house before the clearing I hesitated and took a deep breath. This was where normal would end. In my mind I saw the bridge being stormed and armed attackers crossing the channel in little boats—but it was silent and still.

The former baseball field was now rows of tall, ripening tomatoes, interspersed with cucumbers, carrots, and beets. It all looked so beautiful—and of course tempting. We'd understood all along that it was potentially dangerous to grow food where it was so visible to people on the other side of the channel. My mother said it was like "waving a red flag at a bull," daring them to attack. She was right, but really, there hadn't been much choice. Every plot of land within the community had to be put under cultivation, and this piece was such a big one that we couldn't afford to not put it to use. We had to choose between possibly attracting an attack or certain starvation. A definite gain had to win out over a potential risk.

Beyond that I could see the white bridge over the channel. It was one of the two most likely places for an attack and therefore our best defended location. The bridge itself was blocked by a heavy, tall, thick wall, topped by barbed wire. The thickness was made of three layers—wood on two sides with rocks and gravel in the middle as filler. There was a small gate section that could be removed to allow people to pass, but right now it was secured with heavy wooden bars. The whole thing had been designed by Julian, with assistance from people at the airport.

On top of the bridge were four guards with real rifles. Here, behind the barricade, they could shoot but would be protected from even a high-caliber rifle at close range.

All along the channel ran a fence topped with a metal section and barbed wire, with guard stations at twenty-yard intervals. They weren't much more than the width of a picnic table, which was what they'd been made from. The wood and metal and screws and bolts from four picnic tables had been used to build each station. Again, these were Julian's designs. In his unique way he'd made them not only functional but rather attractive as he'd modeled them after the medieval castle designs Willow's father had shown him.

Each guard station was occupied by two people. While both were in Marine uniforms, only one of them had a real rifle, and the other held a fake. It was reassuring to see that those people who had been pulled had already been sent back to their original posts by my mother. I was reassured, and surprised, to see her up on the bridge. I'd thought she was going to the back gate—or was she only sending people there? Either way, her being here made me feel better.

"Good morning, Emma."

The voice startled me. One of the women—her name was Grace—was on her knees between the rows of tomatoes. There was a basket at her feet filled with carrots and radishes.

"Do you think you should be out here?" I asked.

"People still have to eat."

"I know they have to eat, but it might be better if—"

My words were cut off by a "whoosh." A trail of white smoke raced above our heads, followed by a gigantic explosion right behind us! I spun around in time to see the wood of a house shoot up into the air and then rain down to the ground! It had been completely destroyed!

Stunned, I was shocked back to reality by a second "whoosh" that passed over my head. I watched as something hit the ground, and dirt and rocks shot high into the air and showered back down to the ground.

"What's happening?" Grace screamed.

"Those were RPGs," I gasped.

"What?"

Before I could explain the air was filled with the sound of gunfire! I dropped to the ground as Grace jumped to her feet and started running across the open area leading toward the houses.

"Get down!" I screamed. "Get down!"

She dropped down, her basket flying into the air and then landing in front of her, the vegetables spilling out all over the ground. There was just something about the way she landed, the way she'd thudded to the ground. She wasn't moving. The force of the fall must have knocked the air out of her lungs. Then I saw a dark patch emerging on her cream-colored top. She hadn't fallen. She'd been shot. That was blood. She needed help, but what help could I give? She was out in the open and not moving. Was she already dead? The gunfire continued.

I flattened myself closer to the ground, taking shelter behind the mounds of dirt, hidden by the tall tomato stalks. Shots rang out. Some sounded closer. That was our people firing back. On all fours I crawled along, still protected, until I got to a spot where I could see across the channel.

On the far side were people, and they were firing their weapons at us. On the channel itself little rowboats and canoes had been put into the water and people were rowing and paddling over. I saw one of them get hit and tumble backwards out of the boat and into the channel. He'd been shot. We'd got him!

The first little boat came across and the three men aboard climbed the fence, trying to scramble over the barbed wire strands at the top. One of them spun around, his body absorbing a bullet as he toppled over. Then the second was hit, crumbling into the wire, his arm and foot locked in so he couldn't fall and just hung there suspended. The third man retreated and slid down the bank so that he was under cover of the slope.

More of the boats had made it across the channel, discharging more men. They were now massing on the bank, taking cover in the slope of the incline, throwing more fire at the guard stations. Our guards were huddled down, taking cover, bullets coming at them almost stopping them from being able to return fire at all. They needed to fire. Wait, I had a gun!

I pulled my mother's pistol out of the holster and aimed it toward the bank. I instantly realized that I couldn't hit anything from this distance.

My eye was caught by movement off to one side. There was a mass of people—thirty or forty or more—and they were running along the path on Main Island, firing their weapons and charging toward the bridge!

Up on the bridge rifles were being fired. My mother was up there. And as the men rushed forward along the path some were falling, wounded or killed, but that didn't stop others from continuing to move toward the bridge. The first of them made the base of the bridge and took cover behind the pillars as well as using the curve of the bridge itself for protection. They were inching forward, moving from pillar to pillar, trying to reach the top. Some were cut down but they kept coming. How long could my mother and the others hold them off? How long before they got to the top and then over the wall and—?

Three of our guards ran off the bridge, streaking toward the crops and the houses! They were running away! Where was the fourth man . . . and where was my mother? If five couldn't hold the bridge what chance did two have? She needed help.

I got up, still staying below the level of the tomato plants, using them for cover, and ran in the direction of the bridge. The three men were running toward me, toward the cover that I was trying to leave. We met at the edge—Garth was one of them.

"You can't go!" I yelled. "My mother needs you!"

"She's the one who ordered us to leave!" Garth yelled back.

Before I could think to ask anything else they all dropped to the ground and started firing back toward the bridge. What were they doing—? Wait, they were laying down cover fire.

At that instant two more figures ran from the bridge. One of them was my mother. They were running, zigzagging back and forth, dodging bullets as they ran. Garth and the others were firing at the men on the bridge. Some of them were already at the top and a few were starting to climb over the barricade. We had to fall back. They'd all be over in a minute and we didn't have the firepower to—and then the bridge exploded!

The ground shook as a cloud of black smoke shot up into the air and pieces of grit and rocks—little chunks of concrete—rained down around us! I looked up and saw that where the bridge was—where all those men had been standing—was nothing more than smoke. It was gone except for a few jagged, unconnected chunks of concrete. The bridge was gone and all of those men were gone with it. How many had there been—twenty or thirty?—all of them were dead. No, more than dead. They had been blown apart, body parts and disintegration was all that was left.

I knew the bridge had been wired with explosives—they'd made the explosives from ingredients found in garages and under sinks—but I'd had no idea it would be that powerful, it didn't seem even remotely possible. It was my mother's idea . . . my mother . . . in the force of the explosion she'd been pushed out of my mind. Where was she?

At that instant two figures on the grass struggled to their feet. It was her and the other man!

Then I realized that everything was silent. No gunfire, no shouting—nothing. Had the force of the blast blown out my eardrums? On unsteady feet my mother and the other man were running straight toward us. I was relieved when I heard the sound of their feet against the pavement, and then people around me starting to yell. Then the gunfire began again.

Staying low they scampered along the path and into the field, jumping and landing in a heap almost right at my feet. They were panting, gasping, and wide-eyed, looks of terror on their faces.

"Is everybody all right?" my mother asked. Her voice was strained. She was trying to sound calm, but sounded scared instead.

People nodded, or said they were fine. They sat there, struggling to catch their breath, to regain themselves.

"The—the bridge!" I stammered.

"I think we used too much explosive," Garth said.

"Better too much than not enough," my mother said.

"Are we safe now?" I asked.

She shook her head.

"But they're all dead. They're gone," one of the men said.

"The men who were on the bridge are dead. More people are coming over the channel, and the back gate is under attack."

"It is?" I gasped.

"Our guards radioed that they need more support but there's nobody to send."

"Maybe the explosion will scare people, make them decide to retreat, to leave," Garth said.

"They're still firing so they're still coming. We haven't stopped them. They're still at the channel and at our back door. I don't know if they're trying to land at the beach. We've got to slow them down."

"What are we going to do now?" Garth asked.

"Garth, you and Emma have to get to Ethan," she said.

I knew what she meant. We were going to head for the woods. She didn't believe we could stop them. The fight wasn't over but we'd already lost. The best we could hope for was to slow them down. She wanted us to get to a spot we could escape from, because we were going to be overwhelmed and overrun.

"What about you?" I asked.

"And the rest of us?" one of the other men asked.

"We're going to put up some fire. Our people, our families, need us to do that."

I heard how she emphasized the word "families."

"We're going to stop them, right here."

"And if we can't?" one of the men asked.

"Then we'll retreat into the houses as well," she added. "Garth, Emma, you go, and the rest of you follow me."

She got to her feet, still hunched over so she was hidden by the crops. That was the cue for everybody else to do the same. We all followed behind as she led us to the end of the row. Now it was time for Garth and me to head toward the houses while the others made their way to the channel.

"Come on!" my mother yelled.

She ran, and after a brief second of hesitation the three ran after her—toward the gunfire and the armed men.

"Now us," Garth said. "Are you ready?"

"How could anybody ever be ready for this?"

"Give me your hand," he said. We linked hands. "Let's go."

We jumped up and started running. I had to fight the urge to look over my shoulder, but there was no point. I wouldn't be able to see anything—not even the bullet that might strike me down. That thought gave me more speed. We kept running down the path even after we'd made the cover of the first houses. Still panting, from both the run and the fear, we slowed to a trot and then a fast walk, finally stopping in front of our house. We'd made it. At least this far.

"Go inside and make sure your brother is okay," Garth said.

"Where are you going?"

"To the back gate. I need to help. We need to slow them down there as well."

Before I could argue he was gone, running along the path. I started up the walkway, but before I could get to the cottage the door flew open and Ethan and Willow came running out.

Ethan threw his arms around me. "Mom?" he asked.

"She's at the channel. She's going to meet us. Who's inside?"

"My mother, of course," Willow said. "Jess and little Olivia, Julian, Paula, and Jim just got here. Chris was here a few minutes ago."

"Where did she go?"

"She went to the beach to help."

"Let's head in and get ready to leave as soon as—"

My words were cut off by the sound of gunfire and a woman screaming in terror. Her cry cut through me like a knife.

30

"Ethan, get inside and get everybody ready
to go!" I ordered.

"Shouldn't we all go inside?" Ethan asked.

"I've got to provide some protection," I explained.

"And I'm not going anywhere without you," Willow said.

I wasn't going to argue. I was scared, and I really didn't
want to be alone.

"Ethan, tell Jim to scout the way through the backyard to
make sure it's clear."

He nodded and ran back into the house as more shots
rang out.

"That sounded pretty close," Willow said.

I led Willow away from the house to the edge of the path.
I looked out one way and then the other. I couldn't see anybody, but the gunfire continued. It was very close and it was
coming from the direction of the back gate.

All at once people appeared on the path running toward
us. I recognized them, and was about to call out, but then
there was more gunfire and some of them fell to the ground—
they'd been hit!

The rest of the group scurried forward, and there was
more gunfire, and more bodies fell to the ground. The final

few ran off the path and up toward the houses, taking shelter.

Then I saw them. Five or six men, dressed in dark clothing and carrying rifles. As they walked they stopped and shot toward houses and people I couldn't see. They passed by a body on the ground and one of them fired a bullet into it!

"We have to run," Willow whispered.

"You go and get Julian and Jim," I said. "I'm staying." I pulled out the pistol.

"There's too many of them. They'll kill you . . . they'll kill us all!"

"Just go and get them, have them come here. I need help. I can't do it alone."

Willow, on all fours, crawled up the path and into the house. I was now alone, watching as the men moved down the path toward me. Flopping onto my belly, I hid behind the stone wall that edged the property. The men were visible and I was completely hidden. They wouldn't see me until they were practically on top of me, until after the first shot was fired. I could keep myself invisible until the second shot if the first was done right.

I put the pistol down on a rock beside me ready to use. With my hands now free, I pulled the crossbow off my shoulder and loaded in a bolt. Carefully I steadied it on the top of the wall and took aim at the chest of the man who was in the lead. I had to fight the urge to fire immediately. They were half a dozen houses away—well within my range, but I couldn't afford to miss. The first man had to be struck, had to be killed.

I heard a rustling and looked to the side. Jim, then Julian,

Paula, and Willow appeared. Each was armed—a rifle, a pistol, and two crossbows.

"I've got the man in the middle," I whispered.

"Paula, take the man on the far left, Julian the man on the far right. Willow, take aim at the man to the left of the leader," Jim ordered.

Wordlessly they simply propped their weapons against the wall.

The men were still coming. They were whooping and firing their guns. Two men broke away and ran up the path toward the Reynolds' house. Had they seen us, or somebody else?

"Now," Jim said.

There was an explosion of gunfire, the releasing of the bolts, and three of the men were hit! One of them slumped to the ground, a second clutched his chest, a third—my man— screamed in pain, dropped his rifle, and grabbed his arm where the bolt was lodged. He then turned and started running. The fourth jumped off to the side and took shelter behind a pillar.

I grabbed my pistol as the other two came back into view, almost running onto the path before stopping and taking cover. One of them started firing in our direction. We all ducked as we heard bullets slamming into the stone wall that we were hiding behind. The men had semi-automatic weapons and they were sending out a hailstorm of fire against us. We looked over at each other as the shooting intensified. I pictured them coming toward us, keeping us pinned down and unable to return fire, getting closer and closer until they finally flanked us, firing and killing and—and then it stopped. There was still gunfire but it was in the distance.

Carefully, slowly, I peeked over the wall. There were three people on the path, and to my relief I saw that they were Garth, Ian, and Willow's dad . . . and there were three bodies on the path a few cottages down. It was those men—were they dead?

"It's all right," I said to everybody as I got to my feet.

The others followed, hesitantly, still wisely sheltering themselves partially behind the wall. As they passed the bodies of the men, Garth and Ian reached down and took their rifles, slinging them onto their shoulders. They were both already holding semi-automatic weapons that I knew we didn't have. They had to have taken those from somebody else they'd killed.

I leaped over the wall and ran toward them. Willow did the same, running and throwing himself into his father's arms, practically knocking him over.

"You got them," I said.

"There was no choice," Willow's father said. "They were between me and my family."

"It looks like you got some others," Ian said, gesturing back.

"There were four. We got three of them."

"But there are so many others," Garth said.

"How many?" Jim asked.

"I don't know. They've overrun the back gate and most of them are moving along the shore toward the beach," Ian said.

"These few headed up into the houses. I think we have all of them now," Garth added. "They're better armed, and they were killing everybody they passed."

"Maybe we should just surrender," Paula said.

"You don't understand," Garth said. "They're not letting people surrender. I saw them fire on people with their arms up. I saw people that I know get, well . . . they're gone."

Nobody spoke. Nobody knew what to say. I knew I didn't.

"Here, take one of these," Ian said. He pulled an assault rifle off his back and handed it to me. A second was handed to Jim and a third to Paula.

"These are military issue," I said.

"They're all armed, and many of them have automatic or semi-automatic weapons."

"We'd better get going," Jim said. "It won't be long until they're here."

"It won't be," Garth said. "And that's why I have to go back. I have to slow them down."

"One person isn't going to slow anybody that much," Ian said. "But two might make a difference. I'm going with you."

"No you're not. You have a baby," Garth said.

"And that's why I'm going. You can't stop me."

"Or me," Jim said. "Three of us could pin them onto the beach."

"Until they come up from behind you through the houses," I said. "That's why two should be on the beach and two on the path leading from the back gate in case more are coming in through the houses."

"There's only three of us," Garth said.

"I guess that makes me number four," Willow's dad said.

"No, that makes you number five. I'm the fourth," I said. "Willow and Paula and Julian, go back and get people ready to go."

"I need to go with you too," Willow said.

"You promised my mother and me that you'd take care of Ethan," I said.

"And you need to be there for your mother," his father added.

Willow hesitated, and then threw his arms around his father and they hugged. He released his father and then hugged me! Before I could say anything he ran off toward the house.

"Let's go," Garth said. "Anybody we come across who is alone and without weapons we'll send back here. People on our side who we find who have weapons will come with us."

We started walking back toward the beach. I kept my eyes straight ahead, deliberately not looking back.

"Ian and Jim, I want you to take the path leading from the back gate," Garth said.

"Yes, sir," Ian said.

"And take these," Garth said.

He pulled open a green canvas bag. I hadn't even noticed it. He pulled out two clips of ammunition and handed them to Ian.

"That's all you get. Fire until you're almost out, and then run."

"We'll be the two fastest men in the world," Jim said. They hurried off down an alley.

As we continued toward the beach we ran into three of our men, rifles in hand, retreating. People started to materialize from out of the cottages. We sent those that were unarmed toward Willow's house, while we convinced the three men to join us. We were now six. Six against how many?

More people saw us pass and came running out of their houses. It was mostly older people, women with children, and none of them had any weapons. They were a combination of bewildered, confused, and terrified. We didn't have time to explain much—we simply sent them toward Willow's house.

We came up to the last of the houses and Garth had us fan out. Two of the men went to the left while Willow's dad and the other man went to the right. Garth and I headed straight forward. Hunched over for cover, we came up to a low stone wall that separated the garden of the last house from the open beach. I peeked through a gap in the stones and was shocked by what I saw.

There were bodies littering the sand. I was too far away to recognize individuals but they were all dressed in our sandy-colored Marine uniforms—costumes they'd been wearing to fool the outside world. In the end, nobody had been fooled.

What lay beyond that was more frightening. There, less than twenty yards away, by our outer wall, men in dark clothing were massing. There were already two or three dozen. All of them were armed, many with assault weapons. More were coming up from the beach, through the gate and gaps in the wall. They'd probably come along the shore from the back gate, partially hidden by the wall that was meant to protect us. They weren't simply running toward the houses. They were gathering in force to launch their attack. It wouldn't be long. Soon they'd be coming right toward us.

I had my crossbow and a sheath of bolts on my back. My mother's pistol was back in the holster and I held an assault rifle. I'd never even held an assault rifle before but I was familiar with it because it was standard military issue. I was surprised by how light it was. Somehow I'd expected it to be heavier.

Garth opened up the canvas bag again and pulled out three clips of ammo. "This is all we have. It's not going to be enough. I think there are more of them than we have bullets for. We're outnumbered sixty to six."

"There are more than sixty of them," I said.

"You go to those two," he indicated the two men who had been sent to the left, "and tell them not to fire until we do. I'll go to where the other two guys are."

I nodded. I slumped down on the bank behind a big rock just before reaching them and gestured for them to come in my direction. They seemed reluctant but finally moved over.

"You're Tom and Ryan, right?" I asked.

"Yeah," Tom answered. "Where's your mother?"

"At the channel. She's trying to pin them down there."

"I didn't know they'd attacked there as well," Ryan said.

"There and at the bridge. We blew the bridge up. The explosion killed a lot of them."

They both looked shocked and scared.

"She'll stop them at the channel," I said. "Don't worry about our backs."

They nodded, but neither looked reassured or any less scared. That was a sign of sanity.

"And we're going to pin them here. Don't fire until Garth fires, and get ready to run when we start to retreat. Understand?"

They nodded, but didn't look confident. Why should they be?

There were already many more of the invaders gathered there than we'd seen just a few minutes before. How many of them could I hit with a spray from the rifle? How many bullets were in a clip? How many bullets were still in this clip?

It was then that I realized that I hadn't taken any of the other clips with me. And neither of these guys had an assault rifle. They were both single-shot rifles—.22-caliber. They'd be able to get off a shot or two at most before we drew fire and had to duck and flee for our lives.

"Are you scared?" I asked them.

"Terrified," Tom said, and Ryan nodded.

"Me too, but we can't let that stop us. You both need to target a specific person. Aim right at the chest."

"I've never actually shot at somebody," Ryan said.

"Don't think of it as a person. It's just a target."

"Targets don't shoot back."

"If you *hit* the target it won't be able to shoot back," I said.

"No. But the rest of the targets will still be shooting," Ryan said.

"If we hit a few of them they might be too busy ducking to fire. We just might force them to retreat back to the outer wall. That will give us a chance to retreat. Remember, we're not trying to stop them, just slow them down enough to buy time for people to get away."

"Away to where?" Tom asked.

"Back to the houses," I answered.

"And then?" he asked.

"And then we'll regroup."

I knew what our plan was, but really, was it a plan anymore? The bridge had been blown up. The channel was under attack. There were twenty enemy boats off the beach and the wall had been taken. The back gate had been overwhelmed. We were on an island and there was no way off except into the lake. We had a few small boats stashed in the forest by the point, but there wasn't going to be enough space for everybody.

"Why are they waiting?" Ryan asked.

"I guess they're just waiting until they've all landed. Then they'll come at us in force. They still must be worried about what we have," I said.

"They're worried?" Tom asked, and all three of us laughed in response. How could any of us find this funny?

"The waiting is the hardest part," he said. "I just wish they'd get started."

"I think you're about to get your wish," I said.

They were starting to move up from the wall toward the houses—toward us.

"Make your shots count," I said. I felt like I was channeling my mother.

We all propped our guns against the rocks. I took aim at the first man in the first group. I hoped they were both aiming at somebody else. There was no gain in killing the same man three times.

"Wait . . . not yet . . . wait for Garth to fire," I said quietly.

I kept my focus down the sight of the gun. I looked at the man's chest, right where I was aiming. They were getting closer, moving slowly and deliberately, their weapons at the ready. Closer and closer. What was Garth waiting for? Maybe we should just fire now. They'd soon be on top of us and—the sound of gunfire exploded off to our right and I pulled the trigger.

The lead man recoiled with the bullets hitting him and he toppled backwards. I aimed the gun to the left, spraying bullets as another and another and another man crumpled to the sand! Those to the sides either dropped to the ground to take cover or started running back, retreating, some even dropping their rifles as they ran.

I kept my finger on the trigger and I could hear the sounds of Tom and Ryan firing—single shots mixed with the constant recoils and explosions coming from my assault rifle. Then there was silence. My finger was still on the trigger but there were no more bullets left. My gun was empty.

Out on the beach there were bodies strewn about. How many of them were dead and how many had just dropped for cover? The rest were far back, having taken cover by the wall, where the slope protected them from our fire.

"So do we run now?" Tom asked.

I looked down toward Garth. He wasn't firing but he wasn't moving either. Suddenly he got up on all fours and started scrambling toward me. He stopped before there was an opening that would have exposed him.

"Here," he said. He tossed something—a clip—and it landed in the sand beside me. I grabbed it. I removed the empty clip from the rifle and clicked in the full one.

There was a gunshot and I looked over. Tom had just fired at one of the bodies on the beach.

"He was getting ready to fire," Tom explained, sounding like he needed to defend himself.

"Good . . . thanks . . . keep your eye on the bodies that are closest to us."

There was now complete silence. I couldn't allow myself to believe that somehow we'd scared them away for anything more than a few minutes. They were just regrouping, waiting to charge again, or—they started to move. They were coming up the beach slowly, carefully, practically crawling to keep themselves at least partially hidden. A few would run forward a dozen paces and then throw themselves down, weapons aimed at us as the next group ran forward. They weren't going to just recklessly walk toward us. This time there would be fire directed at us. As soon as we shot there was going to be a hailstorm of bullets coming our way. This time, what we'd done before wasn't going to work. It was time to fall back.

And then the silence was broken by the sound of gunfire. It was distant and steady but also different. I'd been around enough firing ranges to recognize heavier guns being fired. If they had heavy guns as well as the assault rifles, we were doomed. Anxiously I turned my head trying to figure out where it was coming from. Was it the back gate, or the channel?

Then there was another sound. It was an engine.

It got louder and louder, but I couldn't tell where it was coming from or what it was or—an airplane raced over the tops of the houses, almost skimming the roofs. It was one of the Mustangs from the airport—it was one of Colonel Wayne's planes! It dipped down, guns blazing, as bullets carved a path across the beach, right through the men moving up the sand! The sound of the engine, the .50-caliber machine guns pounding, and screams of anguish filled the air.

The second Mustang swooped down, guns blazing, ripping into the ground and tearing the men lying there into pieces! It was almost beyond belief, watching this unfold before my eyes. And almost before it had arrived it was gone, with the second plane, shooting off over the lake.

The men on the sand, those still able to move, those still

alive, jumped to their feet and ran back down toward the wall. Some raised their rifles in a futile attempt to fire off a few rounds at the planes, which had disappeared over the water. I raised my rifle as well and fired at them as they ran. A couple crumpled to the sand, either shot or taking cover.

The planes were well over the lake but had started to bank back toward the beach. As the first of the two came closer it let out another blast of fire, and I could see that it was targeting some of the boats. One of them rocked under the impact of the bullets hitting, and then a second and third vessel were hit.

The second plane made one more pass over the beach, flying so low that I could see the pilot. As he dropped down he started firing and a path of bullets hit the wall. The dip in the beach stopped me from seeing what he was firing at, but whatever was there would be torn to pieces.

I heard movement behind and realized we'd been so busy looking in one direction that we'd left ourselves completely exposed. I spun around and—it was my mother and a few others coming to help us!

And then I saw they weren't alone. There were others—heavily armed—running right after them. There had to be twenty of them. Leading the group was Colonel Wayne! It wasn't just his planes, he and his men had come to help us! We were saved. We were safe. Well, safe except for the armed men still alive at the water's edge, and whoever else was still at the back gate or moving through the houses. This wasn't over. Not yet. But that was more than I could have hoped for five minutes earlier. We at least had a fighting chance now.

31

It was still early enough that the day was calm and quiet. If I didn't look too hard or inhale too deeply it was possible to believe that it had all been a bad dream. Of course, dreaming would have involved sleeping, and there hadn't been much of that the past three nights for me or for anybody else.

The thing I couldn't escape, even if I closed my eyes, was the smell—the lingering smoke, the residue of the fires. The last house fire had been extinguished yesterday but almost twenty homes had been damaged during the attack, and after, when we'd driven out the last of the invaders who were taking shelter in them.

I was heading toward Chris's house, and when I turned a corner I was startled by a couple and a small child coming toward me. I knew them. As they passed, the little boy—Emerson—offered me a smile and a little wave. I waved back. His parents passed as if they didn't even notice me. Their expressions were frozen. It wasn't that they were ignoring me; it was as if they hadn't seen me at all.

That dazed, glazed look was everywhere. So many people had lost loved ones, had even seen them die before their eyes, or had seen things happen that they'd never thought possible.

There was so much death. And that was another smell—the smell of death, the smell of the bodies. There were so many bodies. There was no final count yet but I'd heard the number two hundred and eleven being mentioned. Two hundred—one out of every four people who lived here . . . had lived here. In the end, though, the invaders who had died outnumbered that. The planes had had devastating consequences.

Volunteers willing to collect the bodies had formed a team and started with the people who had belonged to our community, moving on then to the bodies of the invaders who had died in or near the houses. Because there were too many bodies to bury it was decided that we would bury only "our" people. The bodies of the invaders were gathered up, thrown into wheelbarrows and kids' wagons, and brought to the beach, because there were so many of them there to begin with. They were thrown into a big pile right at the edge of the water by the stone breakwater and then soaked with gasoline and set on fire. Fortunately, for the most part the wind blew the smoke and smell and ashes away from the houses and toward the city. Sometimes, though, the wind swirled around and changed direction, and then the odor would reach us.

There was still a chimney of smoke rising above the beach. In the beginning it had been so thick and dark it had stained the sky, but now it was thin and wispy and whitish. There probably wasn't much left to burn. I hadn't been down there. In fact, I wanted to be as far away as possible.

In the end we counted 232 invaders killed. That didn't include the men who had been blown up at the bridge, or those who had died on the boats, or who had drowned trying to escape.

The day before, our people had cleared out the last of the stragglers who hadn't been killed or fled. It was difficult and dangerous, and Colonel Wayne and his men had led the way, going throughout the community house by house, and then into the forest, killing or chasing the invaders. They'd steered them to the beach and then driven them into the lake. Some of them had left behind their weapons and shoes and swum out, thinking it was better to risk drowning than being shot.

It was terrible and tragic that the invaders had made it to the houses before our rescue came. I guess I shouldn't have complained, though. I was one of the lucky ones. If my mother and the colonel hadn't come when they did, the six of us by the beach would have been dead. As we were firing onto the beach, our backs to the houses, other invaders were moving in right behind us. From what I could gather we were no more than thirty seconds away from being killed. And without their help—the men on the ground and the planes in the air—we all would have been killed.

There had been just too many of them, and their superior firepower had allowed them to sweep over our defenses. Guards with fake guns and even real single-shot rifles were no match for them. So many of our guards had been killed. It was terrible, but at least I understood those deaths. It was what had happened next that I couldn't understand or forgive.

The invaders had fired indiscriminately at everything that moved. They'd shot women and children and old people who were hiding or just trying to run away. They took no prisoners. They shot the wounded. And that was why there were so many dead.

The numbers were easy. The real individuals were not.

Everybody had lost somebody. Most had lost more than just one person. In a community this small and tight everybody knew everybody else. Sometimes their families went back together for generations. The dead included friends, neighbors, and family. People who played tennis together, or shared meals, played stand-up bass in the same acoustic group, were chess partners, or shared boat rides over to the mainland, acted in the same plays, sang in the community choir or . . . it went on and on in a thousand different ways.

Nobody was free of grief, but some had more than their share. A wife who'd lost not just her husband but her mother, or perhaps an oldest son or daughter. A husband who had been on the wall to defend his family, and then returned home to find they had been murdered. What sort of person could do that? What sort of person could just murder unarmed innocents?

My mother and Ethan were okay. We'd all walked away alive and unwounded. In some ways I guess I was luckier than almost anybody else, because I wasn't that connected to the people around me. I *knew* them but I really didn't *know* them. We'd only been here a few months. How well could you get to know somebody in three months? I hadn't lost anybody in my family, but I had still lost people close to me.

Jim had been killed trying to stop the invaders advancing from the back gate. Ken had been shot down at the wall. They'd been buried together along with another dozen people. I wasn't sure if it made it harder or easier that the burial was shared by so many families. Shallow graves had been dug in a clearing behind what was left of the back gate. The place where Ethan and his friends had ridden ostriches was now a cemetery. Rows of crudely made crosses marked the clearing. People had promised to make better ones later on, but right now there was no time for that.

When I closed my eyes I could see Paula at the gravesite, trying to be strong, but in the end failing. Julian was the same. I stood well back and looked away, or closed my eyes and let my thoughts go someplace else.

I walked up onto the porch now, moving as quietly as I could, and peeked in through the living room window. Inside, Chris and Colonel Wayne and my mother and a half dozen other community leaders were meeting. Yesterday and the day before had been about death and its consequences. Today was about making decisions.

I'd been invited to join the meeting, and I was half an hour late. I had decided to go for a walk first to clear my head. Part of me was honored to be invited, and I did want to know what was going on. But another part of me simply didn't want to be there. I didn't want to listen to any discussions, to hear any more information, or to make decisions. I just wanted to be a teenager again, whose most important decisions were what I was going to wear in the morning and who I was going to sit with at lunch, who wasn't angry at anybody except maybe a teacher, or some jerk who had said something about me or my friends. I was supposed to be annoyed with my brother and angry at my mother for something she said or did. But as I looked through the window, I saw my mother sitting there at the kitchen table and realized how much she meant to me. How much she meant to this whole community. Even if she hadn't been able to save all of them.

At that instant she looked up and saw me through the

window. She smiled ever so slightly and motioned for me to come inside. There was no choice now. I opened the door and was greeted by nods and hellos as I entered.

"Sorry I'm late," I said.

"I just got here myself," Colonel Wayne said.

I took a seat on a chair set back from the table. Even if they wanted me in the room I didn't deserve a place at the table. That was for the adult decision-makers.

"Were there any incidents last night?" Colonel Wayne asked.

"Nothing really, although there was a false alarm. People are pretty jumpy," Sam said.

"That's to be expected. If you were vulnerable before, you're more vulnerable now."

"But we won," one of the women, Carol, said.

"Nobody won," Chris said.

"I'm sorry, I didn't mean that. I just meant we defeated them."

"We defeated some of them," my mother said. "The rest got driven away."

"How many do you think did get away?" Chris asked.

"It's just a guess but I'd say at least twice as many escaped as were killed," my mother replied.

"But we got lots of the weapons they left behind, right?" Carol asked.

It was so strange to hear her ask that. She had been one of the people most against defending the community, one of the most vocal against taking up arms against others.

"We've ended up with more than seventy assault rifles, plus the ammunition that they carried when they fell," Sam said.

Half of the weapons and ammunition had been given to Colonel Wayne. That had only seemed fair because they'd used up so much of their ammunition in defending us.

"With all the new weapons we're now more able to defend ourselves," Carol said.

People looked toward my mother to answer. She looked down at the table, and Chris jumped in to speak.

"We used up most of our existing ammunition trying to defend ourselves. We did get more weapons, but there are now fewer people to use them," Chris said. "As well, our walls are shattered in places, the gates are destroyed. We're weaker than we were, and the only reason we stopped them this time was because of Colonel Wayne and his men."

The two planes had stopped the invasions across the channel and across the beach. They had sunk boats in the harbor and chased others away. What they hadn't been able to do was attack those coming through the back gates, or those who had already made it to the cover of the houses.

"We owe you so much. We owe you our lives," Chris said.

"Yes, we're so grateful. Without you we would have, well, we would have all died. I know that," Carol said.

"I'm just happy that Sam was able to get through and we got here in time."

"If you'd been even a few minutes later," my mother said, "well, none of us would even be here."

"And I think that's where this discussion has to start," Chris said. "Colonel Wayne, would you still welcome us to move to the airport?"

"The invitation and the terms remain the same."

The terms were clear. People needed to bring with them

all the resources they had to support themselves. They had to be willing to agree to live under the authority of the colonel. This was not going to be a democracy but a strict military arrangement. I'd lived almost my whole life under that structure so it was almost reassuring to me.

"I don't believe that we can stay here any longer," Chris said.

"And if we don't want to go anywhere?" Carol asked, and a couple of others nodded.

"That's your choice," Chris said. "We can't make you go, but you can't make us stay."

"And I need to make one thing very clear," Colonel Wayne said. "If you are attacked again we won't be coming to your rescue. We lost men and we lost ammunition and risked our planes. That won't happen again."

"How long do people have to make their decision?" Chris asked.

"There's no deadline," Colonel Wayne said. "You must decide."

"And we'd be safe there with you?" Carol asked.

"Nobody can make a guarantee of safety. Together we can stand against any foe we've seen." He paused. "At least, any that we've faced so far."

There was something in his hesitation, a slight change in his voice that made me wonder. Were there other enemies out there that were more powerful?

"I don't need more time," Chris said. "I'm going to move."

"You know you're going no place without me," Sam said.

"Count me in too," Garth added.

"And you all know where I stand," my mother said. "I am taking my family to safety."

"I feel like there really isn't much choice," Carol said, and others nodded.

"No, there's always a choice," my mother said. "Come with us and live, or stay here and die."

32

The last wheelbarrows came across the rickety little wooden bridge that had been thrown together to temporarily link Ward's Island with Main Island. With the old bridge blown out it was the only way to get things over. I wondered how many loads had been taken across over the past two weeks. Probably too many to count, and there were still more to come.

The decision to leave had been a difficult one for a lot of people. There were some who'd said they would stay—they'd lived in the community their whole lives and they were prepared to die there. Finally, though, when they'd realized that the dying part was going to come sooner rather than later—maybe in just a few days—they'd changed their minds. In the end, everybody had agreed to move, and that made it so much easier. There was no need to leave some things behind, or figure how to divide up resources, or feel bad about abandoning people.

Everything of value was moving to the airport compound. First people and produce, food and supplies, livestock, personal things, and household goods like mattresses and furniture. Most everything was loaded onto the back of one of the three big military trucks that were part of the museum at the airport. Old trucks—antiques—worked the same way as the old airplanes.

The livestock was brought over on the hoof. They were herded toward the little bridge, but many panicked and just swam across the channel. Gathering them back together on the other side and getting them to the airport was like an old-fashioned cattle drive. It was such a strange little herd—mainly goats, some sheep, the three cows, the zebras, and the ostriches. Ethan rode one of the ostriches like a cowboy. Somehow, for him and for some of the younger kids, it was still just a game, an adventure. They seemed blessed with short-term memory. Two weeks ago for some of them was like two years ago for others. Being younger could be a blessing.

I climbed up onto the back of the truck as the last items were stowed aboard. I settled in on top of the load at a spot perched right over the cab, where I could see anything that might present a danger. Below at the wheel was Warrant Officer Gonsalves. I liked having the military guys around. My mother had her pistol back but I now had a rifle. Everybody leaving the compound was given a weapon that they would return when they arrived inside the safety of the wire and walls.

The rest of the guards, who had been all around in the woods, came back to the trucks. Every trip—and it seemed like there'd been hundreds—had armed guards. The drive along Main Island took over twenty-five minutes, and we had to pass by dozens of little groups of people who were living out there, trying to survive as best they could. None seemed that big or that well-armed but each was still a danger. I always thought back to what my mother had said at the beginning: even good people get pushed by desperation.

That fourth dimension in all of us was never that far from the surface. I'd seen it time and time again. I'd lived and almost died within it.

The Mustangs were in the sky many times a day now. It was reassuring to see them, knowing they were there to protect us, watching everything, prepared to take action. Without those planes we never would have survived this long. They were the reason the attack had been beaten back, the reason we'd lived.

Sam climbed up and took a spot beside me.

"You're coming with us?" I asked.

"What—you don't want my company?"

"No, I just mean you've been staying here on Ward's at night."

Sam, along with up to twenty armed guards, had been staying overnight at the houses. They certainly couldn't stop another big attack—in fact they were under orders to run if one came—but they were there to protect the place from looting.

"We'll come back to scavenge more things, but almost everything anybody might want has been taken. There's no need for anybody to guard the site."

The last few days had been about taking building materials. Fences, sheds, wood stoves—even some of the houses themselves were being disassembled for the wood and parts and brought over to the airport complex.

"But won't people move in here when there aren't guards anymore?" I asked.

"We expect some people to settle in, probably take over some of the houses, but we'll come back and take what we need."

"Wouldn't it be better to just keep them out to begin with?"

"It's dangerous to keep camping out there at night. I'll be glad to spend tonight at the airport so I can get some rest."

"If you really want to rest you might want to sleep outside," I suggested. "It's pretty noisy inside the terminal."

Creating housing for everybody at the airport compound was turning into a big task. It was going to take a lot of imagination, lots of materials, and even more work. Julian had figured out how to turn the terminal into subdivided living quarters, and I'd seen the plans, so I knew it could be done. In the meantime, we were sharing space with the rest of the airport community and we were all assigned small sleeping areas separated from each other by blankets and sheets strung from rope and line. It was a long way from the nice little cottage I'd been calling home for the past few months.

I had started to think back longingly to the tent we used to sleep in, and finally, after a few nights of disturbed sleep, I'd gone and got it from where we'd stored it on the little island. We pitched it behind one of the hangars, and my mother and Ethan and I had been sleeping there. I'd slept well every night since then.

It wasn't the crowding that bothered me. There was lots of noise at night in the terminal. It was only to be expected with that many people in one place. Mostly it was the normal sounds of snoring and talking and coughing. That didn't trouble me. It was the crying that I couldn't handle. I understood it, but that didn't make it any less gut-wrenching.

People seemed to react to loss in two ways. Either they wanted to give up, or they wanted to dig down deeper to survive. Julian was digging down deeper. It might have been a way to honor Ken, or simply a way to be so busy that sorrow couldn't overwhelm him.

Summer was turning to fall but the weather was still good. The days were hot and the nights were cool but not cold. As I rode along on top of the truck, I couldn't help but think about what would normally be happening at this time of year. The whole world would be getting ready to go back to school. New clothes, new haircut, my mother going with me to buy some new makeup, and my father taking us to get school supplies, and . . . I hadn't thought about my father in a long time. What was that saying, "Out of sight, out of mind"?

I knew he had to wonder and worry about us. I just wished I could let him know we were all right. At least as all right as anybody could be going through what we'd been going through. I knew he was okay, though. That wasn't just me pretending or denying. He was a Marine, stationed with a thousand or more other Marines. No matter where they were they would be there for each other. Still, I wished that place could have been here with us.

We rumbled along the path. The trucks were old and the engines spewed out clouds of blue smoke that you could not only see but smell and taste. Not pleasant, but a lot better than walking.

I looked back over the channel to the Ward's community. All that remained were empty houses.

"I'm going to miss living there," I said.

"It's the only place I've ever lived," Sam commented.

"I've lived in nine other places."

"Wow, that's a lot."

"I guess I'm an expert at 'new.' I always thought when I grew up that I'd find a place to live and never move again."

"Maybe the airport is the place," Sam said.

"I hope I don't spend the rest of my life living at the airport." I paused. "Do you believe that's possible?"

"I don't know what to believe anymore."

The brakes of the truck squealed and we slowed down dramatically. Just in front of us were two men standing on the path, rifles on their shoulders, arms waving us down. I felt a surge of adrenaline, and then Sam spoke.

"It's Johnny and Jimmie."

"I wonder what they want."

"I guess we're about to find out." Sam turned around and yelled out, "Everybody be aware. Weapons ready."

"But they're our friends," I said.

"They are definitely not my friends."

Our truck stopped right in front of them, the other two trucks coming to a stop behind us.

"So, Sammy, it looks like you're leaving town," Johnny called up.

"We're all leaving town, but you know that."

"It was a terrible thing that happened," Jimmie said.

"I wish we could have done more than just watched," Johnny said. "All those men and those boats had us pretty worried that we were next."

"But they didn't attack you," Sam said.

"We're small potatoes. They hardly noticed us when the prize was in front of them," Jimmie said.

"So what do you want?" Sam asked.

"Maybe we're just being neighborly," Johnny said.

"In that case we're going to get going."

"Well, there is one other thing," Johnny said. "With Ward's gone we're still in need of some produce, some vegetables and other things."

"Well, as far as I know we don't have anything to spare."

"As far as I know, nobody's asking you for what you think you know. We need you to pass on a message to the people who actually make the decisions," Johnny said.

"Or maybe we should at least talk to who's in charge of this little caravan," Jimmie said.

"You're talking to that person," Sam said. "I can pass on a message."

"Good for you. You've risen all the way from security guard at the marina to a messenger boy!"

It was easy to see why Sam didn't like these two.

"We've noticed these trucks rolling back and forth," Jimmie said.

"Not to mention the planes in the sky," Johnny added.

"Yeah, and your point?" Sam asked.

"Gasoline. You need gasoline, and we can arrange that."

I knew gas was an issue. Obviously they'd figured that out too. They were jerks but they weren't stupid. Sam had said that.

"And how would you two idiots get gasoline?" Sam asked.

"Calling us names? Now that really hurts," Johnny said.

"Yeah, because we care so much what Sammy the messenger boy thinks," Jimmie added.

"Look, let's not make this personal. We have boats. We know people who know people," Johnny said. "You tell us how much gas you need and we'll arrange for it."

"And what do you get out of being so helpful?" Sam asked.

"A piece of the action. Think of us as real estate agents or stockbrokers."

"I think of you in a lot of different ways, but those aren't the words I usually use," Sam said.

"Oh, I think my feelings have been hurt again," Johnny said. "Why don't you tell them that we offered a way to get gasoline and you turned us down and called us names instead?"

"I'll pass on the message," Sam said. "Now why don't you move to the side, or better yet, just stand there and we'll run you over."

They stepped off the path and Sam yelled for the driver to start again. We started rolling.

"You really don't like them, do you?" I said.

"They're both jerks. They're liars and thieves and cheats. Nothing that's happened will have changed that."

"But do you think they can get us gas?" I asked.

"They've always been big talkers." He paused. "But you can put a hat on a pig, it's still a pig."

"I see them more as snakes," I said.

"So do I, but I couldn't figure out how to put a hat on a snake!"

33

I walked to the edge of the channel and took a seat on a large rock. It was my favorite place to be by myself—or at least as "by myself" as was possible inside the compound. There were guards on the wall and there was always a hum of activity, but right now, right here, I was almost alone.

This was the point at which the city and the airport were closest together. There was just a narrow passage out of the harbor and into the lake. Prior to all of this happening there had apparently been talk about building a bridge or digging a tunnel to link the island to the mainland. We had to be grateful that had never taken place.

From here I could see much more than just the buildings. Cars and trucks were infrequent but I could see them as they chugged along Lakeshore Boulevard. At night, across the water, sound traveled far. They weren't the sounds that had kept me awake at night before—streetcars and ambulance sirens and laughter as people came home at night after the bars closed. Instead it was screaming and the occasional gunshot. How they were connected was left to my imagination.

The sun was starting to go down. It wouldn't be long until the city and the entire world vanished into the darkness.

We had more contact with the city than just watching it from across the channel. The colonel arranged for scavenging trips to collect whatever could be found. And there seemed to be lots of stuff there if you knew where to look, and had the firepower to protect your people while they were collecting it. In one way you could call this a necessary action. From another point of view, how was it different from people kicking in our condo door and stealing all our stuff?

One of those trips to the mainland was happening now and my mother was part of it. I would have asked to go along but now, under the colonel's authority, these missions belonged almost exclusively to the adults. I was a bit upset when I'd first heard about the policy, but I was also relieved. I'd seen enough. There were worse things than being inside the wire—being outside, for one. Besides, it allowed me to just be here, to be a teenager.

Willow and I spent a lot of time together. We'd both agreed—without saying a word—that we wouldn't talk about that hug he'd given me. That didn't stop me from thinking about it, though. I thought that maybe we could be more than just a guy and girl who were friends, but I wasn't ready to take the next step. If it didn't work out, I'd risk losing him as a friend. I couldn't afford to risk losing anything more.

The living arrangements had now expanded beyond the terminal itself. My family had left our tent and moved into a small space that been carved out for us in one of the hangars. I was grateful to be inside again, where we weren't stepping on each other. As well, I'd started thinking farther ahead. It was early fall and still warm, but winter would follow. There was no reason to believe things would be better by then. Or ever.

"Good evening."

I jumped slightly and snapped around.

"Sorry, I didn't mean to startle you." It was Colonel Wayne.

"I was just lost in thought."

"Thought or worry?" he asked as he sat down beside me on the rock. I shuffled over to make room.

"Both. Isn't the scavenger party supposed to be back before dark?"

"It's not dark yet."

"So you don't think I have anything to worry about," I said.

"Emma, we both know there's more than enough to worry about out there. We also know it's a good team with lots of experience, well-armed, with a solid plan, and they have your mother in charge as their leader. She's a real Marine."

I knew what a compliment that was coming from him. She had quickly become one of the people Colonel Wayne counted on the most. Not just for leading missions, or for being a nurse, but for giving advice and for communicating things that needed to be shared with the "civilians." Along with Lieutenant Wilson, she was who he relied on the most.

"And remember, even more important, she's not the only Marine here."

"I know, and I'm grateful."

There were over seventy-five people here who had military or paramilitary training. They were either members or former members of the Army or Marines, or the National Guard, or former or present police officers.

"I know you're a little disappointed that you aren't being allowed to go on the away missions anymore. I just don't want to put young people at risk any more than I have to. Besides, I have something else in mind for you."

I waited for him to continue.

"With more missions being mounted outside, I'm leaving the perimeter with less defense than I'd like. I was wondering about organizing some of the older teenagers to receive formal training to be on guard duty."

"Sure, I'd like to be part of that."

"No, I don't want you to be part of it. I want you to lead it."

"You want me to be the leader?"

"Of course, all of you will be under the direction of Sergeant Miller, who's in charge of guards, but you would be his, shall we say, lieutenant, with the teenage guards. If you're willing, that is."

"I'm willing. I'll do it."

"Good. We want to build on the successful missions we've been having, so there will be many more in the coming weeks."

I knew about those successes—everybody did. They had been going through the deserted grain elevators along the lake and had discovered literally tons of flour still trapped in chutes. They had found medicines locked in storage areas in local hospitals—my mother had been instrumental in leading a team through her old hospital. They'd uncovered thousands of cans of food—corn, peas, SpaghettiOs, beans, tuna, peaches, and oranges—in a transport truck that had been buried under the collapsed wall of a burned-out supermarket. Thinking about those canned peaches made me want them.

"If this mission works the way it's planned, we'll have more than enough gas and diesel to run the trucks, planes, and generators," he said.

"Sam doesn't trust our partners very much."

"Sam is a smart young man. I don't trust Johnny and Jimmie much either."

"But you sent our team out with them to get gas just now?"

He shrugged. "We have to be prepared to take reasonable chances and use precautions to balance our concerns. Not trusting them doesn't mean we don't try. It just means we build in enough strength and safety to compensate for our lack of trust."

"And if they don't come back with fuel?"

"Then we'll try through one of our new friends."

It gave me a good feeling to think that we did have more friends. The colonel had established contact with other settlements. And through them we'd connected with even more settlements—the colonel called them "colonies." One of them was a former military base, and another had evolved around an embassy with its high walls, security, and security detachment. They weren't close, but with our planes the distance could be covered. There was talk about how to start trading and even offering support to each other. So far it was only talk, but with that talk came some hope. The real problem was transporting things—like fuel—over those distances.

"We'll always make sure we have enough fuel to keep our planes in the air," Colonel Wayne said.

"Those planes saved our lives."

"And they keep our lives safe now. Those are the only two war birds up there."

"I guess they're the only planes of any kind."

"We've heard reports that there are some older small planes that are still flying. Flight gives you eyes in the sky and the ability to cover long distances. Any plane is a good plane."

"Are there plans to put the other planes in our collection into the air?" I asked. The airport museum had over a dozen planes that sat at the edge of the runway. We were now living in the hangars that they used to call home.

"In time. Some need to be repaired or made flight-worthy. And of course we need more pilots. There are only three of us who can fly, and nobody who can handle the big bird."

The big bird was an old passenger plane.

"We're using a lot less fuel in the generators since we added those solar panels."

"I'm glad they got them up and running."

All the solar panels from our community had been successfully installed and met a lot of our needs for electricity.

"We're in better shape than we've ever been," Colonel Wayne said. "You were right—the first one to see it—the two groups have different skills and abilities, and together we're stronger."

The whole compound was being transformed with fields being plowed and planted. There was hardly an inch of land that wasn't under cultivation or ready for planting in the spring. A big irrigation ditch had been built at the edge of the main fields and had made watering so much easier. The Ward's people didn't know much about defending or fighting, but they did know about planting, baking, weaving, building, and living off the land.

"And we have you to thank for all of this," he said.

"I'm sure lots of people were thinking about it. Sooner or later somebody else would have suggested it."

"Any later and it would have been too late." He paused. "It almost *was* too late."

Colonel Wayne's radio came to life. The away team had come back.

———————

The three big trucks rumbled across the narrow isthmus toward the gate of the compound. This was the only spot where the compound connected to Main Island, and it was where our defenses were strongest. I was happy to see the trucks but I would be happiest when I saw my mother.

The gate opened and the first truck rumbled through. In the growing dark, with headlights leading the way, I couldn't see into the cab. Colonel Wayne waved it over and it came to a stop just inside the gate. The other two trucks pulled in behind and the gate was sealed up again.

My mother climbed out of the cab of the first truck and all my worry was washed away. She and the colonel exchanged salutes. I wanted to give her a hug but knew that wasn't military. She gave me a little nod of the head and I responded the same way.

"Captain?"

"All members of the team have returned, sir."

"Any difficulties?" Colonel Wayne asked.

"We encountered no opposition but we were unable to complete our mission successfully, sir."

"They had no fuel?"

"They had no usable fuel. We tested it on site and it was diluted and contaminated."

"Do you think that was intentional?" he asked.

"I'm not sure, sir. We just knew that it had no value."

"That must have left our trading partners unhappy."

"I don't think any of us were happy, but it was resolved," she said.

I wondered what "resolved" meant. I guess I'd find out later.

"Get yourself and your party fed and then come to my office. I'd like a full report."

"Yes, sir."

They exchanged salutes again, and she turned and headed back to the truck. I'd see her back at our room in the hangar.

———————————

It was getting late but I didn't want to go to sleep before my mother arrived. I sat up in the little common area that twenty of us shared. All the bedrooms led off a corridor from this area.

Chris sat under the one light and read a book. Her bedroom was two down from our room, where Ethan had already turned in for the night. Julian, Sam, and Garth all had their own little rooms in our hangar. Our room was bigger because there were three of us. The biggest one in the building belonged to Ian, Jess, and Olivia, plus Paula, who now lived with them. Since Jim's death she had become the "aunt" and was staying with them. It was nice to have our "family" here with us.

"What are you reading?" I asked Chris.

She turned the book around to show me the cover.

"*On the Beach* . . . I don't know that book," I said.

"It's post-apocalyptic end-of-the-world stuff."

I laughed. Louder than I'd thought I would.

"I know. Here we are living it and I'm spending my free time reading about it."

"Is it good?"

"Rather gripping. Interestingly, a number of the characters choose to give up rather than fight on," she said.

"Cowards quit."

"I've thought about quitting," she said.

"I'm sorry, I didn't mean to call you a coward."

"I just think, at my age, maybe it would be better if the limited food we have, the little resources we have, medicine and shelter, went to younger people."

At that moment, on cue, we heard Olivia start to cry, her voice coming through the thin plywood walls.

"I think Olivia disagrees," I said.

"Or agrees."

"Look, I know you're not young."

Chris laughed. "I haven't been young for a long time."

"It's because of you that my mother and I were able to come to the Ward's community. It's because of you that we came here. You're important to everybody. You're important to Sam. You're important to me."

She smiled. "That is sweet. You and your brother and mother are important to me, too. And don't worry. I'm not going anywhere. I'm just going to read about it." She got to her feet. "I think it's time for me to go to sleep. Perhaps you should do the same."

"I'm just waiting up for my mother."

She came over and gave me a hug and I hugged her back. "Don't wait up too long," she said.

Chris walked down the corridor and into her room. Olivia stopped crying. I was alone.

I wondered why my mother was taking so long. Was there more to report than she'd let on? That thought made me a little uneasy, and that made me want to wander a little. When my head got too busy it was better for my feet to get into motion.

I got up and went outside. It was still warm but there was a cool wind blowing in off the lake. The only sound was from the waves hitting against the breakwater, and except for a few points of light in the terminal leaking around the blackout curtains and the stars in the sky, there was complete darkness.

Out of the darkness I saw some movement. There was somebody walking along the edge of the runway coming toward the hangars. I hoped it was my mother. Instead of staring harder into the gloom, I closed my eyes and sort of willed her to appear. I kept my eyes tightly closed.

"What are you doing out here?"

I recognized her voice and opened my eyes.

"I was waiting up for you."

"You must be wondering what went wrong out there."

"I heard you say that the fuel was tainted."

"Yeah, but I think there was more to it."

I waited for her to go on.

"Something strange happened. When we discovered it, when we told them that we weren't going to trade, the people argued that it was good gas," she said.

"Wouldn't you expect that?"

"I did. I also expected it might lead to a firefight, but I

was able to talk everybody down. I suggested it was an honest mistake and we'd do business together in the future."

"Will we?"

"We do need fuel, and they are in a prime location. They have tanks just off the water. Who knows? But what was more troubling was the way Johnny and Jimmie acted," she said.

"What did they do?"

"They did nothing and they said nothing."

"But . . . I don't understand."

"You can often tell more from what people don't say and don't do than what they do say and do. They didn't react at all. They didn't argue. They didn't look surprised. They kept poker faces, as if they'd known what was happening before it happened."

"So you think they knew that the fuel was bad?"

"I'm fairly positive of that. The question is why would they want us to have bad fuel?"

"Wouldn't they just be trying to make the deal so they could get their cut of things?" I asked.

"That's one possibility, but what if it's more?"

"What more could there be?"

"Do you know what would happen if that bad fuel went into our planes?" she asked.

"It would harm the engines, right?"

"It might cause the planes to stall out mid-flight and crash."

"But why would they want that?" I questioned.

"Those two Mustangs are the most powerful weapons we have. Possibly the most powerful weapons anybody has. With them we're strong. Without them we're much more vulnerable to attack."

"From Johnny and Jimmie and the guys at the marina?"

"They're nothing to worry about. At least not directly. But what if they're working with somebody else? I've been thinking about the invasion on Ward's. When we were attacked, they came straight toward where there were dozens of Marines posted with automatic weapons," my mother said.

"But they weren't real Marines or real guns."

"But how did the attackers know that?" she asked. "If those had been real Marines with real automatic weapons we would have mowed them down."

"Well, you were afraid that somebody would find out it was all fake."

"Johnny and Jimmie knew. We both heard them say something about it. I started wondering why they weren't attacked by the group that attacked us."

"I just figured they weren't big enough to bother with." As I said those words I remembered that's what they had told Sam and me. "You think they were behind all of what happened?"

"I think they played a role. They're still playing a role. At least that's what the colonel and I are starting to think."

"So what are we going to do?"

"At this point we're going to do nothing. We need proof."

"And until you get the proof?" I asked.

"We have an advantage because we think we know what they're doing but they don't know it. There's an old saying, 'Keep your friends close and your enemies closer.' I need you to keep this information to yourself. It's the colonel and the two of us who know what we suspect."

"I won't tell anybody."

"I know you won't. Now, let's go get some sleep."

34

"I thought our shift would never end," Willow said.

"It was only six hours," I pointed out.

"Six hours under a hot sun, wearing way too much clothing, and with a very heavy gun on my shoulder."

"It could have been worse," I said. "It could have been twelve hours with *no* gun on your shoulder."

"Okay, true. How did I ever let you talk me into being a mini-soldier, though?"

"As I recall, you volunteered. Would you rather be working the fields?"

"No, I have to admit that I'd rather have a rifle on my shoulder than a hoe in my hands."

Everybody in the entire compound had work they were assigned or had volunteered to do. There were fall crops still being planted and others harvested, meals being cooked, clothes being washed, repaired, or sewn. Candles were being made, bread was being baked, trees were being cut to clear more land for crops, and the wood was being chopped to be dried and ready to feed the wood stoves over the winter. Fences were being reinforced, guard stations built, and more living quarters were being constructed. Scavenger parties were going to the city to get what they could find or trade for, while others were in the woods gathering apples, digging edible tubers, finding mushrooms, collecting leaves for tea or herbs and spices for food, and collecting acorns and other nuts that could be eaten. The goats were being milked daily and some of the milk was made into cheese and yogurt. There were always hooks and nets in the water and fish to be cleaned and dried.

A school had been set up for the younger kids—kids as old as Ethan. After all, it was time for the school year to begin. It was only a few hours a day but it was a way to try to make things "normal." As well, there was now a barber shop and hair-dresser. There was a woman who did nails. The yoga instructors had started classes again, and pots, cups, and plates were being made in the pottery studio that had been set up in a shed behind one of the hangars. While we hadn't had any plays performed, the artists had still been at work. They'd painted a gigantic mural on the back of one of the hangars. It was a picture of Ward's Island, or at least how Ward's Island used to be. It was painted as if somebody was standing on the baseball diamond looking out at the houses. There, clearly visible, perfectly painted, was Chris's house, the cottage we'd been staying at, two dozen more homes. It swept out in the other direction past the playground all the way to the white bridge that connected Ward's to Main Island—before it was blown up.

People would stand in front of it and gaze at it and talk about things that they used to do, people they knew, memories they shared. It was beautiful and peaceful and wonderful and sad and terrible all at once. All they had was this mural and their memories. I remembered something I'd once read: "Don't cry because it's over, smile because it happened." I wasn't sure if it was Einstein or Dr. Seuss who said it, but either way I tried to smile.

There were so many people doing so much to make the place run. And it was all working so well. Nobody seemed to object to anything they were asked to do. I think seeing death up close the way the Ward's Island people had seen it made them work harder to never see it that close again. And beyond it all, making sure that it never happened again, was the security.

There were, of course, guards on the walls and along the fences and in the guard towers. Twenty-three of us—the teenage guards—had been trained to offer support. We worked day and evening shifts along with the regular guards. Our role became even more important when there were away teams because guards were pulled off the perimeter to go along. Today was one of those days. It was good to have so many real automatic weapons rather than so many pretend guns.

Above everything were the planes, those two beautiful Mustangs. They made regular patrols, going up at least twice a day. From up there they could see anything coming our way. Almost as important was the fact that they could also be seen. They were more than our eyes in the sky—they were our aces in the hole. They had saved our lives at Ward's Island and kept us alive here.

Mechanics were also working on the more "flyable" of the other planes in the collection. I'd been told that the big passenger plane was now almost airworthy, but they didn't have anybody with experience flying something that big. The colonel thought he could possibly fly it but he was too important to risk.

We now had a Navy to go along with our Marines and Air Force. Seven boats of different sizes—all with old pre-computer engines—had become part of our colony. There were always at least two boats and security teams stationed just off shore. Three other boats were used by the away teams when they made trips to the mainland. Jimmie and Johnny and their boats were still being used sometimes, but there was a definite effort made to, as my mother explained it, "marginalize, minimize, and isolate" their involvement.

Finally, two boats were equipped to be fishing boats exclusively. They had rods and reels and nets—and of course they never went out without security. It didn't matter where or for what reason, if somebody was leaving the compound there were always guards and weapons along.

Willow and I had been walking and talking as we passed through the dwindling remnants of the forest. It felt good being out of the sun and in the shade.

"How about we get into bathing suits and go for a swim?" Willow suggested.

"Good idea."

There was a small beach off one of the breakwaters. It was a popular place, and instead of lifeguards we had real guards. We were also protected by the boats out on the perimeter. There was nothing to fear there except getting a sunburn.

We got to the edge of the runway and I paused to survey the scene. Little heat waves shimmered up from the flat, black tarmac. At the far end was the terminal, now almost completely divided into living quarters and a few offices. The control tower sat off to the side and stood well above every-thing else so that it had unobstructed views in all directions. Although there was no way I could possibly see them, I knew there were eyes with binoculars looking over the water, off to the city on one side and toward Main Island as well. There were always people up there, day and night.

Off to one side were the hangars. Some, like ours, had been made into living space. Others still held planes, or were used for storage of food and supplies. On the other side, and between the hangars, every single inch of land had been put into cultivation. There were dozens of people with hoes working, weeding, tilling the land, and picking ripe produce. Before all of this I'd never really thought much about food or about gardens. Food came out of the fridge, or, more abstractly, from supermarket shelves. I'd never really thought about people growing it. I'd never needed to.

"There are the Mustangs," Willow said, pointing up and above the far, far end of the runway.

It took a second for me to pick them out. They were low and coming in for a landing and—"There are three of them!"

"Three Mustangs?" he asked.

"Three planes. There's a Mustang leading and one trail-ing, but between them is a smaller plane."

"But we haven't put three planes up yet, have we?"

I shook my head. "They look like they're coming in."

The three planes were close together, coming in low and slow. They skimmed along the runway; the little plane touched down and then bounced slightly back up into the air before settling down.

The first Mustang pulled up slightly and we both involuntarily ducked down as it shot over our heads and then over the trees. The second Mustang did the same, again causing me to duck.

The little plane kept coming along the runway, straight at us! Was it going to stop before it reached us and the trees? Willow grabbed me and pulled me off to the side but at the same instant the plane jerked slightly, swerved to one side, and then came to a stop.

A rush of our guards materialized out of nowhere. They had their weapons up and they surrounded the plane.

"Hands up!" one of the guards yelled toward the plane.

There were two people in the plane, but neither seemed to react. Then I saw one of them, and then the second, slowly raise their hands. On each side two of the guards came up to the doors while the rest of the guards continued to aim their guns at the plane. The doors were flung open and the two people were grabbed and pulled out of the plane and tossed to the tarmac. One of them screamed. She was a woman— no, a girl, not much older than me!

"Search them!" one of the guards yelled.

I could see them both being frisked, checked for weapons.

"He's clean!" one of the guards yelled.

"The girl is, too."

"There's a pistol on the floor and a rifle inside the cockpit!" another voice called out.

There was the roar of an engine and I looked up to see a truck racing toward us. Colonel Wayne was in the passenger seat. It made me feel safer, just knowing that he was here. The truck's brakes squealed as it came to a stop.

"Let them up!" Colonel Wayne ordered.

"Yes, sir!"

The two were pulled to their feet. It looked as though they were both teens, no older than seventeen or eighteen. Neither of them looked old enough to fly a plane.

"Have they been searched for weapons?" Colonel Wayne asked.

"Yes, sir. And we have confiscated their weapons from the plane."

Colonel Wayne nodded in acknowledgment. "Release them."

They were released. The man—the boy—moved over and put his arm around the girl's shoulders. He was trying to comfort her, trying to protect her. I could see that his face was bleeding.

"You're bleeding." Colonel Wayne pulled a white handkerchief from his pocket and held it out.

The girl took it and placed it against the cut on the side of his face. Now she was comforting him.

"Did you do that in the landing?" Colonel Wayne asked.

"It happened when your men threw him on the ground!" the girl snapped.

I had to admire her. I didn't think there was any way I could have been that brave if it had been me.

"We can't be too careful," Colonel Wayne said. "We aren't used to unexpected guests."

"Guests? Is that what we are?" the guy asked.

"Perhaps 'guest' is the wrong word, but we still need to take precautions when you land at our airfield."

"Your planes forced us to land," he said. "This wasn't our idea."

"Actually, it was mine," Colonel Wayne said. "I gave the order when they radioed in your presence. Seeing your plane over the city caught us unaware."

"Seeing your two Mustangs wasn't what we expected either."

"Please accept my apologies for the manner in which you were forced to come here, as well as for your injury, but we felt it would be wise to talk to you and you didn't respond to our attempts to radio you."

"I didn't have the radio on. It wasn't like I was expecting a call." He paused, and his tone changed. Pointing to the cut on his face, he said, "This is nothing. Apology accepted." He held out his hand. "I'm Adam and this is Lori."

"Robert Wayne," the colonel said as they shook hands.

"Pleased to meet you, sir."

"Do you think they could put down those rifles?" the girl, Lori, asked. "I don't usually expect apologies to come with weapons involved."

Colonel Wayne signaled and the weapons were lowered.

"I think it was equally unexpected that the pilot and passenger of a plane would be two young people," he said. "But since you're our guests, why don't we continue this conversation over a cool drink and some food?"

"If we're guests, are we free to decline your invitation and climb back into our plane and leave?" Adam asked.

That was a good question.

"After that rough landing and hard braking I think it would be wise for our ground crew to have a look at your plane before you take off."

"And if I don't want that?" he asked.

"I'm afraid it would be unwise and inconsiderate for me to force your plane to the ground and then not take responsibility for making sure it was airworthy. As such, I must *insist* that you join me for a drink. I could never forgive myself if I sent you up before the inspection took place and something happened to you. We definitely would not want anything to happen, would we?"

"No, we wouldn't want that," Adam said.

I could tell that his words and his tone didn't match. He was uncertain and afraid. I didn't blame him.

"Take care of their plane," Colonel Wayne ordered the men. "And, please, be more delicate than you were with the pilot."

Our guests, along with the colonel, got into the truck and drove off.

"Wow, that was strange," Willow said. "What do you think is going to happen now?"

"I'm definitely going to find out."

We watched as the truck pulled up to the terminal. They got out and went in through a door that led to Colonel Wayne's office.

"Do you want to come with me?"

"I don't need to know that badly. I'm going swimming. Besides, you'll tell me afterwards. You do tell me everything . . . well, almost . . . right?"

"You know the answer to that."

I left Willow and trotted down the runway. As I got close to the terminal I heard my name being called out. It was Ethan. He was in a bathing suit and T-shirt. I wasn't surprised to see him. He was just as curious as I was.

"I saw the plane land. What happened?" he asked.

"Two people, both not much older than me."

"That's strange. Let's talk to Mom," he said.

That had been my plan all along, although at this point I didn't think there was much more to know. We went inside and as quietly as possible moved down the corridor to the infirmary. They'd set up a little medical clinic where my mother and the two doctors worked. It was the closest thing we had to a hospital, and there were regular hours when patients came to be seen.

I pushed the door slightly open and peeked in. I was relieved to see that it was just our mother, alone, sitting at a desk beside the examination table.

"How did you get here so quickly?" she asked.

"We came when the plane landed," I said.

"You didn't know you were sent for?"

We both shook our heads.

"The colonel and I both thought it would be wise for you two to meet our guests," she said.

"Really?"

"Yes. In a while I'm going to tend to the scrape on the boy's face. I want the two of you to wait out in the corridor until I call you."

"And then what do we do?" I asked.

"Talk to them, answer questions, just be yourselves."

"And find out what we can?" I asked.

"And find out what you can. We think the two of you might make them more comfortable and willing to talk. They might relax and say something they didn't mean to say."

"Like what?" Ethan asked.

"We have no idea. It's not like we get planes landing here all the time. Just be friendly and keep your ears open."

———————————

From down the hall we saw Adam and Lori being taken in to the infirmary, and then as quietly as we could we moved down the corridor until we were right at the door. I shushed Ethan and then tried to listen in. I could hear voices but not what was being said. We waited patiently—at least, as patiently as we could. Luckily we moved back from the door just before it opened and my mother and the two teenagers came out. He had a piece of gauze taped to his cheek.

"I told you they wouldn't be far," my mother said. "These are my kids, Emma and Ethan."

They introduced themselves, even though we knew their names. They seemed friendly. We exchanged a few polite words but it was clear that they were just anxious to get on their way. We walked along with them, down the corridor toward the exit, and I tried to strike up a conversation without success.

Outside their plane was waiting. Colonel Wayne was standing by it, talking to one of the compound mechanics. The colonel came toward us. He had a smile on his face.

"So both you and your plane are all ready to go," he said. "I don't mean to delay you any longer."

"Thanks. Thanks for everything," Adam said as he offered his hand and they shook.

Our mother motioned for us to come to her. We slipped back as the colonel led the two of them toward the plane.

"Sorry, I couldn't get them talking," I said under my breath.

"No need to be sorry. They didn't say much to me, either. They're being very careful about what they share."

We watched as the colonel continued to talk with them. Finally, they climbed into the cockpit of the plane. They settled into the seats, strapped on their harnesses, and put on their headsets, and then the plane came to life. The propellers became an invisible blur as the colonel stepped to the side. He offered a little wave and then a salute as the plane bumped away to the end of the runway.

The engine roared again and the plane started down the tarmac. It picked up speed as it went, getting faster and smaller until it lifted off, easily clearing the trees at the end of the runway. We watched it gain altitude and then bank, heading almost directly toward the city.

"Do you think we'll see them again?" I asked.

"Hard to say," my mother said. "They seemed like decent people, but I've been fooled before."

35

Willow, Ethan, and I stood beside the Cessna. I'd seen it land about an hour ago but was on perimeter duty and couldn't go to check it out until my shift ended. It had been over two weeks since the little plane had first landed, and I didn't think anybody thought they'd ever see it again.

Ethan had watched the plane land and he'd run right over to investigate. It was Adam and Lori and some old guy who Ethan thought was probably their grandfather. They'd got out of the plane and had immediately been escorted into the offices. I assumed they were meeting with Colonel Wayne. Mom was away leading a scavenger patrol on Main Island and I didn't really have a good excuse that would allow me in. Instead we waited out on the tarmac hoping to catch a glimpse or a glimmer of information.

At last the door popped open and an older man walked out.

"That's him," Ethan hissed. "That's the guy who came with them."

The man gave us a little wave and a smile and walked toward us. He was old but his back was straight and he moved crisply. He moved like a soldier. Was he an old soldier?

"Hello, I'm Herb. I'm assuming that you are Ethan," he said, pointing at my brother. "And you must be Emma?"

"I am . . . and this is Willow. But how do you know who we are?"

"You met Adam and Lori the first time they landed here. Your mother is the Marine nurse named Ellen, right?"

"Yes, but how did you know we were them?"

"Lucky guess, I suppose."

"Are you in charge of the other community?" I asked. Colonel Wayne had not learned much from Adam and Lori when they'd first met, but they had let him know that they belonged to another well-established group. I figured that was why he'd been so polite to them when they were leaving—he didn't want to alienate any potential new allies.

"I'm part of a committee that makes decisions. Would you like to know one of those decisions?" he asked.

"Yeah, sure," Ethan said.

"We're making arrangements for your settlement to have all the gasoline you need for your planes, trucks, and generators."

"That's amazing!" Willow exclaimed.

"And what are we giving you in return?" I asked.

"Oh, no, it's not a trade. We're giving you the fuel."

"But why?" I asked.

"Think of it as an act of friendship. We are a very strong community, and our two communities are going to become trusted allies."

"Why are you telling us this?" I asked.

"I figured you'd know soon enough. Doesn't your mother tell you everything?"

I didn't know what to say.

"I tell Adam everything. I trust him the way Colonel Wayne and your mother trust you. He told me you're in charge of part of the guard detail."

"It's only the teenaged guards."

"Only? That's a great deal of responsibility. Now, I'd better get back into the meeting. I just came out to stretch my legs and get a breath of fresh air and to make sure our plane is ready to go. Nice to talk to you all." He went back into the building and the three of us stared at each other.

"Well?" Willow asked.

"I think things are going to get a lot more interesting around here."

———————

The plane taxied for takeoff. I was part of a crowd that had gathered to see them off. There was lots of talk about what was going on, but nobody really knew much. Willow, Ethan, and I knew more than most people. I shared more things with Willow than I did with Ethan, but there were always things that neither of them could know. My mother would find out exactly what had been talked about today and she'd probably tell me, but she wasn't back from her scavenger patrol yet.

Colonel Wayne stood off to one side. There was a cushion of space around him. I often got the feeling that people were at least a little afraid of him, and I understood that. Not only was he large, not only was he in charge, but he had that take-no-prisoners scowl that was almost standard issue for career

Marines. I'd lived on bases enough of my life to not be afraid. Heck, I'd lived with my mother all my life and that was often her default expression.

"I'm going to see what I can find out," I said, and I walked toward the colonel. As I did, there was a ripple of noise from the crowd and I turned in time to see the plane lift off and climb over the trees at the end of the runway. I couldn't help but wonder what it would be like to see the world again from the air.

By the time I'd turned my attention back to the ground the colonel was gone. He must have gone back to his office. I ran, opened the door, and saw him at the end of the corridor.

"Colonel Wayne!" I called out.

He turned and shot me that scowl. Then he smiled and gestured for me to come down the hall.

"Would you care to join me for a coffee?" he asked.

"That would be nice. Thank you."

As we walked by the outer office he requested that his assistant order coffee to be brought. We entered his office. He sat down behind his desk and gestured for me to take a seat across from him.

"You didn't come looking for me because you want a coffee. You want to know what's happening. Correct?"

"Um, yes, sir."

"So what do you already know?"

I almost said nothing but I thought better of it. The colonel wasn't stupid. "Herb is one of their leaders. They have a pretty big community. They want to be our friends. And they want to give us lots of fuel."

"Did you have your ear against the door while we were talking?"

"No, sir! I would never—" I stopped as he started chuckling. "Herb came out and talked to us. Is he retired military?"

"He's former intelligence."

"You mean like a spy?"

He nodded. "Probably he was CIA. You can see it in the way they look around the room, the way they always seem to be watching."

"And that's somehow different from the way you and my mother act?" I joked.

He laughed. "Point taken."

"And you trust him?" I asked.

"Yes, I think I do, but I always put more weight on actions than words. If they get us the fuel he promised then I'll know we have an ally and friend. And if what he said about their battle with The Division is true, then we have a strong ally."

"The Division? Wait, I've heard about them."

"They're a paramilitary group. A larger, better-armed, and even more ruthless version of the group that attacked the Ward's Island community."

I felt a sudden rush of panic. I understood how they could be larger, but how could they be more ruthless?

"We'd heard chatter about The Division, but that talk has died down over the past two months. If Herb is to be believed, the reason for that is the work of his people," Colonel Wayne said.

"They destroyed them?"

"They destroyed part of them. In fact, today on the flight here they were shot at by remnants of The Division. So our new friends could be powerful allies, or powerful enemies."

"But you think they'll be allies."

"I'm hoping. As time progresses we're going to need to gather allies around us because . . . well . . ." He let the sentence trail off. There was something in his expression that suggested he'd already said too much.

"Can they be trusted? Time will tell," he said.

The door opened and our drinks were brought in.

"For now," he said, "let's just enjoy our coffee."

36

We were traveling in a convoy that included six of our boats. My mother was on another boat. All together we had over seventy armed people with us. We hadn't run into much—a few small ships out fishing, mainly—but we knew that dangers could be out here just as well as in the city.

We'd been sailing for almost four hours. I wondered how much longer it would be.

I walked up the stairs and onto the bridge. Sam was piloting our vessel. He was at the wheel, and three other guards were scanning the surrounding water with binoculars.

"Nice color," Sam said.

"What?" I asked.

"Green skin goes nicely with your blue eyes."

"Thanks, I was trying for color coordination. How far do we have to go?"

"Do you see that little tip of land to the right?"

I followed the direction he was pointing. "That's it?"

"That's the breakwater that protects Port Credit. When I was your age I used to take a boat there from the island all the time."

"It's a long way to come."

"There was this girl I liked and she lived there. People in love do stupid things."

"Or stupider things when they're desperate."

"Let's not rule out the possibility that I was both in love *and* desperate. Are you worried?"

"Should I be?" I asked.

"I think being worried is healthy. This could be a setup."

"Do you think it is?"

He shook his head. "I think we're safe, but these people could be good friends or powerful enemies."

They called their community Eden Mills. The way they described it, it was basically a subdivision that had been made into an armed compound. By air it was only an hour away, and so after meeting Herb, Colonel Wayne had arranged for the Mustangs to do a distant flyover, so high and wide that it was doubtful they could even be seen from the ground.

Next, Colonel Wayne, with their permission, had piloted one of the Mustangs and visited their community. He'd landed on a big blocked-off street that bordered their community which they used as a runway for their Cessna. He'd been given a tour by Herb and Adam's mother, who was a police captain.

From what I'd been told it was a settlement that had a lot in common with ours. They had a perimeter wall with watch towers and lots of armed guards. They had cultivated all the land inside to grow crops. They were a little island of calm in the middle of the chaos on the mainland.

There was a cackle of communication over the radio. It was my mother. She was ordering two of the boats—including ours—to go ahead of the four other ships. We'd be the scouts.

Sam pushed the throttle open and we pulled away. The second boat was close behind.

Sam picked up a microphone. "Attention, attention, please," he called out over the speakers. "Please take your stations and be prepared for landing."

Ahead of us was a protected waterway bordered on one side by low-level apartment buildings and on the other side by a couple of piers and what looked like hundreds of boat slips, most of them filled with boats of different sizes. From the clothing strung from some of the rails of the boats it was obvious that they were inhabited.

A big white flag was unfurled from the lighthouse at the end of the pier.

"And there is the signal," Sam said. He spun the wheel and slowly we moved toward the pier, where there was an open slip. Somebody walked onto the pier. It was Herb.

"Throw me a line!" Herb yelled as we closed in.

The man on the bow did as he was requested. Herb grabbed the line and pulled the boat in as Sam reversed the engines to slow down our momentum. The boat snugged in against the slip and a second man jumped off and tied off the stern.

"Welcome," Herb said. Then he saw me. "Emma, I'm so pleased you could join us. Let me help you."

He offered me a hand and I took it, stepping off the boat. Six of our guards moved along the pier and took up positions where they could take cover.

"I see you have your backup in the sky," Herb said.

For an instant I didn't understand, and then I saw two small dots on the horizon and knew it was our Mustangs.

"I appreciate people being careful," Herb said. "I feel the same way myself. If you look hard enough you'll find our Cessna up in the air circling as well."

"Adam is up there?"

"His father is the pilot today. I like to have eyes in the sky."

"You don't trust us?"

"There are lots of bad people out there. I want to make sure we're not taken by surprise by anybody else."

Sam joined us. "So what happens now?"

In answer, Herb pulled a walkie-talkie out of his pocket and ordered "the truck" to come forward. "I'm going to give you the fuel you need."

Almost instantly we heard an engine and grinding gears, and then a big fuel truck rumbled onto the pier.

"We have a whole lot of fuel to give you. We'd better get started."

———————

It was almost midnight when the final load was transferred to our big ship. It was long after our Mustangs had had to go home, but we were still well protected. In addition to our guards, Herb had brought squads with him. He never told us the numbers but they took up positions on the perimeter of the marina to protect us. He allowed my mother to take control of the truck and our guards to control the immediate positions around the pier.

Before the planes had left we'd radioed back to the airport and told them we were going to be late. There was a lot of fuel and it was a slow process to transfer it. I was so happy to be here with my mother. She didn't need to worry about what was happening to me and I didn't have to worry about why she was so late.

Each boat had running lights—green on the starboard, red on the port, and white on the stern. They were the only lights, except for the stars and a crescent moon in the sky. The shore was over to our left somewhere. Out here we were safe. Today had been a long day. It had also been a good day. We'd gained more fuel than we'd thought was possible. And probably more important than that, we'd gained an ally, somebody we thought we could trust.

37

I watched the Cessna take off. Herb was in it, with Adam's father at the controls. When they'd landed they'd gone directly to see Colonel Wayne, and they'd been there for no more than thirty minutes. It was a long way to fly for such a short meeting, unless there was something very important to discuss.

Colonel Wayne stood by the entrance to the terminal watching the plane disappear. I thought he'd just turn around and go back inside so I was more than a little surprised when he waved and motioned for me to come over. I trotted across the tarmac.

"I need you to do something," he said.

"Yes, sir."

"I want you to very quietly find your mother, Chris, Sam, Lieutenant Wilson, and Sergeant Miller. Ask them to come to my office at 1400 hours."

"Um . . . sure."

"Oh, and you should tell them not to mention the meeting to anybody else. I want them to casually make their way here."

"Sure, but, why, if I could ask, sir?"

"I'll explain all of that when they arrive."

"I'm sorry, I didn't mean to pry."

"Oh, did I mention that I want you to be part of this meeting? See you at 1400 hours."

─────────

I settled into a chair in the corner of the room. Even though I had been invited, I wanted to be as much in the background as possible. Of course the colonel sat behind his desk. Sam and Chris shared the couch on one side and Lieutenant Wilson and my mother took the two chairs on the other side. The sergeant stood by the door.

"Thank you all for coming," Colonel Wayne began. "And I appreciate your discretion in keeping this low-key. I would also ask that all of what I'm going to say be kept confidential for now."

"Does this have something to do with the two guests who have just flown off?" Sam asked.

"Yes, it does. They came to tell me about a threat to their community," Colonel Wayne said.

"What sort of threat?" my mother asked.

"You're all familiar with a group that calls itself The Division. They have battled with the Eden Mills community before. They have re-emerged as a threat."

"And what does Eden Mills want from us?" Chris asked.

"They are requesting support in the form of one hundred armed persons for a short period of time."

"That's a lot of guards to put in danger," Sam said.

"The danger should be minimal. They are asking that our people be deployed along their walls while the Eden Mills people go outside their boundaries to engage the enemy."

"There's still a big element of danger," Chris said.

"An element, but less than the community itself is facing," my mother replied. "It's always safer inside the wire than outside."

"I meant for those of us who remain here. With that many guards gone, we're vulnerable to attack," Chris said.

"No question we will be more vulnerable, but we can compensate the same way we do when we send people out to get fuel or to scavenge."

"But that's fewer people and less time," my mother said. "Away parties are only gone for the better part of a day. I'm assuming this will be longer."

"They are asking for people for a period of between forty-eight and seventy-two hours."

"And so you brought us here to discuss with us whether we should send our guards?" Chris asked.

Colonel Wayne shook his head. "No. I didn't bring you to ask your permission. I have already given them my word that we will be providing them with support. This is a command decision and not open for discussion."

The room went silent.

"Really, we're only offering to them what we offered to the Ward's Island community. I would think that those who lived because of our intervention there would be the first to understand," Colonel Wayne continued.

"Although you didn't ask for our permission, I want to voice my approval. I am completely aware of what our fate would have been. How could we possibly object to doing for others what was done for us?" Chris said.

"Thank you, I appreciate your words and support," Colonel

Wayne said. "But it's more than that. We need our allies to stay strong for when we, in turn, might need their help."

"Is there something else we need to know?" Chris asked.

"I'd be a fool to believe that there aren't greater enemies out there, enemies that could destroy us."

"Do you know that?" Chris asked anxiously.

"There has been talk, rumors, reports. This time we're helping the Eden Mills community. The next time it could be us in need. We have to come to the defense of our friends so that they'll be able to come to our defense."

"I understand," Chris said. "I think we all do."

There was a nodding of heads around the room.

"Again, this is for your ears only at this time. I brought you here now to apprise you of what has been requested and what we are going to do, but, more importantly, to work through the logistics of how this can be accomplished in the time frame we're discussing."

"How long do we have?" my mother asked.

"They need us to be there in less than four days."

"A week to ten days would be more realistic," Lieutenant Wilson said.

"They have been given an ultimatum that is time-sensitive. The clock is ticking and we need to act," Colonel Wayne explained.

"Are we going there by boat and then truck?" Sam asked.

"No, I think by plane."

"But their Cessna can only carry three passengers," Sam said. "That would be sixty or more trips."

"We have one other possibility we're going to utilize," Colonel Wayne said.

38

Our big passenger plane sat on the runway surrounded by hundreds of people. Some were getting ready to board. Others were there to say goodbye to the passengers. But most people were there just to watch. It was impressive. The big plane—it was called a Stratoliner—was getting ready to take off.

The mechanics had been working on it for weeks, on and off, getting it ready to potentially fly again. It had never been a priority because we didn't have a pilot to fly it, or a real need to put it up into the air. That had all changed, and over the past few days it had become their only focus.

The pilot was Adam's father, Mr. Daly. He had been a commercial jet pilot before all of this had happened, and he said he'd flown the great-great-grandchildren planes of our Stratoliner. Twice yesterday and twice today he had taken it up into the air for test flights. It was incredible to see it roar down the runway and into the air. Everybody who wasn't on guard duty—and probably all of those who were—watched as it took to the sky. It was both incredible and incredibly scary. It hadn't been in the air for almost forty years, and there must have been hundreds of old parts that could have broken. I felt such a sense of relief when it finally touched back down that first time. With each test flight everybody became more confident, and now it was time to entrust it with the lives of our people.

The first people started up the stairs and onto the plane. This flight was going to have fifty passengers, half of the crew that was being sent to Eden Mills. A second flight, later today, would take the rest.

I moved through the crowd toward my mother. She was standing by the plane, checking people in as they boarded. She, along with Sergeant Miller, was in charge of the mission. They not only chose the people, they would lead them to Eden Mills.

As I got close she saw me and handed the clipboard to Sam. He was going along on this mission, as was Garth, and a lot of those who had military or police training—almost everybody I really trusted. Even Colonel Wayne was going to leave temporarily, as he was going to fly one of the Mustangs. My mother came forward, and before I could talk she motioned for me to follow as she led me away from the crowd.

"How are you doing?" she asked.

"I'm fine. I'm good."

"I need you to remain calm and in charge."

"Lieutenant Wilson is in charge," I said.

"He is, but you have a pretty important role to play."

With most of the guards—and almost all the most reliable guards—being sent away, they had asked the teenage guards to pull extra duty. We'd be on for twelve-hour shifts, then off for six, and then back on for twelve until they returned.

"I'll take care of things. You know that."

"I know you will."

"Are you going on the first flight or the second?" I asked.

"I need to be there when the first group lands to start to get things set up properly. I'll be fine. We'll all be fine."

"You can't guarantee any of that."

"You know there are no guarantees. I'll do whatever I can, and I know you'll do the same."

I nodded. "I have to go. My shift on the wall starts in twenty minutes."

We hugged, and then I turned and walked away. There was no point in watching her climb onto the plane. I'd be able to see it fly off from my spot on the fence.

———————————

It had been a long day. I'd been on the fence while the plane took off and I was still there when it came back for the second load of people. Seeing the plane come back of course told me that my mother was fine, the plane was still in one piece. Willow and I now watched as it took off again. It was so much more amazing when I didn't have to worry about my mother being on board. It soared almost directly over my head, and I watched as it gained altitude and started to bank over the city.

Almost immediately it was followed into the air by first one of the Mustangs and then the other. They were traveling with it as an air escort. I watched as all banked and then disappeared into the distance. I couldn't help but wonder what people on the ground would think when they looked up and saw three airplanes fly past.

"It's time for us to move," Willow said.

"Okay, sure."

Every fifteen minutes we rotated from one post to another, changing places with other guards who were already stationed.

"This is going to be a very long couple of days," Willow commented.

"I hope it seems incredibly long because that means nothing interesting will be happening."

"Something seems to be happening up there," Willow said.

At the next post the two guards were out, standing by the fence, and they were talking to two people on the other side of the fence.

"You go wide," I said, "through the forest. Be in a position to radio for help if it's needed."

He angled off to the side and disappeared into the trees. I pulled the rifle off my shoulder and held it out in front of me as I started forward. Were they being held by force? But then I heard the sound of laughter. If they had been taken prisoner, they really seemed to be finding it amusing. I closed in, but they didn't seem to notice me at all. I recognized the guards. They were both part of the teenage guard brigade—Sarah and Rachel—and they'd come with us from the Ward's community. Due to the angle and the mesh of the fence I couldn't tell who was on the other side. I just knew the tone of the conversation was friendly, even flirtatious.

A twig snapped under my feet, the conversation stopped, and they both looked in my direction. Sarah waved. I didn't wave back and I kept my gun up and slightly angled toward the unseen people on the other side of the fence. As I closed in the angle changed and I saw who it was—Johnny and Jimmie. I stopped in my tracks.

"Hey, how are you doing?" Johnny called out.

"Yeah, you're Emma, right?" Jimmie said. "Your mother is that Marine lady."

I didn't even want to talk to either of them. I knew what they might have tried to do with that tainted fuel.

I turned directly to the two girls. "Why aren't you two at your post?" I asked.

They looked a little bit startled, and then Rachel spoke. "We are at our post."

"Your post is in the guard station, not talking to these two."

"Look who thinks she's in charge!" Johnny said and started laughing.

"I *am* in charge. I'm the captain of the teen guards. You two need to get back to your post, and you two have to leave, now."

Rachel opened her mouth to say something as Sarah grabbed her by the arm and pulled her toward the guard station.

"Wait, where are you going?" Jimmie called out after them.

"Come on, girls!" Johnny added. "Come on back!"

The girls looked over their shoulders but kept walking away.

"You have to leave."

"You think you can give us orders too?" Johnny asked.

"Leave now before I call for Sam to come and deal with you."

They suddenly didn't look so pleased or so confident. I knew they were afraid of Sam, but this was, of course, a complete bluff as Sam was in the air flying to Eden Mills. They didn't know that.

"I think he'd welcome the chance to shoot you two for being a threat." I pulled out my radio.

"We'll go, we'll go. We didn't mean no harm," Johnny said. "We just wanted to talk to a couple of girls we like."

Both girls were three years older than me but Johnny and Jimmie were in their mid-twenties or older.

"I don't care who you like or don't like. You don't interfere with our guards or trespass on our property. Just leave and do it now." I pulled my rifle up and aimed at them.

"Are you planning on shooting us?" Jimmie asked.

"You should leave before we find out."

They didn't move. In fact they both smirked.

"I've killed before. With a crossbow and with a rifle. I've heard it's like everything else, the more you do it, the easier it gets. So, you want to help me find out?"

They hesitated, and then started to walk away—slowly at first and then more quickly, disappearing into the trees. I felt a sense of self-satisfaction. They were unnerved by the idea of me calling Sam. They were even more afraid of me than that. I'd been bluffing when I said what I did, but really, I wondered, did it get easier each time?

I walked over to the two girls and got there just as Willow arrived from the other direction.

"What did you tell them?" I asked.

"What we talk to boyfriends about is none of your business," Rachel snapped.

"Boyfriends?" I asked.

"We used to date them," Sarah said.

"Well, at least we went out with them to a movie, you know, before all this happened."

"That's disgusting," Willow said. "They're so old."

"They're not that old," Sarah said defensively.

"I don't care whether you want to marry them. I just want to know what you talked about right now," I said.

They didn't answer.

"Look, you can tell me what you talked about or you can tell Colonel Wayne when he gets back."

I saw that neither wanted that any more than Johnny and Jimmie wanted to have to deal with Sam.

"We were just talking, about nothing, really," Sarah said.

"Were you talking about the plane?"

"We saw it leave," Sarah said.

"It was hard to miss. It roared almost right over our heads," Rachel replied.

"And what about the plane did you say?"

"Nothing . . . they just asked about it . . . you know, where it was going."

"And did you tell them?"

They both sheepishly looked down. Obviously more was said.

"And what?"

"We didn't tell them anything they couldn't see with their own eyes," Rachel said.

They were lying. It was obvious. It was equally obvious they weren't going to tell me the truth.

"Willow, I want you to stay here with Sarah at this station. Rachel, you're coming on patrol with me."

I expected some argument but there was none.

I started walking and Rachel silently fell in beside me. I wanted the two of them separated in case Johnny and Jimmie came back the minute we were out of sight. I wasn't sure what they could have said to them, or what harm it might do even if they told them everything. Still . . . I couldn't help wondering.

39

"It's impressive to watch the planes take off," Chris said as we stood in the control tower.

"Even more impressive from up here," I said. What I didn't say was that what impressed me most was that we'd made it through the first night without incident.

The two Mustangs were at the end of the runway. Off to the side, parked, was the Stratoliner. I'd been more than a little surprised to see it there this morning. Apparently it had been brought back during the night, and then Adam's father, along with Adam, had flown their Cessna back home. There was no room for the Stratoliner at their location, and the colonel wanted it back here, safe and secure and under his control.

"I'm glad to be here," I said, "but I wish I was there instead."

"At Eden Mills?" Chris asked.

"That's where the action is going to happen."

"I think I've had enough action for a lifetime."

The Mustangs taxied out onto the runway and came to a stop, awaiting instructions. There was chatter between the air traffic controller and the two planes. It hardly seemed necessary to have an air traffic controller when there were so few planes to control.

I recognized Colonel Wayne's voice over the radio. He was in the lead plane. He had insisted on going on this mission because he needed to be there for "his people." I think that was a big part of the reason, but I think he also didn't want to be left out of the action. I understood that. The action was addictive.

"Mustangs Alpha and Bravo, you are clear for departure," the air traffic controller said.

"Roger that," Colonel Wayne replied.

"Affirmative," the second pilot answered.

Even through the glass on the control tower I heard the roar of their engines as they opened the throttles and the planes started moving along the runway side by side.

If all went as planned, the Mustangs would be back in less than four hours—about an hour there and the same back, and a couple of hours patrolling in the middle. It couldn't be much longer since they only had enough fuel capacity to be in the air just over five hours. Then, if everything went as anticipated, the first planeload of our people would be back, possibly even before dark or early the next morning. And hopefully my mother would on that flight. I wanted her back. I needed her back. Even more important, Ethan needed her back.

He never did all that well when Mom wasn't around. He had trouble getting to sleep, and he'd wake up a few times during the night. That's why Mom wanted me there with him. Of course, her not being with us wasn't so different from her being out all night on duty, or being pulled out of bed to go to the clinic to deal with somebody who wasn't well. But this time she wasn't even at the compound, and I could feel myself getting more anxious too; it wasn't just Ethan who missed her.

The compound did feel strangely empty with Sam and Garth also away and Colonel Wayne about to be. Lieutenant Wilson was a good person and I trusted him, but it wasn't the same. At least I still had Willow. He wasn't protection but he was good company. He was my friend, somebody I trusted, somebody I cared about. And the more I was around him, the more he meant to me. I knew he felt the same way about me. At least, I thought he did. It wasn't like something I could ask him . . . or could I? Maybe I could, but today wasn't going to be the day.

The planes picked up speed as they created distance from us. They were taking off over the trees and over Main Island. They both lifted off and soared over the forest and into the air.

I looked at my watch. It was now three hours and fifty-nine minutes until they returned.

"I guess there's nothing to do now except have some lunch," Chris said.

"If it's a fast lunch. I'm due out on perimeter duty soon."

———————

We'd hardly sat down with our meals when the walkie-talkie cackled to life. "Chris." It was Lieutenant Wilson.

She fumbled with the buttons. "I'm here."

"Can you come to Colonel Wayne's office?"

"I'm just having a quick bite with Emma. I'll be there in fifteen minutes."

"There isn't time for lunch, and bring Emma along. We have some guests who are being brought in and need to speak to us," he radioed.

"Guests?"

"Yes, and please come quickly. They should be here within a few minutes."

I followed Chris to the colonel's office and we met Lieutenant Wilson there.

"So, who are the guests?" Chris asked.

The lieutenant gestured to the door, and we turned in time to see Johnny and Jimmie being led in.

"What are they doing here?" I demanded.

"They said they have something they need to say, but they wanted Chris here when they said it."

They both nodded.

Chris gestured for them both to sit beside her. "It's good to see you boys."

They both looked down at their feet.

"Um . . . look . . . we need to tell you something," Jimmie said.

"We were hoping to get here before the planes took off," Johnny said.

"But we were late and we were nervous, like, actually scared to tell you. We don't want nobody being mad at us."

"We don't want nobody to shoot us," Johnny said.

"My goodness, boys, of course nobody is going to shoot you—wait, what did you two do?" Chris asked.

"We didn't mean for things to go the way they're going to go. It's just that, well, I don't know how to say this," Jimmie added.

"The best way is to just spit it out," Chris said.

Jimmie and Johnny exchanged a look, and then Jimmie spoke. "There's going to be an attack."

"An attack where?" Lieutenant Wilson asked.

"Here," Jimmie said. "You're going to be attacked."

"And how do you know this?" Wilson asked.

"We, um, just sort of know things."

Wilson got to his feet and came around the desk until he was standing directly in front of them. It was then that I noticed he'd taken his pistol out of the holster and it was in his hand by his side.

"You said you hoped you wouldn't be shot," Lieutenant Wilson said.

"Please, boys, we're not going to shoot you," Chris said. "Just tell us what you know and how you know it."

"We were there when they planned it," Jimmie said.

"When who planned it?" Chris asked.

"They're from the city. They're powerful," Johnny said.

"And there are still lots of them left," Jimmie added.

"Still?" Chris asked. "What does that mean?"

I wondered the same thing, and then the answer came to me. "You've been talking to the same people who attacked Ward's before, haven't you?"

They didn't answer—which meant I was right.

"Why would you cooperate with those people?" Chris demanded. "You saw what they did to people you've known your whole lives."

"We didn't have any choice," Johnny said.

"There's always a choice," Chris said.

"Not if we wanted to stay alive. It was work with them or be killed," Jimmie said.

"You could have come to stay with us in the community. No matter what bad opinions people might have of you, you were still part of our Ward's family. There was a place for you."

"We knew you couldn't last, that you didn't have the weapons. Sooner or later you were going to be destroyed. If it wasn't them, it was going to be somebody else."

"So you sold us out," I said.

"We were just doing what we needed to survive. They told us they'd just chase you away, not that they'd try to kill everybody."

"I can't believe you did that," Chris said. "I feel so . . . so . . . disappointed, so betrayed."

Jimmie shrugged and Johnny looked down.

"But now, after seeing what they did, what they're capable of, you're still helping them. How could you meet with them again?" I asked.

"We're just trying to live," Johnny said.

Lieutenant Wilson raised his gun and pointed it directly at them. "I guess you're going to find out what happens next. Traitors can only be dealt with in one way. Both of you, get to your feet and—"

"Stop!" Chris said as she stepped between them. "Let's just sit down and let's take our time and—"

"There isn't much time," Jimmie blurted out. "We thought it wasn't going to happen for a few hours, maybe even tonight, but we saw them coming ashore and gathering in the trees. It's going to be soon. I guess they were waiting for the planes to leave."

I felt like I'd been kicked in the stomach.

"This couldn't have happened at a worse time," Chris said.

We had to do something and do it fast.

"Can we radio Colonel Wayne and get the planes back here to defend us?" I asked.

"Negative. They're flying at low altitude to avoid detection and that puts them out of radio range," Wilson said.

Our timing, our luck, couldn't have been any worse. And then I realized that luck and timing had nothing to do with it. It all made sense.

"They're attacking now because you two told them all about what was happening here," I said. "You two knew how weak we are right now with everybody gone, with the planes gone. You didn't just hear about them making plans to attack, you went and told them this was the perfect time. That's the only way they'd know to attack right now."

They didn't deny it.

"I really should put a bullet in both of you," Lieutenant Wilson said as he raised his gun.

"Please!" Johnny said. "We did come to warn you! Doesn't that count for something?"

"Doesn't matter. We wouldn't have needed a warning if you hadn't told them," Lieutenant Wilson said.

"Chris, please, you can't let him do this!" Jimmie looked terrified.

"I'm not sure I want to stop him."

"We have more to say, please, let us tell you!" Jimmie pleaded.

"It's important, really, just hear us out!" Johnny said.

Chris and the lieutenant looked at each other, and he

nodded and lowered his gun. Had he really been getting ready to shoot them, or had it all been a bluff?

"Thank you, thank you," Jimmie said. "We know their plan and we're here to tell you."

"They're going to attack from Main Island!" Jimmie jumped in.

"But there's more," Johnny added. "They're going to radio you, tell you that if you just have everybody go into the terminal they won't hurt you, that they just want to take your stores and then they'll leave!"

"But they won't leave," Jimmie said. "They're going to capture the passenger plane so that you can't use it to get your guards back. They're going to block off the runway so the Mustangs can't land when they get back and they'll run out of fuel and crash into the lake."

There was silence. Finally they'd run out of things to say.

"Why should we believe anything either of you has said?" I asked.

"Because we're telling the truth, honestly," Johnny said.

"Honesty isn't something I expect from either of you anymore," Chris said. "But I can't imagine you coming here for any other reason. I believe you."

"Then you're not going to kill us?" Jimmie asked.

"We don't work that way," Chris said.

"So we can go?" Johnny asked.

"We also don't work that way," Lieutenant Wilson said. "You will be put in our security room until the colonel returns."

"What if he can't return?"

"You'd better hope he does," Lieutenant Wilson replied.

"There's one more thing," Jimmie said. "They're listening in on your walkie-talkies. They know the frequencies you're using."

"Something else you told them?" Chris asked.

"No, honestly, we didn't," Jimmie protested. "They just know. They're like you, they're military too."

"How many of them are there?" Chris asked.

"Two or maybe three hundred," Jimmie said.

"That's a big difference. How many are there?" Wilson demanded.

"We don't know. We just know there are lots of them— probably too many of them."

There was a knock on the door, and the colonel's assistant barged into the room. "There's a call coming in from the control tower. There's somebody on the radio who wants to talk to whoever is in charge."

"Tell them we're coming and we'll speak to them," Lieutenant Wilson said.

40

WE MOVED QUICKLY TO THE CONTROL TOWER.
Johnny and Jimmie had been led away at gunpoint and put
into lockup.

"What are we going to do?" Chris asked.

"First things first," Lieutenant Wilson said. "We need to
talk to them and—"

"No, we don't," I said, cutting him off. He looked shocked.
"Sorry, sir, but let me explain. We already know what they're
going to say. We need to act first and use these few extra
minutes to start to get ready."

"What do you have in mind?" he asked.

"We need to send a message to the off-duty guards, and
do it in person, tell them to get ready and get out."

"And tell them not to use the radios," Chris added.

"But if there's no radio chatter then they'll be suspicious,"
Wilson noted.

"We'll use the radios, but only to our advantage. We'll let
our people know that the enemy is listening in so we can
feed them false information. We'll figure out a signal to let
our people know if what they hear is real or pretend."

"That's brilliant," Lieutenant Wilson said.

"I also think we should take precautions," Chris said.

"Those who are not able to help defend should be moved to safety."

"I'm not sure there will be any safe place on the compound."

"I'm not talking about the compound. I'm talking about sending them to the boats," she said.

"That can't be done without possibly alerting our enemy that we're on to their plan," Lieutenant Wilson said.

"He's right," I said. "You're both right, and it might buy us more time. Let's get to the control tower and I'll explain."

"Is this the commanding officer?" the voice asked over the radio.

"This is Lieutenant Wilson, and I am in charge."

"And can you make decisions?" the voice asked. "Life-and-death decisions?"

"That sounds like a threat," he radioed back. "Can I at least know the name of the person who is threatening us?"

"My name isn't important, but the threat is real. We are just outside your compound and are prepared to launch an attack."

"You know we are more than capable of defending ourselves."

"Not as capable as usual. You are short on defenders, and your planes are gone and will not be back for hours," he radioed.

Wilson took his finger off the button and spoke to us. "They do seem to know things. I'm going to wait a few more seconds before responding. He'll expect us to be surprised that he has that information."

"You are wrong," the lieutenant finally replied.

"I am right. Two planeloads with fifty guards per plane left yesterday. Your two Mustangs have just left—"

"And have been called back. Leave immediately or face the consequences!" He sounded convincing.

"If you persist in your bluff we will simply attack now. No further discussion."

Before responding, Lieutenant Wilson took his finger back off the button, as if thinking through the threat.

"Obviously you're calling because you want to talk to us. What is it that you want to say?"

"You have food and supplies that we want. We can either break through your defenses and kill people, or you can simply let us take what we want," he said.

"And why are you making this generous offer to spare our lives?"

"We're not savages. We don't want to kill unless we have to, and we really don't want to have some of our people killed in the attack. We know we can overwhelm you, but there will be a cost to us."

"How do I know that you have the overwhelming forces you claim to have?" Wilson asked.

"We are prepared to move our forces into a position where your guards at the gate can see us. This is a sign of good faith. If there is a single shot fired, then all negotiations are over, and in retaliation we will simply attack and kill every man, woman, and child in the compound. Do I make myself clear?"

"Clear. Give me a minute to have the guards stand down."

He let go of the button so we could talk. "Okay, I'm assuming that our people have passed on the word to the guards by now, so let me radio them."

We had sent Willow and Ethan, along with four off-duty guards, to talk to the different guard stations. All the other off-duty guards had been scrambled and were waiting, ready to head for the fences and stations. They had all been briefed about the situation, about the plan, and knew to be aware that they were being monitored on the radio but to act as if they weren't. There were fifty-five guards plus the twenty teen guards for a total of seventy-five people to protect the perimeter. It wasn't enough.

The guards were also made aware of a message within a message, a secret code that we knew and our enemy didn't. Any communication that either started or ended with the lieutenant identifying himself was an actual order. When he didn't do that, he was speaking for the enemy to hear and they were to disregard what he was saying as false.

The lieutenant picked up the walkie-talkie. "This is Lieutenant Wilson speaking to all guard stations. I need all guards along the island fence to stand down, there is to be no use of weapons, I repeat, no use of weapons at this time. Do you all copy?"

One by one all the stations, including the three stations by the fence, reported that they understood.

"There will be people appearing on the land bridge from Main Island. I need to know from the gate guards how many of them there are and how they are armed. But you are not to fire upon them unless you are fired upon. Understood? Lieutenant Wilson out."

"Understood," came the various responses.

I looked at my watch. It was now three hours and fifteen minutes until the Mustangs were scheduled to return. They might be back a little early, or up to an hour late, but they'd be no later than that because they needed to refuel . . . unless they landed at Eden Mills to refuel and decided to stay longer. I couldn't think of that because I had no control over it. I just had to think that when they returned they'd make short work of anybody attacking us—unless they'd already reached the buildings.

The walkie-talkie sprang to life. "There are lots of them!" I recognized Willow's voice. He sounded panicked. "I can't count that many but there have to be close to two hundred, maybe more, and they have semi-automatic weapons . . . we could never stop them!"

"So far," Chris said quietly, "everything that Jimmie and Johnny have told us has been correct. It's time to put the rest of the plan into effect."

The lieutenant walked to the radio and pressed the call button. "Do you read me?"

There was static and then a response. "So you saw our forces?"

If he'd been listening in to our walkie-talkie conversations as we thought, he already had the answer to that question, but he was pretending not to know.

"Our guards reported to us. We are aware that you have a large, well-armed force. If you have your forces retreat we are prepared to bring a quantity of food and leave it outside our fence and—"

"That is unacceptable," he said. "We want you to open the gate and withdraw your guards. We will decide what food and supplies we will take."

"If you tell us what you require then we will bring those supplies and—"

"And poison the food?" he asked. "We will take what we want."

That actually made sense from their point of view. Most of all, though, it was an excuse to get inside.

"We want all of your people to withdraw to the terminal. If they remain inside that building and don't fire on us we will not attack."

If they still had more RPGs then putting us in the one building meant they could cause mass death with a few well-placed grenades. This was putting all of us in one basket, making us one target.

"We will take what we need from your stock and then withdraw," he continued.

"That is completely unacceptable!" Wilson snapped. "We need to talk about—"

"There will be no talk," he radioed. "You withdraw your guards and go into the terminal or we will simply attack and kill anybody and everybody. You will force us to kill not only the guards but everybody."

The lieutenant had removed his finger from the button. "So far it's exactly how we were told it was going to go."

"So far," Chris said. "Tell them what we want to do."

He nodded and pushed down the button. It was now up to him to put into place our counter-plan. "How do we know that you won't harm our people if we open the gate and withdraw?"

"I give you my word."

"Excuse me, but we need more than your word. We have a condition."

"You're in no position to make conditions."

"Hear me out or we'll have no choice but to try to stop you. We may lose but there will be a cost to you as well."

There were a few seconds of silence. "Let's hear it."

"I want to have time for our people to be evacuated onto our boats and anchor in the lake where they will be safe."

"Do you think you can delay us enough to allow your planes to return?" he asked.

"We only need thirty minutes," Wilson said. "We will then wait off shore until you have taken what you want and have left."

There was silence from the other end.

"They're thinking it over," Chris said quietly. "That's a good sign."

The radio came back to life. "You have thirty minutes. Not a minute more. If the gate isn't opened at that point we will launch our attack."

"That's all we need. Thank you," Wilson said. He released the button. "Chris, you have to get the evacuation started."

People had already been alerted and were preparing to head down to the docks while we were negotiating.

"I'll get everybody down to the pier area so if they're watching they'll believe we're evacuating like they think."

"I want it to be more than a pretense. I want people loaded on the boats and I want the boats to leave," Lieutenant Wilson said.

"But we have a plan to stop them."

"And if that plan doesn't work I need to know they're safe," Lieutenant Wilson said.

"But crowding that many people into so few boats, there's a real danger that—"

"There's a greater danger staying here."

"But what then?" she asked.

"Either we repel the attack and you return, or the boats sail to Port Credit and you make your way north to Eden Mills."

"I don't think that we should—"

"Chris, we don't have time for this. You need to get the people evacuated while we're still able to do so."

From the control tower we had a view past our boats and out onto the lake. Our six boats were the only ones in sight. There was a way to escape, but for how long? The invaders had to come over to the island by boat, and we knew they had boats the last time. Would they move to block any chance of our people escaping by water?

Chris looked as though she was going to argue, but then didn't. She nodded in agreement and turned and left the control tower.

"I'm going to lead the guards to the fallback position," Lieutenant Wilson said. "You get the teen guards down to the pier to provide assistance in getting people onto the boats, and then evacuate along with them."

"You want *us* to leave?"

"I can't risk your life and the lives of the others."

"You need us. With us here we have a much bigger chance."

"I can't risk the lives of children in a direct attack."

"We're not children. We're soldiers. We've been trained. We're not running. Let us be part of it. Besides, leaving is no guarantee of anything better. Out there, with no home and no food, a lot of us would die anyway," I said. "This is our home. We need to defend it."

He didn't answer, but his intimidating Marine glare faded.

"Okay, we're in this together. Let me send out a radio message." He picked up the walkie-talkie. "Can I have the attention of all guards, at all stations." He paused. "We are in the process of evacuating the compound. Guards on the perimeter are to hold their stations until that is clear. At that time I will give the order for the guards to withdraw and come to the pier to join the evacuation. Roger and out."

He hadn't used his name at the start or end of the message. Everybody on our side knew this message was just for the attackers.

He turned to me. "Let's get going."

41

Lieutenant Wilson and I hurried to the guard
station at the gate. We ran to the last open space, aware that
we were easily within the range of a sniper scope, but also
that our time was almost up. As we ran I looked beyond the
fence and the gate out onto Main Island. There, among the
trees, I caught glimpses of them. They had withdrawn but
they hadn't gone far.

We took cover behind the shelter. There were four guards
already present, including Willow. Ethan—under the threat that
I'd kill him myself if he didn't—had left and gone to the pier.

"We're glad to see you two," Willow said.

"I'd like to say we're glad we're here, but we're not. How
much time do we have?" I asked.

"Two or three minutes. It's time for the signal," Lieutenant
Wilson said.

He took the walkie-talkie.

"This is Lieutenant Wilson," he began.

That introduction meant that this order was not only for
outside ears but was to be followed as well.

"All guards, I repeat, all guards are to leave their perimeter defenses and retreat. I repeat, all guards are to retreat to
the assigned site. This is an order."

The invaders would think this meant going to the pier to evacuate. The guards had all been briefed in person and knew where they were really going to go.

Lieutenant Wilson let out a big sigh and now spoke directly to us. "You four guards need to retreat to the backup position as well."

Three ran away immediately. They didn't need to be told a second time.

"You too," Lieutenant Wilson said to Willow.

"I'm not going until Emma goes," he said.

"Are you disobeying an order?" Wilson said.

"Um, yes, sir . . . if that's all right, sir."

He nodded his head ever so slightly.

"Thank you, sir."

Willow reached out, took my hand, and gave it a little squeeze. I didn't know how or why but it made me feel safer.

"They would have heard and now seen people retreating. That probably buys us a little more time," Wilson said.

More, but not enough. The planes were still almost three hours away from their return.

"I'm going to go and open the gates and then we'll fall back," Lieutenant Wilson said.

"No, it should be me," I said.

"Negative, it has to be me. I can't put you in rifle range like that."

"They're not going to shoot somebody going out to unlock the gate," I said.

"But they might shoot you after it's been opened up."

"Which is why it can't be you," I said. "If you're killed, who will lead the defense?"

He looked as though he was thinking through my words.

"You know I'm right. Besides, I'm a smaller target, and I move a lot faster than you. As well, seeing a kid doing this will make them even more confident, and that confidence will work against them. So, do I go?"

"You've thought this through."

"I have."

"You really are a Marine at heart." He reached into his pocket and pulled out a large metal key. "I'll wait here."

I leaned my rifle against the wall of the shelter and turned just in time to see Willow snatch the key from his hand and start running for the gate!

I started after him, and Lieutenant Wilson grabbed me by the arm and stopped me.

"There's no point in two lives being risked."

I wanted to argue, but he was right. Besides, by that time Willow was almost halfway there. He was running across the open ground directly toward a mob of people with guns who wanted to kill him and everybody else here.

"Why did he do that?" I demanded.

"He wanted you to be safe," Wilson said.

That was more insane than anything else that had happened over the past six months.

Willow reached the gate and I felt a sense of relief as he slumped down behind the wooden barrier, a series of wooden beams that had been laid down to stop anybody attempting to ram through it. I watched as one by one he moved them. With the fifth one pivoted to the side he was now free to undo the lock. He was fumbling around.

"What's taking him so long?" I asked.

"It's not long. Be patient."

He took off the lock and started to pull a thick length of chain free from the fence. Next he took the gate and slid it over to the side, all the way, until the space was wide enough to allow a vehicle to pass through—or hundreds of heavily armed men.

"It's open!" Willow yelled toward the trees. "Just let me leave . . . let me get to the boats . . . that's all I'm asking . . . please!"

His words sounded desperate and scared and pleading, which they were. But it was probably good for them to hear that desperation, to think that they had nothing to fear from us.

Then he turned and ran.

He reached the shelter and I grabbed him and wrapped my arms around him.

"Don't you ever do anything like that again!"

"I think the correct response is, like, thank you for risking your life for me," he said.

"For me?"

"I didn't want you to risk your life," he said.

"Thank you."

"We have to go," Lieutenant Wilson said. He handed me and Willow our rifles and then together we turned and started off.

I looked back over my shoulder and saw the invaders starting to come out of the trees. A rush of adrenaline surged through my body. They were coming, and there was nothing to stop them except us.

We followed the path through the forest and quickly reached the fields surrounding the runway. A few weeks ago these had been filled with crops—tall stalks of tomatoes and cucumbers and beans that would have provided cover. Now they had all been harvested, and there was nothing but open space all the way to the irrigation ditch that marked the edge of the runway. It had been dug to save us the work of bringing water to the crops. Now it was going to save our lives—at least I hoped it would.

All along the ditch were our guards, stretching out in a line, standing, waiting, shuffling around. They had all abandoned their spots on the perimeter wall and this was the agreed-on fallback position.

"Everybody listen!" Lieutenant Wilson yelled. "On my command, you are to spread out along the line. Our lives depend on you staying silent, staying low, until I give the order. I want to alternate, teenage guard and adult guard, all along the line. Weapons are ready, but nobody is to fire until I fire."

They all looked so scared, so uncertain. Exactly the way I felt. They needed more.

"We can do this!" I called out. "They're not expecting us to fight. They're not expecting us to be here. We have surprise on our side. That's why we're going to live and they're going to die."

The lieutenant nodded in agreement. "We're going to win. Now take your positions!"

All along the ditch people started running and then climbing or jumping or sliding down into the ditch. It was muddy and at the bottom was a shallow pool of water. Lieutenant Wilson and I took up a spot in the middle. I was right beside him, and Willow was right next to him on the other side.

"Thanks for doing that. They needed to hear it," Lieutenant Wilson said.

"I'm not sure if I was talking to them or to myself."

He took out the walkie-talkie. "The perimeter has been abandoned. Please await evacuation until the final guards have arrived. All of the guards will be at the pier within two minutes so we can completely abandon the base. Do you read me?"

"We read you." It was Chris. "Four boats have left. Two will remain until your arrival."

"Roger that," he said.

We all knew that message wasn't real because he didn't use his name.

He turned to me. "A little more false information and false confidence for our attackers. I don't think we'll be waiting for long."

Lieutenant Wilson took the angled scope—the periscope—and positioned it so he could see out of the ditch without having to peek up and reveal himself.

I leaned back so I could see along the ditch in one direction and then the other. On both sides were people I knew, people who had come to be my friends. Some were seniors and some were my age or a few years younger or older. They used to be farmers, yoga instructors, actors, retired government employees, or just high school students. Now, together in this ditch, we were all soldiers. We were just here trying to stay alive—and to do that we'd have to kill other people.

There was complete silence. It was so quiet that I could hear the wind blowing through the leaves of the trees. And then I heard something. They were coming. I clicked off the safety on my rifle. All along the line I caught glimpses of people doing the same thing. Everybody was low and silent.

"They're coming out of the trees," Lieutenant Wilson whispered.

"All of them?"

"So far only a few."

That was what we'd feared. We needed to get more than a few advance scouts. We needed to surprise the main body and mow them down. If that didn't happen the rest would flank our position, moving off to the sides, and this ditch would become our graves.

"There are more now," he said. "And more. It looks like they're all coming."

The bluff had worked. They were so positive that what they'd heard on the radio was true, that we were all retreating, that they weren't taking any precautions.

There were voices now. They were loud, and there was laughter mixed in. This was a joke to them. We were a joke.

"The first are within twenty yards and closing," the lieutenant said quietly. "We need to let them get a few steps closer . . . another few seconds."

The time seemed to tick by in slow motion.

"And now!" he yelled.

The lieutenant jumped to his feet and I did the same. Now others along the line rose up, and his gun and my gun and theirs all exploded in fire. Out there, the enemy was just a few feet away, so close I could see the surprise and terror in their eyes as the bullets ripped into them. Bodies were spun around by the impact, tumbling to the ground. Others were falling to take cover, turning and running away, and still being cut down! We fired and fired and fired, the smell of gunfire overwhelming, the sound pounding in my ears.

"Cease fire!" Lieutenant Wilson yelled.

The gunfire slowed and then stopped. The ringing in my ears was the only sound that I still heard. In the distance I saw a few people running off into the forest. I waited for more but there weren't many. The rest were stretched across the field. There were bodies, lying in the mud, twisted into grotesque piles. Except for a few last twitches they were still. Except for the few who had fled they were all dead.

"We did it," I said.

Most of us were still in the ditch, guns at the ready and aimed out, waiting for a counterattack that never came. We weren't going to be caught by surprise.

After more than an hour of simply waiting and watching, and tending to the three of our people who had received minor wounds, Lieutenant Wilson led a detail of ten guards out through the killing field, into the woods, and out to the gate. It wasn't until he radioed back that they had all fled, and that he had resealed the gate, that I felt we were free to let down our guard even a little. It had been almost three hours since that first shot had been fired.

I climbed out of the ditch, out of the mud and water. I was cold and wet but I was alive. I felt alive. In front of us were hundreds of what had once been people but were now simply bodies. There was no point in looking any more. I turned away, toward the control tower and beyond that to the pier, where I could see the boats had berthed. They'd been radioed to return and were now letting people off. Soon the Mustangs would be back. Soon my mother would be back.

"It feels good," Willow said.

"What feels good?" I asked.

"The sun. It feels good to have the warm sun shining down on us."

"You're right. It does."

I raised my face to the sky and took in a deep breath. The sun felt good on my skin. The air felt good in my lungs. We were still here. We were still alive. We had survived. At least for now.

ACKNOWLEDGEMENTS

The character Chris is based on my grade 5 teacher—to whom this book is dedicated. In February 2017 she turned 93 and I went down to have a cup of tea with her at her place. She lives half the year on Ward's Island. The island in my story is called Ward's Island. When I pictured the events of my story happening I pictured this community. When I wrote about my character's cottage in the book it was her cottage that I pictured. More importantly, when I crafted this character who is wise, kind, decent, and caring, I pictured her.

My mother died when I was very young. My life circumstances were often desperate and difficult. Thank you, "Miss Gay," for being there at an important time in my life and believing in me. Thank you even more for continuing to be there and continuing to believe in me.

With love,

"Ricky"

Don't miss

ERIC WALTERS'

action-packed

THE RULE OF 3 series!

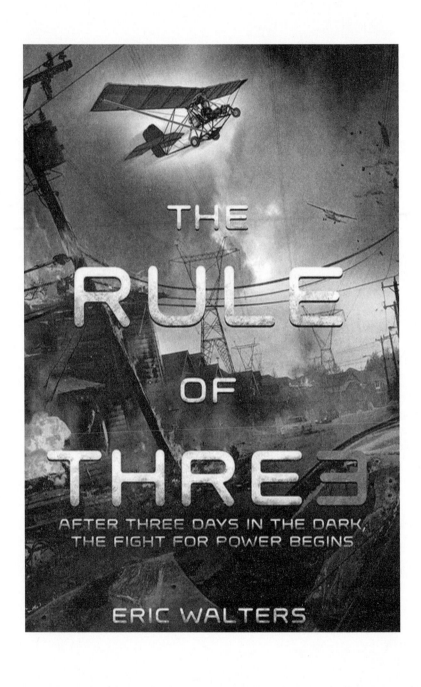

THE RULE OF THREE

OF

THRE3

AFTER THREE DAYS IN THE DARK, THE FIGHT FOR POWER BEGINS

ERIC WALTERS

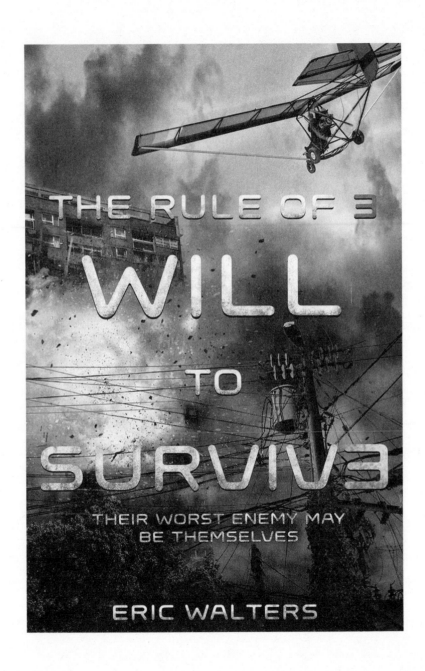

THE RULE OF 3

WILL

TO

SURVIV3

THEIR WORST ENEMY MAY BE THEMSELVES

ERIC WALTERS